SECRET LIVES

SECRET LIVES

Stories by

CATHERINE BROWDER

SOUTHERN METHODIST
UNIVERSITY PRESS

Dallas

Requests for permission to reproduce material from this work should be sent to:
Rights and Permissions
Southern Methodist University Press
PO Box 750415
Dallas, Texas 75275-0415

Some of the stories in this collection previously appeared, in slightly different form,
in the following publications: "Fusuda the Archer" in *Kansas Quarterly;*
"Silver Maple" and "Amnesty" (as "Jesús and His Brother") in *Shenandoah;*
"Animal Heaven" (as "Triptych") in *Farmers Market;*
"The Missing Day" in *New Letters;* "Snow" in *Potpourri;* "Soap"
in *Number One;* and "Good-night Mr. Johnson" in *The Kansas City Star.*

Cover photograph by Catherine Browder
Jacket and text design by Kellye Sanford

Library of Congress Cataloging-in-Publication Data

Browder, Catherine.
 Secret lives : stories / by Catherine Browder.— 1st ed.
   p. cm.
 Contents: Fusuda the Archer — Silver maple — Pizza man — Animal heaven — The
juice-seller's bird — Girls like us — The missing day — Center zone — Secrets — When
Luz sings her solo — Amnesty.
   ISBN 0-87074-480-1 (acid-free paper)
   1. Title.

PS3552.R6827S43 2003
813'.54—dc21
                                                                                2003042720

Printed in the United States of America on acid-free paper
10   9   8   7   6   5   4   3   2   1

For R.M., with love.
And for my students in the Don Bosco English Program
whose lives are a testament to the resilience of the human spirit,
my admiration.

ACKNOWLEDGMENTS

Help came from many directions: from the National Endowment for the Arts in the form of an individual grant in the 1990s that freed me to complete several of these stories and begin others; from the Missouri Arts Council, which gave support early on; from my editor, Kathryn Lang, for her faith and good judgment; from David Remley and Carol Black; and from many writer friends and colleagues, including Dana Carr, Mary Eaton, Donn Irving, Pat Lawton, Loring Leifer, Margot Patterson, Michael Pritchett, Christine Shields, Ann Slegman, Wyatt and Roderick Townley, Gloria Vando, and reader *extraordinaire,* Donna Trussell. To all, my thanks and gratitude.

CONTENTS

FUSUDA THE ARCHER

B ad luck had everything to do with it. That much I had already decided. My performance, such as it was, was scheduled for the last day, and I had made my promise over a year ago. I'd lose face if I pulled out now. The conference was a large, tedious affair that somehow, to my continual amazement, attracted linguists from several countries. It was always held in Tokyo, and like some harbinger of summer, it was always held in May. Whenever I went—taking in the panels and papers and introductions and pointless arguments over tea—I felt as if I were collecting lint from the corner of a familiar pocket. I rode up on the train the day before it started, renewing my oath never to go again.

Conference officials had arranged room and board, as they had every year for the last four. I expected to be placed in the usual university dorm or rooming house, which was fine as long as I was alone. Instead, I was informed two days before I left Kyoto that I would be staying in a private home. Had I met my host, named Fusuda, at some earlier date? Was there some special link between us, now forgotten? Mostly, I wondered why I hadn't been consulted.

My visit to the Fusudas' took place during my fifth year in Japan. Through chance, good timing, and the kindness of friends, I landed a job at a national university after my first year. The university seemed glad to have a man of my qualifications, and thanks to a handsome salary and favorable exchange rate, I had even been back to the States for two holidays. In fact, the current job was better than anything I might expect at home. So I resigned myself to a long stay overseas. I taught my share of dull, basic English classes, as did everyone else, but I had a sensible plan: establish myself in the linguistics field, improve my Japanese, and be invited home to something more secure than an assistant professorship in a competitive and poorly funded department.

There were other foreigners at Kyodai—Kyoto University. We all shared departmental chores: the meetings and speech contests and tutoring, sponsoring the bicycle and kendo clubs, pouring tea. Japan is kind to bachelors like me, and I was seldom bored, except at the annual conference, which I attended out of obligation—my *on* to the University.

I phoned the Fusudas as soon as I arrived in Tokyo to announce I was on my way. I spoke to Fusuda's mother, who had been briefed on my visit. Most likely, she would know more about me when I arrived at her gate than I would know about Fusuda. The mother informed me that "Kei-san" would meet me at the station. Probably Fusuda's wife. I found the right suburban train and arrived within half an hour.

The station was old and shabby. I had no sense of Tokyo, spending most of my time in the western part of the country. A dense, oppressive network of exits, stairs, walkways, tracks, and underpasses converged in a single block. I wanted to leave as soon as I stepped off the train; there was no place to stand still. Here was commuting reduced to its appalling essence. I gripped my small bag, which contained papers for the conference, clean clothes, and a novel. Then a blond Western woman, easily six feet tall, approached me, took my hand, and shook it before I could respond.

"Hello, Corelli-san. I'm Kay Fusuda. I know, I'm not what you expected," she announced as if it were a set piece. "I believe we were once on a panel together. It's been several years."

I didn't remember her at all, and certainly she was not a woman one could easily forget. As I followed her away from the station, she explained the house was less than a mile, and we walked through a crowded neighborhood that smelled of diesel fuel and burnt fish. I struggled to keep up. Her only remarks concerned the neighborhood, when to take a left or a right, how much farther to go.

The Fusuda family home was traditional, with weathered wood and a blue tiled roof. A stone wall protected it from the street, and over it leaned a flowering cherry, now heavy with blossoms. The old woman I'd spoken to on the phone met us at the door. After an interminable greeting, during which she kowtowed, making me feel glum, she took us to a verandah off a large uncluttered tatami room, where we sat in incongruous overstuffed chairs. I looked back into the room we had just walked through in our stocking feet, back over a thick Persian rug covering the tatami. Only two pieces of furniture stood in the tatami room: a long, low table and a tall, heavy Korean-style chest with round brass fixtures. Both were made of hardwood, lacquered and expensive. Instead of the usual hanging scroll or porcelain vase, a tall archer's bow leaned inside the alcove. The bow was covered in a dark blue folk cloth like denim, and a leather quiver of arrows stood beside it.

"I've been here forever, it seems," Kay began. "My husband is an engineer. We met years ago in Minneapolis when we were both students. Where are you on the agenda?" she asked.

"The last day," I said. "The luck of the Irish."

I'd hoped for a laugh, but she nodded seriously. "Yes, that would make one tense, waiting to the bitter end like that."

We sat there quietly until I thought I would lose my nerve and so asked where we had met, confessing I didn't remember. Had she confused me with someone else, in which case I was staying in her house under false pretenses.

"David Corelli. I never forget names," she said flatly. "I'm not surprised you don't remember. It was two years ago. I became sick during the meeting that year, and a friend read my paper for me. Nerves, I suppose. It was the first year the conference had invited translators. Before that, they treated us like illegitimate children. Anyway, I remember your paper. I remember it well."

I found this remarkable, since I didn't remember my own paper at all. Silence settled over us again, like the cherry petals that had settled over the garden stones. Thankfully, the old woman arrived with tea. Without losing track of the conversation, perhaps having only held her breath, Kay went on. "When I discovered you were coming, I asked someone at the university if you'd made any special arrangements. You hadn't, so I asked that you stay with us." She stopped again, and I took the opportunity to thank her. Much more pleasant to be in a home than a dormitory room, I said, sipping tea and thinking of my friends who would soon be hitting the small bars and fun palaces of fluorescent Tokyo.

Kay stared into her cup and then gave me a short history of our friendship. As it turned out, I was the one who had insisted she sit down when she thought she was going to faint, during that first year. How could she forget? she said. I had practically caught her. At the time, she'd laughed at me and commented about the worried look on my face. I gathered few men ever asked her how she felt, as few men doubt the strength of an elm or the force with which it could fall.

"In the year I met you, the year I got so sick with nerves, I heard you give a paper unlike any of the others. Do you remember it now? Criticism was mixed. Your reviewers called it 'eclectic,' 'careless,' 'witty,' 'needing tighter controls.' All the hard-line academics were jealous of it, but it was the high point of the conference because it was so unexpected. How could you have forgotten?" she asked and almost smiled.

The mother-in-law reappeared and invited me to use the bath. Afterward I was taken to the guest room, where I read late into the night. *How could you have forgotten?*

Her remarks followed me in. I never would have imagined a conference paper, which I had probably written in haste, could have fired so much interest.

At breakfast, I met Kay's husband, who had not returned from work by the time I'd gone to bed. Seiji was a company man, and dining obligations kept him out late most nights. Throughout the meal we jockeyed for languages. An American-trained engineer, Seiji spoke English well and was determined to use it. Whenever Kay lapsed into Japanese, he started up again in English. What happened when they were alone, I wondered? Did they each use the other's language then? I had seen this happen when couples shared European languages. They formed a new language in the random mix of tongues. Perhaps this method kept all languages alive. But I always suspected it was something saved only for guests, like a silver tea service or fine Spode china.

The house belonged to Seiji's parents; it was his mother who cooked and served the meals. Not once did I see the father, whom I assumed must be away on business, although I did hear someone coughing in the bathroom early one morning. I wondered what the old woman thought of her daughter-in-law. Kay had none of the older woman's compact grace. If any conflict existed between the two women, it was as hidden as Seiji's father.

After breakfast, the three of us walked to the station. Seiji would take a northbound express while I waited with Kay for the local. I couldn't help but watch them together. Seiji was unusually tall, but Kay was slightly taller, a blond spectacle, with startling dark blue eyes. Otherwise, I found her rather plain with an unremarkable figure that was not lean or large or curved but more like an unfinished birch plank.

The train jerked from station to station, and by pushing a little, we found seats.

"Who's the archer in the family?" I asked, remembering the bow in the alcove.

"I am. I've studied for eight years now. It's my life, or my other life, you might say." She smiled and her face was suddenly transformed into that of a surprised mare whose teeth were being examined for age. As if she knew its alarming effect, Kay stopped smiling and looked away. It was the first and last time I saw her self-conscious and the only time she let me see her smile.

"Eight years," I repeated without looking at her. "I haven't done anything for eight years except work and eat out a lot." So, everyone has a life beyond the one at hand, I thought, something to look forward to while translating bad textbooks or teaching bored students, something we can tell ourselves lends meaning to our lives. Something, anything, to give us an edge over the tired housewife dozing beside us on the streetcar.

"I started practically from the moment I arrived," Kay went on. "This was at the beginning of that craze for martial arts at home. It's difficult to remember how one gets started with something. Chance, I suppose. You meet someone who knows someone who teaches and will take you on. Which is exactly what happened in my case."

She stopped while the train emptied and filled before going on.

"I study with a man named Yomura. He taught classes on the second floor of a martial arts dojo when I first met him. They taught kendo and judo upstairs. It was really like a community recreation hall or a YMCA. They even had a basketball court in the basement and a Little League baseball diamond in back. A few yards behind the back fence of that field was an expressway. When the wind blew from the northeast, the kids couldn't hear themselves yell. Yomura's moved now. Two years ago, to a swankier hall and farther away.

"Anyway, Yomura Sensei taught upstairs in that hall. I would come to the lessons with butterflies in my stomach. I changed into my tunic in a closet I shared with one other woman. After we'd changed, we'd come out into the hall, bow to the flag at the far end, come onto the padded floor and do warm-up exercises. Then Yomura Sensei would come out, and we would all bow to him and line up on the mat, all of us sitting on our heels. First we did breathing exercises, ending with a shout. I always felt too self-conscious to shout. I only pretended.

"The second floor walls were really all windows. Some of those windows were cracked, and others had slivers missing or a whole pane. I never remember any heat up there. We were tested regularly. Sensei and his assistants put us through our paces and evaluated us. All very mysterious at first. But I can remember the first test. It was winter and I was sitting on my feet, shaking from the cold.

"When it was my turn, I remember standing and seeing our reflections in the cracked panes. One figure stood out from the rest, and I laughed, thinking, 'who is that giraffe?' Then I turned and sat down. When it was my turn again, I got to my feet, and for a fleeting second I saw the giraffe once more. And I realized with a shock it was me. I never *felt* tall when I went to my lesson. Maybe it was only from spending so much time on my knees. Yomura and his helpers seemed like giants from that perspective. Yomura never appeared short. Never. And whenever he demonstrated an exercise or stretched his bowstring, he was taller than anyone else in the room . . . Well, Corelli-san, here we are."

We walked from the station to the university, a distance of perhaps half a mile. In the hall of an old Meiji brick classroom building, which had somehow survived the firebombs, the conference was tightly organized. With as many helpers as participants, no one could wander off unattended. No one could possibly get lost, and so no official could be accused of insensitivity. All that was missing were the young tour guides with the yellow flags and a sheep flock of tourists. Kay arranged to meet me at 5:00 for the return and took off in a whirl of excitement. I soon ran into friends from Osaka and drifted out for a long, beery lunch, without attending anything for most of the day.

The week progressed exactly as planned, daily activities ending at 5:00 and beginning the next morning at 9:00 or 10:00. I was unable to hear Kay give her paper. The one man I felt compelled to hear was scheduled for the same time. During the breaks my friends collared me and complained I was being unsociable. I pointed out that I had a hostess to consider, while they were footloose. I wanted to invite Kay to join us, but they were an unpredictable lot, used to the flatteries of bar hostesses. Any one of them could be a boor if he felt like it. So instead I took her and two of her colleagues out to a restaurant one night before catching the train back to the Fusudas'.

When we returned each evening, Kay's mother-in-law brought fruit or snacks, even though we usually returned right after dinner. She wanted to hear about the day's activities, and Kay obliged her in great detail. After I retired, Kay waited up for Seiji, often until nearly midnight.

Late on Friday I took the night train back to Kyoto. I couldn't sleep even though the lights were dim. I was kept awake by a haunting sense of exclusion, not just from the Japanese—I was used to that. It was more like being the only "Gentile" in a happy group of Mormons. I wondered with bewilderment if I were the only foreigner in Japan who hadn't seized one of the native arts or crafts for my own redemption.

A week later I sent a note of thanks to the Fusuda family. I didn't hear anything from them until the first week of the New Year, when Kay sent a cable. She would be arriving on the thirteenth of January for the annual archery contest held at Sanjusangendo Temple. Panicky for details, I made a long-distance call that night. Seiji's mother answered. No, Kay was not at home. She was at her lesson. Every night she goes to practice, the old woman explained. I gave her my telephone number and a message for Kay to call when she arrived in Kyoto.

She telephoned from her lodging soon after she arrived. Kay, her teacher, and two more of his students had taken the bullet train from Tokyo that morning. The old man would shoot in the contest while his protégés held his robes, so to speak. Kay spoke excitedly, her voice revealing the importance of the event: her *sensei* had actually invited her. This was the first time she'd been invited to Kyoto in the eight years she'd worked with him. She'd gone to other contests, small regional affairs, but never to Kyoto. It was as if she'd finally passed an initiation, which had lasted for years.

I suggested we meet for dinner the next night, and she agreed. I gave her the address of an old restaurant near the Keihan train station, one that specialized in noodles and soups. It was a two-storied wooden, provincial place, not particularly cheap but usually crowded. The food was excellent, and it was easy to find from the inn where she was staying.

I arrived early, waiting near the restaurant where I had a good view of the street. After a few minutes, I saw her walk away from the bus stop, a giraffe moving head and shoulders above the crowd. She hadn't seen me yet, and I watched her move single-mindedly along the sidewalk, ignoring a young man with bleached hair who was jumping up behind her, trying to make himself as tall as Kay for the amusement of his friends. When she was just across the street, I noticed her face. My God, I thought. So we all put on that city face like a mask, as if putting it on could ward off the imminent disaster we know follows Westerners through the streets of Asia. I waved and she crossed the street.

Beyond the thin sliding wall inside the restaurant, a group of men sang and clapped while we tried to talk. I resented the noise. I always did. Company men exercising their right to be rowdy when drunk. Kay didn't seem concerned.

"I'm sorry about the noise," I said. "If I'd known we'd have this much competition, I might have suggested a different restaurant."

"No bother. Nothing to be done."

"Are you comfortable here?"

"Oh, yes. The food's excellent." She answered quickly, to reassure me, I suppose. "I know how it looks, like I'm folding myself in half. But really, I'm used to it."

"Actually, I meant, are you comfortable in Japan?"

"That's a different story now, isn't it?" she said slowly, putting down her chopsticks. I knew it was abrupt, but it was a question I frequently asked as if looking for the answer to a simple problem, which some day I might solve.

"This is where I belong because this is where Seiji is," she said. "Of course, if you mean how does a tall blond female *gaijin* get along here—"

"I wasn't thinking so specifically."

"—I do. But when you make concessions, you are compensated in other ways," she said, and I waited. I was familiar now with her deliberate approach to a story, the long pause after the introduction. This time there was no story. She picked up her chopsticks and pulled one long, fat noodle out of her bowl.

"You don't plan to stay much longer, do you?" she said.

"No, I don't."

"The future's at home, isn't it?"

"Yes."

She nodded. "You know, I've lost any sense of that home. And what is the future, Corelli-san? Something imagined that will only bring us closer to the end?"

I was in no mood for this. The drunks next door were singing maudlin songs, my ankles hurt, and Kay sat across from me without evident pain, hovering on the edge of metaphysics, or worse, something vaguely and dismally Zen.

"Are you coming tomorrow?" she asked.

"Yes, if you're inviting me."

"Absolutely! Do come for some of it. Sensei is scheduled for the morning. He's one of the old-timers. Some days I wish away that old man's years. Wish them down to forty or fifty. Yomura is seventy."

"Someday you'll be in your teacher's place," I said, thinking later it sounded patronizing.

"Probably not. I'm not Japanese."

"Well, surely, if you're good enough."

"No, Corelli, I think that's too much to expect. You know this country as well as I do. I'll always be someone's assistant. What's that expression? The token *gaijin*?"

So, hope had been given up along with the future in one sweeping act of resignation. It seemed as if Kay were clutching Fate to her bosom like a convert, and I felt suddenly restless and suggested we go to a coffee shop. It would be quieter. She declined, saying she would have to get up early to help Yomura. One of the men in the next room yelled rudely for more beer. The waitress, a round matronly woman I'd just paid, scurried away.

I walked Kay to her bus stop, and we waited there in silence.

"Will I have a chance to speak with you tomorrow?" I asked, making conversation.

"Of course. You'll be able to find us."

Her bus arrived, and I waited, as local custom required, until it was out of sight. *You'll be able to find us.* She'd said this without a trace of irony, or perhaps I'd simply missed the humor. It struck me as odd, how matter-of-factly she used her improbable height and color as a reference point. I couldn't accept that she'd simply gotten used to being a freak. No one ever did. With my small build and dark features, I usually blended in. Yet even I had been frowned at once by a very old, frail man who muttered as he passed me on the street, ". . . so ugly!"

My alarm didn't ring the next morning, throwing me out of kilter. I dressed quickly and flagged a taxi, knowing the buses would still be jammed with rush-hour passengers. The air was damp and bitter, a poor season for outdoor sports.

I paid the fee at the main gate and entered the grounds of Sanjusangendo. Few tourists milled inside the temple, where they kept the buddhas. Interest was centered on the outside corridor of the main hall. I'd missed the opening ceremony, and I couldn't see Kay for the crowds. Both archers and spectators came and went. The available space didn't allow everyone to watch at the same time. Stands had been set up to accommodate the crowd, but they were filled at the moment. I couldn't see anyone handing out programs but later picked one up off the ground.

I spotted Kay finally. Her teacher was about to shoot his arrows, and she sat behind him with the two other protégés. At one point she stood up, towering over her teacher. A ripple ran through the stands. She was an odd sight, reaching straight up like a wild fir among the bonsai. I felt nervous for her, the way I felt at departmental meetings when forced by protocol to keep quiet. So I waited, holding my nerves in my hands, vigilant for those imprecise words that would define her strangeness, her lack of beauty, anything to justify my sudden anger at the crowd, forgetting an old man who admired her skill had invited her. I even forgot I didn't share Kay's problem. No one bothered to stare at me.

Kay's behavior was utterly ordinary. For all my exhausting attention to the crowd, I heard only one remark: "Tall, isn't she?" Nothing more. When her teacher had finished, I left to have a cigarette in the front courtyard. I didn't hear Kay come up until she spoke my name.

"I'm glad you could make it," she said.

"Is there always such a crowd?"

"Yes, unless it's colder." The very mention of cold weather made me feel the chill through my jacket. I noticed she was only wearing a quilted exercise tunic, and over this the traditional long blue culottes.

"Don't you have a coat?" I asked.

"No. I'm not cold. Really. Excitement, I guess."

"Not even a sweater? Long underwear, perhaps?" I joked.

She turned her head away to laugh, shaking her head.

"You'll catch cold if you aren't careful. It's very damp, you know."

"Did you see the old man?" she asked.

"Yes, he's very impressive. But I'm afraid I don't know much about all this."

"Who does?"

"How long are you staying?"

"We're leaving this evening."

"So soon? Well, have a safe trip back."

"Thanks," she said quietly. "You know, you're the first man in years who's asked me if I was cold and shouldn't I put on a coat. My moth-er-in-law asks, of course. All the time. But it's not the same thing." Her cheeks were flushed, and for a moment, I was afraid she was going to cry. Instead, she turned and walked away. I saw people step aside, heard the embarrassed titter of a young woman, but Kay didn't notice.

I noticed on her behalf and kept score, feeling shabby for it afterward. I left the temple and walked home, wanting to tire myself out, to push my expatriate's malaise into the pavement and leave it there. The walk was long enough to sort through this free-floating discontent, and I wondered where Kay had so painstakingly stored hers. It never occurred to me she might not have any.

The following evening I was about to leave my apartment for dinner when the phone rang. I was afraid one of my friends was calling it off, so I made the effort to answer, fumbling with keys, rushing back in, shouting rudely into the phone.

"This is Kay Fusuda," she said softly.

"I'm sorry. I thought you were someone else. What's happened?"

"Something came up and we stayed on."

"I see."

"I thought, perhaps, we could meet somewhere for dinner or coffee. If you would let me treat. Believe it or not, I seldom get a chance to talk to fellow *gaijin*." She gave a nervous laugh.

"I'm meeting some friends for dinner. I was just on my way out. Would you care to join us?"

She didn't answer right away. "No, that's all right. I don't want to impose."

"You wouldn't be. Not at all."

"Thanks anyway. Please call us when you come back to Tokyo." She said her good-byes quickly and hung up.

I locked the apartment and took off briskly for the bus stop. In my haste, I couldn't think of one reason for her shyness about joining my friends. And why was she so eager to get off the phone? I was halfway to the bus, turning over these questions, when I stopped abruptly. I'd suddenly remembered how soft her voice was on the phone and the remark she'd made in the temple. My head filled with images of Seiji holding forth at breakfast, of the old woman kowtowing at my feet, of Kay sitting absolutely still, and alone, with her hands folded in her lap. I needed more than ever the company of my friends and hurried toward the bus.

I didn't attend the May conference that year. My dislike of it had come to a head in the months since I last saw Kay Fusuda. I found an escape hatch and begged off to continue some fieldwork I'd begun during the winter vacation. I rationalized to my department head, who was suspicious of shirkers, if this research could be completed soon, I would have a first-rate paper for the following conference. To my surprise, he agreed. He wasn't usually an agreeable man.

Then Kay wrote, inviting me to stay with them once more for the May conference. She was looking forward to seeing me. Reluctantly, I wrote back and explained why I wouldn't be coming. That was last I heard from her for six months.

I was suddenly busy. I continued my field trips to Hyogo Prefecture, not far from Kyoto. I was studying a regional dialect there, and research was proceeding normally, if not well. As I feared, I would need several years to accomplish what I had originally planned. Faced with my promise, I trimmed the fat off the project, trimming away the most interesting parts in the process.

So we moved through the rainy season and into the summer vacation, which I also spent away, and finally into the long, clear fall. In late October a chance to return to the States for Christmas came up when I was invited to give a paper. I approached my department head once more. Wada had no control over my holidays, and I didn't need Wada's permission to go home. In getting his approval, I was only being wise and respectful. I explained this would be a dry run for the next Tokyo conference, and Wada was pleased someone would be representing our Kyodai in Chicago. Only tact prevented Wada from guessing aloud I would also be looking for a job in the States.

I wrote the Fusudas, telling them I would be leaving December 14 for the holidays. I wanted to take them both out to dinner. I would call when I arrived in Tokyo. Within days Kay telephoned, inviting me to stay with them. I declined, having already made overnight plans. She seemed so disappointed by this that I readily agreed to come for dinner the night before I left.

As soon as I stepped off the train, I felt a constriction of the heart. Nothing at the station had changed: the limited view, the web of stairs and exit signs, the lonely kiosk in the middle of the platform that sold sex magazines and orange juice pep-ups. As quickly as possible, I walked down into the narrow streets. I remembered the way, but there was no need to rush. I stopped first at a neighborhood market and phoned ahead. While there, I bought a gift box of oranges for Seiji's mother, each individually wrapped in green tissue paper.

The streets were full of smoky dinner smells. Housewives threw water over the streets in front of their doors, settling the dust. When I reached the Fusuda gate, I pushed the bell. In spite of its age, the house had been wired with an intercom so Seiji's mother could turn away the greengrocers she didn't want to face. I identified myself to the voice on the other end, and within seconds Kay opened the gate. She led me into the house and up to the familiar chairs on the verandah. Glass doors had replaced the screens that used to separate the verandah from the garden in spring. A gas stove stood on the floor, throwing out its pale heat for a yard or two.

Seiji was home early. He was bathing, Kay said, and would join us shortly, which he did, dressed in his dark house *yukata*.

"Has Kay been bothering you about archery again?" he asked in a jocular voice.

I stood up and bowed, then took his outstretched hand.

The old woman served an elegant meal on heirloom lacquer ware. Talk was polite and dull, and later I decided it was so because of Seiji. He asked me about my field trips, my paper and research, interrupting from time to time to offer suggestions on historic sites and restaurants in areas of Hyogo where I would not be traveling. Surely Seiji was more interesting in Japanese. Maybe some paralysis develops while playing host in a second language. Meanwhile, Kay remained unusually quiet.

Since my flight was scheduled for 8:00 in the morning, I left the Fusudas early, amid protest. Kay sprang up.

"I'll walk you to the station, if you don't mind. I've been cooped up all day."

The evening was crisp, and I thought of how cold it could be in January when I returned. In front of us our breath condensed into thin pillows. I didn't want to hurry. I could see us standing on the platform with nothing to say until the train arrived. That was the moment when every word became rushed, saved up until the bitter end.

"You know, Corelli-san," she said abruptly. "I found a book for you. On archery. It's not like those English-language, macho, martial arts books they manufacture in the States. You'll have to struggle through the original Japanese. But even my teacher approved. It's only sixty pages. I hope you don't mind."

She handed me a small parcel carefully wrapped in pale blue paper and ribbon. I took it from her hand, amazed, and stumbled about until I found my wits to thank her. She merely nodded.

"There's a story in it which I'd never heard before. The records for the contest in Kyoto go back over three hundred years. As far as I can make out, it was always held at Sanjusangendo. Anyway, in 1696 a warrior from Kii Province, wherever that was, shot over thirteen thousand arrows. His name was Daihachiro Wase. Over eight thousand arrows went the full one hundred twenty meters—the length of the outside corridor. You remember? I tried to figure out how fast he would have had to shoot them, and I figured one arrow every two and a half seconds. It made me so dizzy I had to sit down. I realized, finally, maybe he hadn't shot them all in one day. He might have had a week or two. A test of endurance would be appropriate for a warrior, wouldn't it? Thirteen thousand arrows! And today the contest lasts one day. By invitation only."

We turned the corner and the station appeared before us like a reproach. I felt suddenly grateful she had come. A few people were already waiting on the platform, and I was glad it was dark. We wouldn't have to see the station in its sad shade of daytime gray. We faced the tracks and the brick backside of a long, windowless railroad building.

"The thing I try to imagine is Wase sitting on his heels," Kay went on. "I have an image of Wase the Warrior—a certain stocky physique and that disciplined samurai bearing—waiting for the right moment to raise his bow, insert the arrow, and shoot. It's not just like target practice, with a bull's eye at the end. There's a proper moment, you know, like a Quaker meeting when the Friends wait until some spirit moves them to speak and not before. So I imagined Wase waiting for the right moment. But when that moment arrives, Corelli, the world could come to an end, and the archer knows it doesn't matter."

We heard the train, at first invisible, until it crept slowly into the station.

"Have a safe trip," she said. "And a Merry Christmas."

She turned and quickly took my hand and shook it, allowing herself a tiny, closed-mouth smile. I suddenly began talking and joking, prolonging my good-byes, overwhelmed by a perplexing sense of sorrow. I climbed aboard, turned to face Kay through the train window, and waved. She shoved her hands into her coat pockets and walked beside the slow-moving train, walking with it for several yards until it picked up speed and left her behind. In her eyes I saw how resistant she was to the empty platform. The bleak mood of it, which had crawled into me like a hermit crab, hadn't touched her. In spite of the harsh light, her face radiated warmth.

The train twisted out of the station, and she receded from view, telescoped into a lone tree on a distant field, until that disappearing sight of her made me feel like a stranger to myself.

SILVER MAPLE

M ildred had never meant to create a spectacle, but there hadn't been time to do much else. Certainly no time to dress. Besides, Trask always said a person was obliged to finish what they'd started.

She told Trask she might have heard them sooner if the kitchen sink hadn't plugged up. In her flight from cupboard to sink, Mildred had caught a glimpse of her neighbor standing on the sidewalk, uncharacteristically still, while her dog whined and tugged at its leash. It was at this point of annoyance with both sink and dog that Mildred heard the catarrhal wheeze of a truck.

When Mildred opened the front door, she saw the city truck parked in front of the house. As she puzzled over this, an extension ladder emerged slowly, noisily from the bed of the truck, stretching up and up until it tottered ominously over the front maple. So focused was she on the ladder that at first she didn't notice the arrival of the second truck. Meanwhile, the ladder jiggled slightly, then stopped. Doors opened and slammed shut. Six men in green city uniforms stepped out of both vehicles and began to assemble at the base of the maple.

Nothing in the scene unfolding before her made a lick of sense. One man was talking but she couldn't make out the words. Several looked straight up while another workman took something off his belt and seemed to be taking measurements from the trunk, five feet up, out to the shade of the lowest limb. The man who appeared to be in charge slapped the trunk and said something that made the others laugh. When one of the men went to the second truck and returned with a long-handled pruning blade, Mildred panicked.

She tightened her housecoat around her and hurried off the porch, down the steps, and across the grass toward the group. The man who'd made the others laugh identified himself as the head of the work crew. The name MULDOON was emblazoned on his pocket—the very man who would later file the complaint. A person, Mildred thought at the time, incapable of explaining in plain English why six grown men were poking at her tree.

When she asked to see the work papers, Muldoon told her the foreman had the papers, but at the moment the foreman was several blocks away.

"We'll just wait here till he comes," she said.

"No, ma'am. We won't wait."

"Why ever not?"

"We got three trees to do by noon."

"'Do?' I don't understand."

"We gotta cut them down, and that's no small potatoes."

"What's the matter with this one? Is it diseased?"

"That's not the reason for its termination."

"Well, what is?" Her voice quivered.

Muldoon pointed glumly. Mildred followed the line of his arm up to where the leaves of one outstretched limb stroked the power line. Incredulous, she stared at him.

"Call him. Please. You may use my phone."

"No, ma'am. I won't."

Mildred froze, utterly lost for words.

"You need to get out of the way, ma'am. Now."

"No, sir. I will not."

They squared off at distance of a yard, and she saw in his swollen face the mirror image of her own. She remembered thinking this must be how a pressure cooker behaved, before you released the steam. All the while, stalled workmen wandered away, hunkered on curbs, smoking. She heard a deep, rich, throaty laugh, a black man's voice. Against the landscape of his crew, Muldoon stood out flushed and white. Two men strolled away from the scene with such studied indifference you'd think such scenes happened everyday. When they reached the second truck, they stopped and began to examine the equipment. From the corner of her eye, Mildred glimpsed another man walk slowly out into the quiet residential street with his hands in his pockets, whistling a tune so plaintive Mildred was afraid she might cry.

Again she suggested they contact the foreman and inform him of their problem. Muldoon threw his baseball cap to the ground.

"Lady, you're the only problem I'm having."

"I just want to know one thing." Mildred raised her arms straight up. "Why don't you just give it a haircut?"

"Because."

"Because what?"

"My orders are these—are you listening, ma'am? CUT THE TREE DOWN. That means all of it."

Mildred lowered her arms until they stretched out in benediction above the crabgrass and clover. "We cut the lawn, trim the hedge, and prune the limbs. And we planted that tree. It's mine."

"Then you can tell me in what size lengths you'd like it cut, so you can burn it in your fireplace this winter."

"Don't anyone move," she said furiously and ran toward the house.

Her neighbor dragged the small white dog to the safety of a screened-in porch as Muldoon instructed his men to get on with it. Long pruning blades and sturdy saws scraped the bed of the truck. Their voices followed her across the porch and through the house. Someone had started the truck, and she could hear the engine growling in the background. The ladder gave off a flat, gray clank as it extended downward, notch-by-notch.

Backs turned, heads bent over power tools, Muldoon foraging in the cab, no one saw Mildred return. As a chain saw began its peace-obliterating whine, Mildred released the safety, pointed her husband's shotgun straight up in the air, and to her own amazement, fired once.

"Lord 'a mercy," a voice screamed.

Two workmen dove beneath the first truck. Another flopped, belly down, into the bed of the second vehicle. One had fallen face first onto the grass, and then crawled hurriedly on all fours toward the curb. Yet another crouched pathetically behind the condemned tree. Next door, Marge Brown's dog yapped wildly without any sign of letting up as Muldoon sank to his knees, covering his head with his hands. Mildred stood as if in shock, the blast ringing in her head.

"Don't shoot," Muldoon yelled. "Put the gun on the ground."

Still clasping the shotgun, Mildred inched backward toward the house, until her calves touched the porch step. Muldoon got to his feet cautiously, his arms stretched out at his sides, horizontal to the ground. He looked crucified, Mildred thought, and unreal, like something from a bad dream. Slowly he made his way backward toward his truck. When he reached it, he dropped his arms and shouted, his words coming at her like a second gun blast.

"Lady, in half an hour I'll have the law down on you."

"You do that," she yelled back, startled, and sat down heavily on the step, the gun across her lap.

The work crew scrambled aboard the two trucks. She heard loud cursing, doors slamming, engines racing, gears grinding, and one long, hysterical peal of laughter. All men aboard, both trucks left the neighborhood at ambulance speed. She lost track of how long she sat there—a moment? an hour?—until her vision cleared and the pounding in her

ears subsided. Hands trembling, she took up the empty gun and gingerly carried it indoors, lowering it like a corpse onto the dining room table.

So, he'd have the law down on her, would he? As if it wasn't enough
to live with, Law would summon Law against a blundering wife.
She could see the disconcerting headline now: MAINTENANCE CREW
ATTACKED / SHERIFF'S WIFE ARRESTED. She could even hear Trask laugh,
see him clipping out the article and attaching it with her raspberry
magnet to the refrigerator door.

It was a careless thing to do, rushing down to Trask's basement den.
The War Room, she called it, a foreign and disturbing place, strewn
with a man's deliberate clutter: stacks of magazines on pistols and hunting; a shelf of wooden decoys; walls heavy with fishing rods, posters,
firearms. Ever since Trask had grumbled that she misplaced things,
she'd refused to clean it, for years coming only as far as the door to
announce, "Dinner's ready."

In the bedroom Mildred changed slowly out of the old terry-cloth
housecoat and into a dark, suitable dress. They'd call Trask, she felt sure
of it. They'd come back, and she'd be waiting.

The tree had been her mother's idea, all those years ago. They'd gone
down to spend a weekend at the farm southeast of Springfield. Emmy
was not yet three.

"Take it!" Mama had said and pointed at a leafless stick struggling
against the milk barn. "It'll give that porch of yours some cool shade."

A last-minute gesture, at once spontaneous and familiar, a way her
mother had of keeping them with her another thirty minutes. Mildred
didn't mind. There was time, since Trask had taken the baby to say
good-bye to the old, lame pony, once Mildred's. Mama had thrust the
pitchfork deep into that lion-colored, southern Missouri soil and
slapped the side of the barn.

"If it's got a hold on life here, it'll live in your front yard."

"What've you got?" Trask asked when he saw it in the bed of the truck.

"A silver maple. For the front."

"Soft maples are junk trees, Millie. First strong wind will bring her down."

Mama walked them to the truck, holding Emmy tight against the faded overalls. The sight of yellow mud clinging to the gumboots made Mildred suddenly homesick.

"You put that tree deep in the ground, and don't go puttin' it closer than twenty feet from the house."

She reached through the open door and patted Mildred's stomach, round and tight as an apple.

"Take care of this one too."

Mildred wanted to leap out of the truck and join Emmy in her mother's arms. After they'd moved upstate, her mother seldom visited, seldom could, unwilling to leave her forty cows—each one named and pampered.

"You got a good man in Trask," Mama said. "Not like some."

She knew Trask was meant to hear, but it wasn't a man she needed then, uncomfortably pregnant, chasing after Emmy, and Trask never home. "Mama's girl," he called her, just to make her mad. It was true, but she never could think fast enough in the face of Trask's teasing to say what she felt: "That's right, I am. What of it?"

They'd planted the tree thirty feet from the house, in what must have been the right-of-way, close enough to the street at least for the city to take an interest. As it grew, Trask pruned back limbs that drooped like willow arms. It was a glorious tree, full and strong, now seventeen years old, the same age as Cara, three years younger than Emmy.

If they came back with anything sharper than a piece of paper, she'd have to fire again, finish what she hadn't meant to start.

No one was on the street when the vehicles turned the corner, a patrol car and a paddy wagon. No sirens. Everyone inside, she thought, peering out living room windows. Two police officers emerged with such deliberate nonchalance she couldn't tell whether they were simply cautious or annoyed. One of them looked as young as Emmy. The older one, balding and paunchy, stopped halfway, bent down with noticeable difficulty, and picked something out of the grass. It took them forever to reach the porch.

"Mrs. Trask?"

Behind him, she seemed to hear another deeper voice say, *Do it right!*

"I'm coming, but I want to know one thing first. No one's to touch that tree while I'm gone. The gun's inside if you want it."

"Won't be necessary," the older man said, grinning. "I got the shell."

She read the document he gave her, and locked the house.

"Where am I to ride?"

"The wagon, ma'am."

She stepped up and thought she'd entered a can. The seat was hard. Metal, she thought, but couldn't yet see. It was better this way, not having to sit in the patrol car, handcuffed probably, making small talk. Thin grids of sun poked through the meshed eyelids of the back window, a tease of light that seemed to rob the dark of honor. The wagon turned and swayed, tossing her to one side. She hadn't counted on this ride, but she hadn't counted on the workmen either.

Maybe it was a case of too much planning, too much holding back. Of all her girlhood friends she'd been the most careful. Franny had never held back. She'd taken up her life as though it had handles for carrying. How easily she'd written Mildred off, all because she'd stayed home to teach, loving it and loathing it with equal force until she met Trask. Fran, the closest friend of Mildred's childhood, had willingly put her life in someone else's hands and spent the summer of '64 marching through the South. Fran had glowed with confidence because she'd been wise enough to sew a comb and a tiny bar of soap into the hem of her granny gowns, just in case she was arrested in Hattiesburg or Selma or McComb. (Mildred looked inside her pocketbook. No comb, not even a dollar. Only a small flattened brush, loose change. Her money purse had been left as usual in the cabinet above the sink.) Mildred had received letter after letter, written fast, the pitch both fevered and euphoric as if living in the Southland produced an altered state.

And she had missed it all. Mildred felt the air inside the wagon grow turbulent and hot, as though a hundred restless beings breathed beside her. It made no sense, being tormented now by this host of regrets. Perhaps adventure was only something people thought they ought to have, mixing it up in their minds with wisdom. All she'd ever craved was a quiet, steady life.

Mildred heard an uneven surge of traffic, felt the gears grind down as the wagon slowed, then sped forward through an intersection.

Trask. It seemed funny now she'd never called him by his Christian name. She hated it as much as she hated her own, two stumbling blocks to marriage. *Xavier Meriwether Trask.* What misguided grandeur would make a mother hang that on a child? What viciousness? Trask's mother was ambitious, a woman with small even teeth and deep-lidded, coquettish eyes. Mildred had known a student once with just such treacherous eyes.

On the day Trask told his mother they planned to marry, Mildred overhead them in the kitchen. Mrs. Trask spoke in a hushed voice that might as well have been a scream.

"Esther Pruitt's daughter? I haven't seen Esther in church in over ten years. I don't believe the woman owns a dress. Well, I must say I'm surprised."

"Millie's a teacher," he said, too quickly. "In town."

But the unhappy seed was planted, which was all his mother had intended in the first place.

It was just they were both so old, Mildred thirty and Trask thirty-three. Trask hadn't told her about the three hunting dogs, the two shotguns, and the deer rifle with the telescopic sights. It was small comfort when he reassured her the guns were seldom used. ("A gun is a tool, Millie," he drawled like Alan Ladd. "No better or no worse than the man who uses it.") The dogs prowled the yard, dug up the tulip bulbs around their rented house, bayed for hours until she burst into tears. He tried to console her, even took two of the hounds to his brother's the following week. He kept his favorite (now long dead), the young blue-tick bitch named Tess.

From meager savings, she bought a Singer sewing machine to make his shirts, brought up her grandmother's bone china so they could have quiet, sit-down meals. Mama gave her the only thing of value at the farm, the Lalique bowl Daddy had given her. Yet day after day she watched the dog root and burrow, listened as Trask fed Tess and petted her and crooned.

"Is she my competition?" Mildred said through her grief. "I want a pretty house, Trask, and you've brought along a female dog who can do any damn thing she pleases."

The period of adjustment stretched out in time like a flat, unplanted field. Trask tried so hard, his mother tried so little, and Mildred, trying to please everyone, had accepted all the invitations to tea where Mother Trask repeatedly called her Millicent.

"Meriwether once loved a truly beautiful woman," Mrs. Trask told her when they'd been married five months. "But she dashed off with some soldier boy instead. To the sorrow of her parents and poor Meriwether. He was never the same."

Mrs. Trask's eyes grew moist and bright. Malice, Mildred thought. A dry, leopard-spotted hand reached for the silver pot and poured tea into thin, rose-bud-patterned cups.

His mother kept close tabs even after they'd moved up to St. Joe. When Trask ran for sheriff, she summoned Mildred back to the old homestead, for no other reason Mildred could discern than to tell her a man who ran for public office absolutely required an attractive and attentive wife. As if Trask were running for mayor or Congress.

"But I'm sure you'll do just fine, Millie," she said. "You have such excellent posture."

"How did you get on with her?" Mildred had asked him, since in their first year together she couldn't detect a single outward sign of affection, or disaffection, between mother and son.

"Okay, I guess," he said. "She always made us take off our boots before we came in the house. Right there in the kitchen. 'We don't live in a barn, boys,' she'd say. It made her happy, so we did it."

She imagined the Trask men, forced to enter their own home through the rear, shoes left humbly on the step, three pairs of nightly offerings.

No one fussed over floors at her mother's, and it made her proud to take Trask to the farm. By then, Mama was running the operation alone. In the presence of her mother's gentle teasing, Mildred saw Trask in a new and reassuring light, jaunty and comfortable with women. When the women were alone in the kitchen, Mama had asked her, "How does he treat his mother?"

What was there to tell? Mildred scraped along the bottom of her observations for something civil.

"He's polite. I guess you could even say he's kind."

"Good. A man who's kind to his mother will be kind to his wife. But you don't care much for her, do you?"

Mildred didn't know how her mother had gleaned this, since she could never bring herself to speak of Mrs. Trask. She couldn't even bring herself to say the words that came so easily to mind, that his mother was cold, extravagantly unkind, fearful that invoking the words might implicate Trask.

"She's difficult," Mildred said.

The wagon stopped abruptly, and Mildred lurched backward. A shriek of metal hinge, a wash of white light, and the door stood open.

"How long have I been in here? Seems like hours."

"Eleven minutes. Traffic was bad."

Mildred inched her way to the glaring entrance and took the offered hand.

"Now what?"

"You'll wait inside. We'll write up a ticket. You'll post bond. Then you'll go home. I'll take you."

"I'm afraid I don't have any money with me." *Not even a comb or a tiny bar of soap sewn into this hem.*

He led her to a high wood counter, around to a desk where she sat contemplating the astonishing immaturity of his face.

"Care to make a statement?" the young officer said.

"There's nothing much to tell. The city sent some men out to cut down a tree, but I couldn't see the need. It's my tree, mind you. I planted it, but I couldn't get anyone to listen. So I went back inside and got Trask's gun and fired one shot, straight up into the air over everybody's head. Seemed the only way to get the man's attention. Trask always says guns have that effect, but I wouldn't know. Never fired one until today." Mildred folded her hands in her lap. No one spoke until she grew afraid she might drown in his bewilderment. Once again she heard the deep voice whispering, *You have to see it to the end.*

"I know it's against the law to discharge a firearm in the city, but I wasn't quite myself at the time. But here I sit, and I'm ready to take the consequences."

"Ma'am, I don't think anything else is required."

A hot spring of anger surged up, and in her haste to stand she knocked a Styrofoam cup of coffee off his desk.

"Am I receiving preferential treatment?"

Speechless, he moved twenty feet to a small, dim cage, opened the wire door and pointed.

"Thank you." Mildred rushed in, and the door was left ajar.

The force that had come on her so suddenly vanished. She crept forward to what appeared to be a ledge protruding from a wall. A television blared. Canned laughter rebounded through the open space beyond the cage like a single voice in a tub. The station was a plain green room with shallow offices adjoining, the work space compressed by rows of file drawers, desks littered with coffee cups and tattered desk pads, a locked cabinet of shotguns and dust-gathering riot gear. Off to one side an ancient typewriter clacked, its rhythm broken by the impatient, ringing phones.

She could see half the front desk, occupied by a large blond policewoman. A tall, exasperated lady in a black pantsuit came in to sign a complaint about a neighbor's dog, her urgent voice having no visible effect on the stolid woman behind the desk. Later, two baffled motorists, sent to the station to file their accident reports, hesitated at the entrance as though their presence were an admission of guilt. All the slow, unexcited purposefulness of the station confounded any sense she'd ever had of crime and justice. Except for the smell in the cage. Someone must have spent the night, leaving his sour alcoholic mist behind.

"Mrs. Trask?" It wasn't the boy this time. This man was dark and fierce-looking and middle-aged. "You're free to post bond."

"I'm sorry, but I haven't got a dime."

"Maybe you'd like to call someone."

"That's all right. I'll wait."

"But you can't wait here long. We'd have to take you to Headquarters, then over to the County. It's not a nice place, Mrs. Trask. Holding tank cells."

He left, murmuring something to the desk sergeant before moving out of her line of vision. A telephone rang, then another. The boy officer returned. "You've got a phone call."

Mildred stared.

"Well, you're entitled to a call. They don't say whether it has to be going out or coming in."

He led her to a desk and punched a button on a phone. She took it, breathing in without a word.

"Millie? You there?"

"Yes, Trask."

"I'll come right out and get you."

"Have you been to the house? Did you know the city wanted to take my tree? 'Terminate it,' they said. I'm not budging till I know about my tree. And if it's not there, I don't think I even want to come home."

"I'll call you right back. Don't move."

"Who can move? I'm incarcerated."

She thought she heard him laugh and felt her blood rise.

"You're the one who always says, 'fish or cut bait,'" she said and hung up.

When she turned back, the young policeman was standing just behind her, embarrassingly close, the distance of a breath. He needed a haircut, and his dark red mustache was cut too high.

"You don't have to wait in there," he said softly.

Mildred closed the cell door herself.

Trask may have taught her how to fish, but no one had to teach her to cut bait. Never squeamish, she'd dug worms out of the garden and manure heap when she was a child, selling them to the bait shop down the road for a penny apiece. Before the girls were born, and for a short time after, Trask and Mildred had driven down to the farm and fished the nearby river. They would park the car along a bumpy clay road, cross a stubbled field where cattle browsed and red-winged blackbirds warbled from the fence posts. At one point the river narrowed into a sheltered inlet, rich with fish. Grass and golden weeds grew along the bank. Farther back, pampas, willows, and scrub oak shielded the inlet from the pasture.

Once, when the fish weren't biting, Trask had told her to reel in. He threw an old army blanket across the weeds and took hold of her waist. The blanket was narrow, and she found herself flattened against the grass, fully clothed at first and then their garments strewn around them in a nest of cotton. A cool river breeze licked her hair and hands and feet as the rest of her warmed under his weight. She'd always thought Cara was the product of that unrehearsed moment.

When they'd reached the farm, Mildred straightened herself hurriedly, missing some dry grass and the smudges on her trousers. She turned to grab her tackle, and Mama whistled at her through her teeth.

"Glad you had a good time."

"We generally do when we fish."

"More than that, I'd imagine."

"I don't know what you mean."

"Why, honey. You got roses in your cheeks and a grass stain as big as the state across your backside." Mama threw back a mane of gray hair and laughed. All Mildred saw were the holes where her mother's molars used to be. Mama walked back to the milk barn, shirttail flapping, a frayed red flannel from L. L. Bean.

"Why don't you go into town and get yourself some proper clothes!" Mildred shouted at the broad, departing back.

"I can't abide shopping, Millie. You know that."

"Ma'am?" The redheaded boy stood in front of the cage. "Someone here for you," he said and ducked away. Trask appeared, hat in hand.

"Millie? I've bailed you out."

"Thank you, but I'm not sure I'm ready."

"They can't keep you here, y'know."

"That's a pity. Just when I was starting to like it, too."

"It's a whole lot nicer at home."

"You wouldn't say that if you'd heard all those chain saws."

He was watching her, staring at her hands folded primly in her lap. He entered the cell and sat down.

"I called the girls," he said. "They're worried."

"Ashamed, you mean. I can just hear them now. 'Gawd, why'd she do it?'"

"They said no such thing. Your Cara said, 'Thatta girl, Mom!'"

"She's your Cara. Not mine."

She was sorry she'd said it. She'd never thought of themselves as the kind of folks who chose up sides, each parent singling out a favorite and leaving the rest unclaimed. It had never been their way. Now you would have thought she wanted to release them all and stand apart, the one unchosen.

"What do you propose to do here?" he asked finally.

"For the moment, sit and think."

"Okay. So they let you sit here and think. Then lunch time comes and afternoon and evening and Cara will miss your fine dinner."

"Don't toy with me, Trask. I've made enough fine dinners to last me a lifetime. And I don't have that much time anymore."

"Mildred? Are you sick?"

"I don't mean it that way."

She watched a pattern of striped light on the floor. An hour ago it was a narrow rectangular patch. Now it had spread out like a carpet, filling the cage. She'd liked her world much better when it was small, back when the guns were left unloaded and Trask guarded the house with a Louisville Slugger he kept beside the bed. She wanted things simple

again, the girls little, the tree no threat to the city. A world within easy
reach, where all the possibilities that had slipped away were recent and
easily reclaimed.

"They ought to bring in a couch," Trask muttered.

He realigned himself on the cot, pushing out his legs until his boots
lay across the stripes of light. The toes were scuffed, the right heel worn
smooth inside. She'd known a day when those boots were so bright
they'd give you back a mirror image if you stooped to look. It was the
only part of his regimen he'd slacked up on. Couldn't stand the smell of
polish, he told her. When she offered to do it for him, he'd looked at
her as though she planned to clean them with her tongue. "No wife of
mine has to clean my boots," he said. "You got better things to do."

He crossed one boot over the other, the worn heel as visible as an
infirmity. She'd stopped lamenting the clumsiness of his footwear after
the tall boots saved his leg. Trask had gone out to a farm south of town
because no one had seen the old man in several days. When Trask had
walked inside the barn, a field rake struck like a guillotine across his
legs. A vagrant, Trask said, and not quite right in the head. When he
finally got home, she saw the torn, red trousers, saw the limp, and cried
out in pain and rage at his complete disregard.

"Honest to God, Millie. It's nothing."

Mildred wondered if Trask would have told her anything about what
happened on the farm, except the wound made telling necessary. The
rudiments of the case were spelled out over a late supper, the girls studying in their rooms. Her carefully prepared accusation—"You can't protect us from your life, Trask. What do you want us to do? Read about it
in the papers?"—was never made because he answered all her questions.

"When I come home," he told her later, "I don't like to bring all the
dirt home with me. You understand? I figure my family deserves better."

The brittle words lingered in the air until they seemed to group themselves around Trask in a fence that didn't so much shut her out as shut

him in. Perhaps this was the way some men preferred to live, each case
unconnected with his own life and, when done, no longer thought of
since something new had come along to take its place. It seemed an odd
and chilly way to work.

"How's your leg now?" Mildred asked.

"My leg?"

"You don't limp."

"You know I don't."

"I'm glad."

She looked at the scuffed boots, her eyes traveling up to the where the
socks would end beneath the trousers. She knew the scar by heart, long
and smooth as a blade.

"That was five years ago, Millie. The leg's fine."

"Do you know what the doctor told me when he phoned the house?
'Lucky man, your Trask. Given a sharper blade or a shorter boot, Trask
would have lost his leg.' I never cared much for your doctor after that."

"Why in the name of heaven are we talking about my leg?"

"I was just thinking about it, is all. In the last twenty years I haven't
had twenty minutes stuck together just to think."

He moved in close and put an arm around her shoulders.

"Come home with me now, Millie."

"I need to know about the tree first. It's important."

"You're taking up their time and space."

"I don't notice a crowd, do you?"

"You've done what you had to do. So now it's time to go home."

"Why, you're not listening to a word I say."

"But it's your home and you're its caretaker."

"This is what comes of care-taking, Trask." She banged the cot with
her fist. "This is where they brought me because I care so much."

Mildred felt the tears, always arriving out of spite when she wanted
them least. She hadn't meant this to be a game, nor had she meant to

hold him accountable for every tiny hurt. The uncharitable words appeared of their own free will. They were never meant for Trask, nor for any person, but for something that had no shape at all. She looked up, contrite, and found him smiling.

"If you don't come home," he said, "there won't be anyone to pet the dog or iron my shirts, and then the cats will go off their food."

Mildred fixed on him a look of such reproach his neck turned red.

"I only meant to make you laugh. What d'you want me to say?"

"You'll know when it comes. I can wait. God knows I'm an expert on waiting."

"You're not a waiter," he said indignantly. "You're a planner. What's wrong with that? And when I did come along, you sure didn't say no."

"But I was just so old," she whispered to the floor. He ignored her.

"I remember when we met," he said.

"How could anyone forget? At a high school basketball game. Chaperones, they called us. Prison guards is what we were. Both of us bearing down on a skinny little boy because he tried to sneak his Coca-Cola into the gym. Nice way to start a marriage."

"Hell, Mildred. It didn't start then. You didn't even like me at the time."

"No, I didn't. I didn't like the uniform. Too many buckles."

"But I noticed you."

"That wasn't hard. We reached the boy at the same time. What a hateful pair we much have seemed."

"Not hateful, Millie. Just doing our job. I remember how your hair bounced and your face was flushed. You were pissed, but I thought you were the prettiest thing I'd seen."

"That's because the only things you generally see are other men. Ugly ones, too."

Trask hurled his head back until it hit the cell wall behind, the laugh coming out in a high-pitched string of coyote yips. He swatted his leg with his hat, and Mildred felt the infuriating tears again.

"So why did you wait twenty-one years to tell me you thought I was pretty?"

"I didn't know there was any need. Wanna know something else I remember? Right after I was elected, you came up to me and touched this very buckle you hate so much, and you said, 'Don't you be one of those old boys with his flesh hanging down over his belt. You won't let that happen, will you?'" He slapped his stomach, solid but taut, room for expansion built into the frame. "In all these years, I've loosened this belt just one notch. I want you to know that."

An uneasy quiet settled between them. She became aware of his hands traveling the circumference of the hat brim. A telephone rang and someone answered, calling out irritably, "Hey, Jim. Get it." The typewriter tapped out a fast, staccato line, fell silent, and started up again. Her eyes followed the slow progress of light across the floor: shadows had receded to within inches of the cell.

"You know what's funny?"

At the sound of her voice, he pulled his feet back and leaned toward her like a man at prayer.

"I've never touched one of your guns before. It must be that I'd seen you cleaning them, watched you show Cara how to handle the shotgun. I hated it, you know, encouraging her to take an interest."

"I didn't encourage her. She asked on her own."

"I know. She's always tried so hard to be your boy."

"What are you saying, Millie?"

"Just I knew more than I thought I did. At least I knew enough to release the safety and hold it out of harm's way."

She'd begun to glimpse why it was she'd grabbed his gun, the reason appearing like a small smudge on the horizon, bound up with other small things: the age and height of both her children, their favorite foods and beloved pets, the hours of the day they were most cranky or forgiving.

Then the specklike reason vanished, as unexpectedly as it had come, slipping over a distant edge. There was no reason after all. Counting was all she'd ever done, a human recorder, a hoarder of children's forgotten trinkets, of red maple leaves pressed between book pages, faded news clippings and honor-roll lists, a re-election poster with Trask's picture—a dreadful likeness that made him look as though his jaw were swollen.

Mere tidbits, nothing of consequence when she measured them against the world her daughters would soon enter, the heavy weave of outrage and confusion that Trask confronted every day. This was the unkindest part, making a place for the girls and Trask without being invited into theirs. That was her job, wasn't it? Making a place. Being their place. And now that place seemed bereft.

"Trask, have you ever had a 'running' dream?" she asked. "I have, time and again. I never seem to change in the dream. Even the scenery is the same. There are streets and traffic and tall buildings all around. Up ahead, there's someone I have to reach. I can see them but I have to run to catch up, and my feet are turning into lead. I keep moving—left, right, left, right—but my legs keep getting heavier, each step slower. Like I was moving through a pool of tar. Then I realize I've only been running in one place, and suddenly I can't lift my feet at all. When I look up, the person is gone."

Trask was staring at her, his back straight, smile gone. The young policeman called Trask to the phone. When he stood, she felt his presence grow larger in his imminent departure than when he sat beside her. The officer gazed at her, long enough for Mildred to think again how very young he looked. A child still. Like Emmy.

Sunlight had receded to the windowsill, the cell now lit by fluorescence seeping in from the open office.

"Mildred?" She looked up. Trask had put his hat on. "I'll be back shortly. Will you be ready?"

She didn't answer, and he turned and walked away.

Was a body ever ready? Trask was, always. So was Cara, favoring the father. Only Emmy's movements resembled her own. But Emmy, struggling so hard toward freedom, had taken a job and chosen to live away from home. She might plant a different tree to mark the year of Emmy's departure or in memory of the first, but somehow it seemed silly to turn one tree into a monument for another.

Mildred left the cell abruptly and walked up to a young black woman wedged against a computer terminal.

"I'd like to use the phone."

The ringing had an unfamiliar, abstract sound, like a recording of a ring. Cara answered, a woman's voice, full and low like her own. The sound of it left her jarred, as though she'd heard herself.

"Honey, I want you to take that chicken out of the freezer. Just put it in the sink."

"Mom? Is that you?"

The grown-up voice slipped back into the recognizable pitch of a daughter. Suddenly she wanted to ask Cara about the tree, whether it was standing or mutilated beyond remembrance.

"Where are you?" Cara asked, her voice suppressed, half-woman and half-child. She would have liked to tell Cara, to find the proper words, but no words came.

"When are you coming home?"

Yes, that was the question, wasn't it? "As soon as your daddy picks me up."

Her daughter sighed, relief made flesh, soft and unbearably lightweight.

The desk sergeant pointed to a plastic chair, one of three, beside the narrow entrance.

"Wait there, if you like."

Her handbag arrived and she signed a form that stated she'd received all her personal effects intact: wadded tissues, the brush, a worn-out tube of Chap Stick among the loose pennies and nickels and dimes. Under her hands the old brown bag felt as rough as homemade pumpernickel.

Take the chicken out. All she had to show for this time away from home was a command given to a daughter who could just as easily prepare a meal, if she had a mind to. Mildred's dress felt tight around her hips and arms, as though her joints had recently expanded. She'd put on more weight in twenty years than Trask had. Emmy said she still had a nice figure, but then Emmy always told you what she thought you wanted to hear.

Put it in the sink. A sink she'd cleaned every day for seventeen years, since Emmy was three and Cara a babe, scrubbing out coffee stains, carrot peelings, lumps of unwanted dinner and rejected pet kibbles. Her sink had received the stubs and threads from countless bushels of beans. It had filled with cornhusks, peach pits, cucumber skins, tomatoes whole and sliced, jams pressed and seeded, pulp she had rinsed and strained and thrown back upon the compost heap to be plowed into the garden she'd tended since the house was theirs. All those years of planting, hoeing, chasing off blackbirds and rabbits, picking the fruit and canning it in scalded jars that stood in tidy rows along a tidy pantry shelf Trask had built her.

So much feeding going on, and for people who would leave her anyway, as if eating were a method of departure. She saw the homegrown food washed away on a fast-moving bore of water, carrying off cats and dogs and children and bicycles and a husband older than herself, who left each morning for work that had nothing to do with her. Nothing had stayed close by, except the tree.

Mildred stared through the thick plate glass. Outside, the parking lot was bathed in such strong light the surface glared. A battered pickup turned noisily into the lot and parked. She watched the man get out, saw the boots appear first, one, two, plunked down like tree trunks. Then the man himself, a tall figure, blanched by sunlight. He removed a handkerchief from his hip pocket, wiped the brim of the hat and then his forehead. Quickly, he ran a comb through hair that had receded slowly but never grayed. The comb came and went so suddenly she was reminded of the swift, nervous grooming of a high school boy. She knew exactly where that comb was kept: behind the wallet in the right rear pocket.

She waited for him to put the hat back on. The arm holding the hat began to move, then stopped. The hat had always pinched his hair in a single uniform crease, as though he wore a bowl around his head. He hated that crimp. She knew.

He turned, sailing the hat through the open window of the truck, and she felt something inside her lift in ineffable sadness and joy. Whatever waiting was left to do would be there again tomorrow, to be picked up or put down for all eternity, if she chose. She watched him coming toward her, across the shimmering asphalt, unaware of being watched, moving with an unfamiliar spring, a young man's light, heart-lifting stride.

PIZZA MAN

〰️

The bus was late. He glanced at his watch again and thought of Mischa. At least it was Mischa who seemed to look back at him from the watch face, not time, as if Mischa were somehow responsible. Across the parking lot, a dozen men and their wives talked and gestured and examined their own watches, crushed out cigarettes and impatiently lit others, and for a moment Vladimir thought he would laugh. They should rename the apartment complex. Call it Little Kiev, not Briarwood Heights.

The heat was intense. They'd arrive for class, beaded with sweat. Even the few Kansans who lived in the complex had said it was unseasonably warm. "If you don't like the weather," they joked, "just wait a sec and it'll change." Vladimir unbuttoned a second shirt button, then a third. He missed his handkerchief. Four-year-old Yelena had taken all the handkerchiefs out of the drawer, pretending to iron and fold each one, and both he and Stella had forgotten to look on the girls' bedroom floor.

He wished Stella would come with him. She had come the first week, but when Yelena began to cry at the babysitter's, she wouldn't leave the child alone. The babysitter had urged Stella to go to class, but she was too upset and stood arguing with the woman—an Afghani—until someone sent for the director.

Stella. His glittering, laughing star. If he closed his eyes he could see her the way he loved her most, her smart boots striking the Kiev pavements with rhythmic taps, tossing fiery tendrils of hair, her eyes squints of merriment, a joke ready on her lips. When had she turned so fierce? *What is the matter with this country?* she'd asked him. *Don't they like children? Do they think it's all right to leave them alone in a room and let them cry?* She'd refused to come back to English school. When Susan, the social worker, told her how important it was, Stella had burst into tears.

"Later, Vlad," Susan had said, on her way out the door. "It will be all right later."

Nearly two months had passed, and it was not all right.

Vladimir could see Mischa and his wife through the window when the bus finally pulled into the lot. They had gotten on at the first stop, at the complex in Lenexa. Such a long ride, from suburbs to city. Forty-five minutes. Too long for the little girls, Stella said. *Tell me, my love,* he wanted to ask, *how often did the girls stand with you? And for how long? How many queues did you wait in, holding their hands?*

The seats around Mischa and Marina were taken. Mischa was slouched against the window, dozing. As Vladimir passed, Marina smiled and held out her hand, softening the blow of Mischa's silence, his eyes shut tight. He glanced at Mischa again and saw for an instant what it was Stella didn't like. The nostrils. Too arched and flaring. The nose like a knife.

Of course, Mischa was an arrogant man, but then, why not? Hadn't he earned it? Hadn't he come to America with as little as anyone else, and flourished? Wasn't he large enough to extend a helping hand? Hadn't he and Marina taken them to the Lenexa Spinach Festival in their bright red Mazda? But Stella had been so quiet in the car, so pulled in upon herself and not the Stella he knew, as though all her energy was being hoarded. When he told her later arrogance can make a man generous, she laughed at him—what a relief to hear her laugh—and pulled the strand of blond hair that coiled around his left ear, calling him her *durak*—her little fool. "Valodya, my love. Your 'friend' Mikhail would sell you the shirt off your back."

Reluctantly, Vladimir took the empty seat beside Bella. So lugubrious, this Bella, who lived with son and husband in the apartment next door. His behind had not reached the sticky green upholstery when she began to moan.

"Ah, Valodya, when it's hot in Kansas, it's wet. They say when it's cold in Kansas, it's wet too. My nose and eyes and neck, all swollen. You'd think a balloon lived inside. Tell me something. Does it ever dry out in Kansas? Not like Kiev, huh? Ah, Kiev. I tell you something, Valodya. I take a walk there every night in my dreams."

"But what about your Leonid," he asked. "Was his job so good there? His health?"

"I know, I know," Bella said, her great weight spilling over onto his seat. "'Better to be rich and healthy than poor and sick.' But Leonid is not so young, and an engineer has many masters."

"He was lucky," Vladimir said. "Remember this. They sent in the Jewish engineers first to clean out Chernobyl. Anatoly Perel went in. Did you see his pictures? The suit he had to wear?"

The yellow school bus lurched and swayed. Small fans feebly stirred the air, and most of the passengers had opened the windows. Bella's head began to bob, her body swaying forward and back as she moved.

"And what about your Sasha?" he went on. "And the grandchildren? What about my Yelena and Larisa? What about them? How could we possibly stay?"

Bella sighed and stopped rocking, leaned away from Vladimir toward the window and shut her eyes.

"Ah, my head," she muttered. "For three months now it aches."

The school occupied the top floor of an old brick church building, up steep and dirty marble stairs. Sometimes his feet stuck to the floor. Mischa and his wife had already reached the third floor, and Vladimir saw them speaking with the teacher, a tall young man whose curls spilled around his ears and forehead as though his hair led an independent life. Vladimir was always glad to see John. Such a jolly person, even if Vladimir couldn't understand his jokes.

He took a seat across the room from Mischa. It was best that way. John would only separate them if they sat down together, hoping to reduce the chatter by spacing out the languages into a jumbled patchwork quilt: Russian, Vietnamese, Spanish, Chinese, and then Russian again. Classroom perestroika, he thought with amusement, except it never worked. Vladimir felt as puzzled as the other Ukrainians at this odd rule that silence was golden. What on earth was a classroom for if not to talk? Never in his life had a teacher shushed a class, but the rules were different here and rather foolish. If he learned nothing else, he could tell Stella he'd learn to mind his tongue. He gazed across the room. Clever Mischa, with his back to the window, and here he sat, Vladimir Katsov, with the sun in his eyes.

John moved the exercise around the room, each student answering in turn, except Mischa answered for everyone, continuing to speak out of turn until John lost patience. ("Please, Michael. Your name isn't Thao. It's not José or Marina either. Keep quiet, okay?") Mischa nodded and said, "Sorry," even if he didn't mean it. Vladimir looked at his watch. He'd give Mischa three minutes before Mischa spoke out again.

John continued around the class, one by one, and Vladimir fidgeted in his seat. A diminutive man named Bui was speaking. He listened as the unrecognizable words came out in blocks of sound, with sharp edges in front and nothing behind. Bui stumbled over his sentence, floundered, retreated, and then midstream stopped completely. Across the room Mischa laughed out loud, and Vladimir looked down at his watch.

"*Lubimaya*—my love," he said and embraced his wife. "This school is the world in miniature. English lessons and free entertainment. You

must come back." He stepped away from her and let her continue scrubbing the counter top with her bright green sponge. "Think of what
you're missing."

Stella raised her arms and eyes to heaven, took the sponge, and threw
it in the sink. "Valodya, we have two girls. Have you forgotten?"

"Larisa is in school until two. Bring Yelena back. It will be good for
her English."

She turned her back to him angrily and picked the sponge back up.
"They speak every language under the sun at the babysitter's. Except
English." Her shoulders drooped, and he thought he was watching a
tree wilt. Stella slid into one of the chairs beside the small round table,
put her head down over her folded arms, and cried. He rushed to her
and placed his hand against her thick, red hair.

"What have I done, Stella? Tell me. What did I say?"

Stella lifted her head long enough to release a sob that flew out like a
shrieking bird. "*Durak*," she wailed.

"Please, Stella. Enough of these names. Enough."

She buried her face against her arms while he stroked her hair and
waited for the sobs to die down. She finally lifted her head. "I'm sorry.
It's just that I'm so tired. It must be the heat."

"Why is it you only want to stay inside this apartment? It's not the
heat, Stella. This isn't good. You had work once. You were a wonderful
designer. Such an eye for color. Why not do it here, too?"

The sobs renewed themselves, an engine revving up. He pulled up
another chair, put his arms around her, and held her tight while she
buried her face against him and cried. He gazed across the modern
white kitchen and rocked her gently back and forth. How she loved all
the clean white enamel, the white counter and cabinets, and how desperate they made him feel. The large colorless appliances—bleached
stones in a desert. He didn't know why the white kitchen made him
think of Israel. It was as close as they would ever come. Stella hadn't

wanted to go to Israel, even when he'd pleaded. "Don't you want to be a Jew among Jews? At last?"

"Who do we know in Israel?" she'd asked.

"Who do we know in America?"

"My cousin and his wife."

"Yes, but they are divorced now, and neither of them can sponsor us."

The argument had grown fierce, words piling up, Stella's face blotchy with anger and grief.

"They send you to the occupied territories," she shouted. "To be killed by angry Arabs. You want that for your children? No jobs. Tiny apartment. Nothing. Nice Ukrainian girls are becoming prostitutes out there on your West Bank."

Such a foolish thing to say. Of course he wanted only the best for them all. But now there was no possibility of a West Bank, or Kiev either—their beautiful, contaminated city—everywhere the silent pollution. There was only Kansas now.

He had just gotten Stella to lie down when the doorbell rang, and he rushed to the door before the bell sounded again. Mischa stood outside in the long gray-carpeted hall. Startled, Vladimir hesitated, his mind on Stella, until Mischa spread out his hands, his lips curling into the unfortunate smile.

"May I come in?"

"Of course, of course. It's just that Stella is sick. Here. The kitchen. Some tea, Mischa? A little bread?" The words tumbled out, hiding his embarrassment, the lapse of hospitality, and his worry over Stella.

"A little tea, please, Valodya. With lemon, if you have. No? Some strawberry preserves. No? Well, you know my Marina. She cannot have her tea without the lemon or her bread without preserves, so we must keep them in the cupboard. And the English biscuits too. I can tell you that Aldi's has the cheapest English biscuits."

"We don't buy them, I'm afraid."

"No?"

"Stella doesn't like too many sweets in the house. The girls, you know."

"Marina always keeps sweets for our little Valentina." Mischa laughed. The tall, arched nostrils flared back until there was hardly a nose at all, only a long thin shaft. Then Mischa's smile collapsed, the lips pursed thoughtfully.

"I think, Valodya, you're looking for a job."

"Yes, of course. Aren't we all?"

"I have the perfect job for you. Everyone who comes to America takes this job first. It's customary."

"And what job is that?"

"You drive?"

"Of course. You know that. I was a taxi driver for six months. Before emigration."

"From chemist to cabbie," Mischa said in a soulful voice, shaking his head slowly and allowing his eyes to flutter shut in sympathy.

"What can we do, eh?" Vladimir moved uncomfortably in his chair.

Mischa nodded. "Some are lucky. Some are not."

Stella's oft-repeated words returned to him. *And do you think it's only luck that your friend Mikhail did not lose his job? Think, Vladimir, think! A few rubles in the right hand? He's a Muscovite . . . Not one of us.*

As Mischa leaned toward him, Vladimir leaned back, uneasy.

"You're lucky you drive," said Mischa. "Many opportunities present themselves, but let me tell you about his job. The one so many new Americans take. I myself had this job, you know. And my boss said to me, 'Mike, if only I had some more drivers like you.' So I told him that I'd find him some. Reliable drivers, I tell him. 'Soviet workers know how to work,' I said."

"And who doesn't?" Vladimir said in a soft voice, "If you want to eat."

"So how long have you been here, Valodya?"

Vladimir glanced at the calendar Stella had put on the wall above the kitchen table, the one with pictures of baby animals. For the girls.

"Sixty-three days, today," he said.

"Just think. You'll be employed before anyone else who's been here two months!"

"What is this job? And what will I drive?"

"Today we only need to discuss the preliminaries. Come to our apartment on Saturday. I'll have the details then. Next week I'll take you to meet the president of the company, your future boss." Mischa tapped the tabletop with his fingertips in confirmation.

"Why so much mystery?"

"What mystery? I only wanted to find out if you would like a job."

"Of course. Who doesn't? But perhaps a few details now would help."

Mischa shrugged and hurriedly ran through the briefest of facts—food delivery, good hours, good tips.

"Come Saturday," Mischa said in a bare whisper and got up with purpose. "We'll have some tea. Maybe your little girls would like to come, too, and play with Valentina."

"Thank you," Vladimir answered quietly. Stella would not let them come, he felt sure, begging off with some excuse. *But Valentina is too old for our girls and too haughty. A true Muscovite, like her father.*

Vladimir didn't speak of it to Stella until after supper, when her headache was gone, the chores of the day behind her, the girls playing quietly and not yet fretful with fatigue. He could hear them in the background. They loved their room, enchanted with the space even if Susan said it was rather small. She hadn't seen the Kiev apartment, which had been nice in its way, with tall ceilings and good wood and ample light, but small. So small. One bedroom with an alcove, everyone shoved in together, he and Stella waiting to go to bed until after the girls were asleep, touching each other only when they could hear the soft purr of their daughters' sleeping breath.

When he told Stella about Mischa's invitation, she said, to his surprise, "Take Larisa. She's old enough to hold her own."

"Ten dollars an hour," he said. "Plus tips."

"What is this 'tips'?"

"The extra. The gratuity."

"You're going to be a waiter? My Valodya?"

"No."

"What then?"

"A driver. Mischa will give me the details Saturday."

Stella sighed. A house-sized sigh, a lifetime worth of sighs, as though
she might rid herself of every contaminated breath ever taken.

"Enough for now," he said and held up his hand.

For the third time Vladimir rang the bell, but still no one answered.
He took Larisa's hand, hesitated, and rang again. Perhaps they had gone
to Aldi's supermarket in Mischa's new car. "Come," he said to his
daughter, and they turned and started to walk down the corridor to the
stairs.

"Ah, there you are, my friend." Mischa's voice boomed out behind
them, and they turned. "I thought for a while you weren't coming."

"But we're right on time," Vladimir said. "As you can see."

"And this is . . . ?" Mischa looked at the girl. A smile pushed slowly
across his lips like paste from a tube.

"Larisa. My oldest daughter. You suggested . . ."

"Ah, of course, I did. But I'm sorry. Valentina went with her mother
somewhere." He closed his eyes and shook his head, as if *where* were of
no importance. "Come in, come in. Perhaps they'll be back soon."

Vladimir remembered the invitation, the promise of tea and English
biscuits, and felt himself sinking. He glanced at Larisa. The little girl
had taken a seat on the edge of a long white sofa that stood in front
of the window. A beautiful sofa, and new. Not like the cast-off green

couch and love seat that stood like boulders in their own living room.

"If this is a bad time, I can come again," he said, still standing.

"No, no, no. Now is the right time. Sit." Mischa pointed to the sofa, and Vladimir sat down slowly at the other end.

Mischa eased his tall frame into a plump black chair and pushed a lever. His body leveled out abruptly, parallel to the floor. An odd position to do business, Vladimir thought.

"Now, Valodya. You have a driver's license?"

"Yes. You know I do."

"Good. For many months I've worked for Paesano's. It's the best first job an immigrant can get. You know, Valodya, all new Americans with smarts, they first work for Paesano's."

"What is *Paesano's?*"

"Pizza," Mischa said, the word intoned as though it were holy. "You phone in your order, you tell the clerk where you live, you wait twenty minutes, and voilà! A driver brings your dinner to your door. You will be a driver for Paesano's," Mischa announced and slapped his thighs.

Vladimir felt his pulse quicken and his hands grow moist. Something about Mischa's smile.

"If you're smart." Mischa's lips parted, showing an even line of white teeth, and Vladimir felt himself disappear into the pure white sofa. "Remember. Ten dollars an hour, plus tips."

"When do I interview and meet the president?" Vladimir asked.

"This is your interview. Nowadays I only drive sometimes. Paesano's has made me the chief of the drivers, the finder of drivers. And now I have found you, my friend. You won't regret it. I only choose the best."

"With a driver's license, of course," Vladimir whispered. "And when do I start?"

"You must come to the office first, fill out the official papers, the tax forms."

"Tax forms?"

Mischa closed his eyes, offered up his grand shrug, his disdainful shoulders and smile. "Only a formality. Monday? Three o'clock. You can get there?"

Mischa pulled the lever on the chair. The recliner jumped forward, hurling him into a sitting position. Mischa reached across the space and handed Vladimir a card.

"It's not far from you or from me. Halfway in between. That's the address." Mischa pointed.

"I can find it." Vladimir examined the card a moment longer before placing it in his shirt pocket. "Three o'clock, Monday."

"I'll be waiting."

Vladimir paused a moment and glanced at his daughter. The Russian tea with jam. The English biscuits. He'd mentioned these to Larisa. If Mischa's wife were here, then perhaps. He rose to his feet.

"Thank you. Come, Larisa. We'll go now."

"*Da svidanya,* my friend." Mischa stood up slowly and remained standing in front of the reclining chair, bowing a good-bye while Vladimir and his daughter made their way to the door and out.

"Back so soon?" Stella looked up from her book as they walked through the apartment door.

"Valentina wasn't there," Larisa said.

He let the girl explain. Her story was more charitable than his would have been. She was merely disappointed. No Valentina, no Marina, no tea and English biscuits.

"What did you expect," Stella muttered, as much to herself as to them. "And the work?"

"I sign the necessary papers on Monday," he said.

"And what is the job?"

"Pizza delivery."

Stella nodded. "I hear this is a good job."

He stared at her. "What is this? My Stella thinks I've done something right? My wife, who can only think to call her husband *durak*?"

"Please, Valodya. Not now."

"Why not now? Since when did *not now* stop my Stella from calling names? Day and night, I hear the names. Needles and knives could not hurt me more, Stella. But now is 'not the time'?" He felt the anger mounting, hot and full and frightening.

"Sit. Please," she said. "Now is the time for some tea."

She took the stool and brought it over to the sink, climbed up, and opened the small cabinet overhead. Her arm disappeared into the dark recess of the cupboard, and when she stepped down, she held a small tin of tea and a long thin rectangular package.

"My secret," she said and held the two items out to him. "The things you thought this house would never have and your rich friend Mikhail's would. But you see? And we are not even rich."

The anger stopped before it peaked, receding like a wave pulled back from shore. Vladimir sat down without a word, watching her fill the kettle and put it on the stove. She unwrapped the anonymous package and removed a carton of tea cookies. With a teaspoon, she opened the lid on the small tin and measured two spoonfuls of loose tea into a pale green and pink flowered teapot—a wedding gift from his mother to Stella, carefully wrapped in her lingerie and brought in the luggage from Kiev. Stella folded her shapely arms under her ample breasts.

"English biscuits," she said. "From Aldi's. I got them for your birthday. But sometimes it's better not to wait."

She smiled, and for a moment he thought he might cry with relief.

He got lost once. He parked in the small lot behind the pizza parlor and saw Mischa's red Mazda near the back door. He wandered through the quiet restaurant until a teenaged clerk asked him what he wanted and took him finally to an office at the back. Mischa was sitting down, his right foot resting on the knee of his left leg, his back to the door.

"Mischa?"

Mischa lowered his leg, turned in the chair to look at him, then stood like a flag unfurling upward.

"There you are, at last," he said, with unnecessary briskness. After all, Vladimir thought, he was right on time.

Two other men stood in the office, and Mischa dismissed them without an introduction. He pointed Vladimir into a chair standing next to a small corner table that appeared to function as a desk. Mischa handed him a pen. Papers were whisked in front of him so swiftly he could scarcely read them. Mischa's hand never released its grip from the edge of each sheet, as if it didn't matter whether or not anyone read the documents. Vladimir's hand shook as he placed the point of the pen against each paper.

"Is there some urgency?" he asked and signed his name.

"Oh, no, no. Just boring details," Mischa answered.

Vladimir lifted the pen, and the paper disappeared from sight. Mischa walked across the room, opened a drawer in a tall black file cabinet, and the document disappeared a second time. Gone forever, he thought. Mischa gave the file drawer a snappy shove.

Vladimir felt his stomach drop, felt the hollowness that remained. So many files in so many cities. Everywhere a manila file, somewhere even a black one. He'd dreamt about a black file. His file. Was it the special color for Jews? Or only for those who'd announced their treacherous plan to emigrate?

And you say you work as a chemical engineer, said the man in his dream. *But your firm has asked you to step down?*

His life and that of his family contained in a slim black file. As soon as he'd applied for the exit permits, he was asked to leave, shunned by people who had worked with him every day for years.

You must find a job, said the man. *The State cannot support vagrants.*

But I had a job, and they took it away.

Perhaps you were a bad worker.

No, I'm a very good engineer, but that isn't why I have lost my job.

Impossible. The State does not release good workers.

We all know why I've been released, don't we?

Even Stella had supported and reassured him. He'd find something, she said, she was positive. *Valodya, my love, you are doing the right thing.*

And so he had worked for a publishing firm, translating educational texts from German to Russian, until he was summoned into a different cramped office and informed, for the second time, that he was being released. When he asked why, the editor shrugged. It wasn't for him to say. It was for him to follow directions, specified by his superior in the somewhat larger office upstairs. The man pointed over his head, his face sagging, inflamed with the colors of vodka.

Am I to finish the day's work?

You are free to leave now.

Free? Vladimir had laughed out loud, the sound coming out in one short, outraged blast.

The editor pretended not to hear and removed a chit, an IOU, which would allow Vladimir to collect his small translator's salary and bread coupons in one month's time. He doubted he would ever see the money or the bread. Would they allow Stella to collect the bread if he were arrested for vagrancy?

His thoughts had moved in unfamiliar loops, back again and again to the chit. Whenever he shaved, took off his socks and shoes, washed his hands, or turned off the light for the night, the words came back, repetitive and obsessive, like the shrill notes of a penny whistle played by a very young child. *You are free to leave. Free.*

"Valodya, my friend," Mischa said in a loud English voice. "You are sitting there, gathering wool."

Vladimir stood up and spread his arms in a shrug. "And now?"

Mischa reached out and took Vladimir's small hand in his long, confident fingers, and shook it. "Welcome to Paesano's Pizza!"

He would work from four to eleven, four days a week, Thursday through Sunday, the busy days. He would drive a Paesano hatchback. At first he was afraid he'd have to use his own unreliable old car, but Mischa had placed a hand on his shoulder, threw back his head with its thatch of black hair, and laughed. A short, round man in a baseball cap stuck his head through the office door and called out, "Hey, Mike, you got keys?"

"This is Al," said Mischa. "He'll break you in."

Break you in? He must ask Mischa about this odd expression, as if people were locked and keyless doors. Before he had a chance, Mischa took his hand off Vladimir's shoulder, walked to the desk, removed a set of car keys, and threw them gamely in the direction of the driver. The keys fell short and dropped at the small man's feet. Al bent over and picked them up, saying, "I'm taking out a load now. You want this guy to come along?"

Wondering if he oughtn't first call Stella, Vladimir was ushered out to the small delivery car. The back seat was folded down, and an aluminum box rested on the flattened surface.

"For the pizzas," Al said. "Keeps 'em warm. So, tell me, Vlad, how d'ya like Kansas?"

"So-so," he said seriously.

"'Auntie Em! Auntie Em!'" Al shouted in falsetto, laughing in a voice like a tropical bird. Eyes twinkling, he looked at Vladimir, as if to gauge the effect, and burst out again. "'Run, Toto! Run!'"

Vladimir stared at him hard. So Mischa hired lunatics as well, one fact he would not share with Stella.

"Guess you don't know about the Land of Oz and all that jazz."

"No. What's this *Oz*?"

"Ooooh, boy," Al muttered. "You'd better ask Mike."

Al backed the car out of its space with the force of a rocket, then shifted forward. The car shot into the street, veered drunkenly left and right whenever Al turned a corner. Vladimir threw out his arm and braced himself against the dash. It would take some practice, driving like Al. Perhaps he wouldn't even try. When he was a taxi driver in Kiev, his boss had given him the only compliment he'd received in months. *You are a smooth and careful driver. But now you must learn to drive a little faster so we may increase our fares.* He never learned to drive faster. The exit permits came instead, and he and Stella and the little girls left for good. When he told his boss—a thin, gray man with no strong feelings for or against Jews—the man had shrugged and wished him well. *You will always find a job as a driver, Valodya. But do yourself a favor. Speed up.*

When he returned to the store with Al, Vladimir phoned Stella to tell her he was "in training." He wouldn't be home until 10:00 or 11:00.

The next afternoon he arrived early, filled with expectation. Today Mischa would turn over a car and orders for pizzas. Mischa told him to sit down and wait until his shift began. *Shift.* Vladimir listened to the word and smiled. What was he to shift? Where was his shift? His neighbor Leonid walked through the door, followed by his son. A complete expatriate community, waiting for their shifts to begin. For a moment, the job felt tarnished. Mischa was everyone's best friend.

What was it Mischa had said, this was the best first job for newcomers? *Newcomers.* He liked the name and rolled it silently across his tongue. A good shape, round and confident, and he whispered it to himself again.

Mischa was striding toward him now, a set of keys in his hand. "Follow me."

Back and forth Vladimir drove, through the well-watered suburban neighborhoods without sidewalks, around the endless shopping malls. He walked less briskly as the night wore on, from car to house to car. By the end of that first evening, he'd made over twenty dollars in tips. ("You don't tell me about the tips," Mischa said, "and I won't ask.") During that first week Stella waited up, steeping tea, eagerly watching him place the tips down on the kitchen table. They separated the bills by value, stacked the coins, and gleefully moved the piles around as if they were children's building blocks. Stella took ten percent for family treats, and the next day before work, Vladimir deposited the remaining tip money in the bank.

"So what do you think of your *durak* now?" he asked one morning before Stella was fully awake.

Her full lips turned down. She pulled the edges of her bathrobe together at her throat and stared at him blankly, and his bright morning mood drained away. He wanted to tease her, reach across the table and pinch her round, soft cheek. But he'd grown afraid of her, afraid of her new, fierce feelings and disconsolate moods. All the names that crossed her lips these days, when once they had been names reserved for shopkeepers, inept repairmen, government apparatchiks. How easy it had been for her, here in Kansas, to find a new target in him.

"I'm teasing," he said quickly.

The tea was ready. Stella got up and poured them each a cup without a word, the silence filled with reproach.

"So," he said softly, as his fear of her took hold of his tongue. "What will you do today?"

Not answering or even looking up, she stared into her cup. How sad she looked, how wildly beautiful, her thick red hair still tangled with sleep. For a moment she reminded him of one of her own sketches.

"Maybe you'll start drawing again."

"With what, Vladimir?"

Where were those proud and merry eyes? They looked at him now as if from the bottom of a well. His new fear dwindled away in sorrow.

"We'll get you the materials you need. Now that I'm working, we'll get them. I promise."

"It's time to expand our reach," Mischa said in English.

The address was in Missouri, he explained. The same street ran east and west, through both states. A long, long street. Mischa spread the map across his desk and traced the street from end to end while Vladimir watched.

"Somewhere over here." Mischa inhaled deeply, noisily, pinching his nostrils in contemplation. It became clear Mischa had no idea where the address might be.

"Let me take the map along," Vladimir said and folded it.

The caller had ordered two large pizza "supremes." Vladimir went into the kitchen to collect them and carried them out to the waiting hatchback. He slid the boxed pies into the warmer, closed the hatch, and climbed into the car. Carefully, he opened the map and folded it into a square, the section he needed facing up at him from the passenger's seat. He left the parking lot and turned onto the long east-west street, traveling at a deliberate, leisurely pace.

A light turned red, and Vladimir eased to a stop, realizing he'd crossed out of Kansas and into Missouri. How odd, to slide from one state to another, with nothing to mark the passage except the color of the street signs. He glanced down to the map. Five, maybe six blocks more, then he had to turn right for a short while, then east once again.

The street he wanted rushed by him before he was ready. Not much traffic held him up, and at the following intersection he turned left, hoping to turn around. He inched the car along the street, looking for a drive. The asphalt rolled down on either side, into shallow culverts. There were no sidewalks in front of the modest bungalows. The driveways appeared narrow and full of large, well-waxed American cars. He had gone into the next block before he found a driveway where he could easily pull in and turn around. As soon as he'd put the car in reverse, a large knot of teenage boys tumbled out of a house. Fussing with the rearview mirror, he hadn't seen more than a blur out his windshield. He pulled the hatchback into the street parallel to the house and straightened the tires. One boy approached the car and waved his hand to stop him. Vladimir waited, paying scant attention to the others who were beginning to disperse up and down the street, while two of the boys went back inside the house, laughing and raising their arms in some sort of triumphal gesture.

"Hey, pizza man." the boy shouted at the closed window. "I wanna talk."

Vladimir rolled down the window.

"I wanna make an order."

"Please call the store. Here." He handed the boy a Paesano's promotional menu through the car window. Instead of taking it, the boy grabbed his wrist and bent his hand back until he thought it would snap off. Vladimir gasped. The boy brought his other hand through the window and covered Vladimir's mouth.

"Outta the car, man," he said and released Vladimir's wrist.

He felt faint with pain, and it was all he could do to make the twisted arm open the door. He stumbled out, leaving the door ajar.

"Over here," the boy commanded, and Vladimir moved against the side of the hatchback, down to the trunk. With his foot, the boy slammed the car door shut while his right hand disappeared inside the pocket of his jacket. Vladimir gazed at him.

"I got a piece in here." The boy raised his jacket by the hidden hand in the pocket.

"A piece of what?" he asked.

"You think you a comedian, man?"

"I'm sorry. I don't know these words." His voice sounded more heavily accented than ever, the newcomer's voice of two months ago.

"Jeez! Got us a retard here," the boy said with scorn, rolling his eyes. "Okay. Listen up. I want all your money. Got that?" The boy, no taller than Vladimir, danced up on the balls of his feet, his head held back while his chin jutted out toward Vladimir, his eyes narrowing. "And I want it now." He grabbed Vladimir's arm with his free hand.

"No money. First stop." Vladimir stared at him, pulled up his shoulders, and shrugged as best he could, since the boy still gripped his sleeve.

"Okay, man. You gonna gimme all the pizzas you got in the van."

"Not so many," Vladimir whispered.

"Now! The gun is in the pocket. You got that?"

Vladimir walked slowly around to the hatch, the boy following behind. How old was he anyway? Fourteen? Fifteen? With his black hair built up in a wedge, his jacket too large, his huge white and purple shoes encasing his feet and half his shins like orthopedic tubs. Vladimir opened the rear while the boy stood at his shoulder and peered over it to the aluminum heating box.

"Oh, man. Two pizza! That all ya got, you fuck? Two pizza?"

Enraged, Vladimir turned and stared at the boy. Was it a national hobby to hurl names about? Or was it something in the air? Now this juvenile delinquent, with no hair on his face and a skyscraper of hair on his head, was calling him names, mauling him like a criminal, and at the same time whining over the food! Two pizza? Ha! Vladimir nearly laughed.

"*Tupitsa!*" he spat out in Russian. The word for idiot. "You want? I give."

Swiftly, furiously, he removed the boxed pie, opened one end before the boy could stop him, turned like a dancer, and wrapped the still warm pizza over the boy's head.

The boy let out a muffled cry and staggered back. Vladimir gave him a shove, and the boy fell sideways, tripping over the enormous shoes, legs strangely crossed like a monk at meditation.

"You fuck," the boy yelled through the crust. "What'd you do?" The crust slid off his head. Cheese, tomato sauce, and black olives slices clung to his hair and eyelashes while a small round of pepperoni slid down one cheek. Vladimir ran to the front of the car and climbed in.

Through the rearview mirror he saw the boy crawl over onto his knees and shake his head. Why, he was only a child. Vladimir turned the key and raced the engine. The car didn't move.

Vladimir yelled at the car and then jammed it into gear. The hatchback lurched forward, and he sped away, retracing the route to Kansas.

His heart banged against its bony cage, tires shrieked, and he wheeled the car into the Paesano parking lot. He slammed on the brakes and felt himself lurch first front then back, the little car moving like a steel hammock. For a moment he lay his head against the steering wheel until he realized the horn was blaring and lifted himself, leaning back against the headrest. He turned off the engine and removed the key, his body so loose and thick he felt as though his limbs were made of jam. When he finally opened the door, he felt such light-headed relief he was afraid he might leave the car headfirst. Vladimir shut his eyes. When he opened them, Mischa was standing beside the vehicle, leaning toward him.

"My friend, I think you're not well."

"No, Mikhail. I've never been better," he said bitterly. "I've traveled across two states and survived. I'm sorry, but I must go home now."

Vladimir rose out of the car, took one step, and sank. Mischa grabbed him under the arms, pulled him up, and leaned him against the side of the hatchback. For the second time in less than ten minutes, he felt himself pressed against the cold steel of the car. He laughed, but the sound coming out was strangled.

"What is it?" Mischa whispered. "Tell me, Valodya."

"Please. If you are truly my friend, don't ask."

He gazed into Mischa's face and saw the bladelike nose, the dark and penetrating eyes, only then feeling Mischa's hands on his shoulders. He hadn't expected Mischa's hands to be so strong. These were hands that knew how to hold onto things, how to take. Had Mischa ever been afraid? Or was it fear that made a man grasp and climb and hold on to this strange new life? Vladimir steadied himself, gave Mischa a weary smile, staring at him until Mischa finally released his shoulders.

He didn't know how long he'd stayed at Paesano's or what it was Mischa had given him to drink, forcing him to come into the office and sit down and talk. He couldn't remember what he'd said, could scarcely remember driving home or parking the car or walking up the stairs to the second-floor apartment. He thought he'd closed the door quietly, but Stella called out anxiously from the bedroom. "Valodya?"

He couldn't answer but moved toward her voice and stood in the doorway to the bedroom where she'd been resting, his arms and hands hanging down as if they'd been badly attached. Stella quickly came to him with arms outstretched, folded his small frame into her full, soft flesh, drawing him toward the bed. "Mischa phoned. He told me everything."

Trembling and pale, Vladimir lay on his back, staring toward the ceiling, seeing nothing, hearing nothing but the steady drone of the air conditioner in the south window. He turned his head and looked at her. Stella smiled. He remembered those lips, the full, defiant, and humorous mouth. Had she come back to him at last?

"Where are the girls?" he asked suddenly, his voice urgent.

"They're next door with Bella. They're fine."

She began to smooth his hair away from his forehead, and he shut his eyes. Her hand felt so cool. He heard her murmuring something. *Lubimaya*. Was that it?

"Newcomers," he said at last.

"What's that?"

"What they call us. The nice name anyway." His mind raced over the other names he'd so recently heard, and he shuddered.

"What's in a name, huh, Valodya? Larisa tells me that she's now called Lara at school, and your little Yelena is now Helen." Stella laughed lightly, her hand stroking his hair. "Maybe we should both change ours."

"And why would you want to change yours?" he asked. Her name sounded to him like a healing balm: *Stella, Stella, my star.*

He didn't want to talk but rolled toward her, burying his face in her lap, shutting out the room, the sun, and all of Kansas while the small west window brimmed with hot summer light.

ANIMAL HEAVEN

n her large clinic play room—the Children's Room, with its bright lights, cheerful posters, soft furniture, and rugs and toys—Ronnie Watanabe sat patiently in a contoured chair. The six-year-old boy coiled at her feet was humming as if he had a cicada trapped inside his chest. Ronnie got up and went over to the gaily painted toy box. She removed a Snoopy doll, a large soft toy with basset hound ears. She cradled the doll and hummed. The boy peeped at her from his half-closed lids while she sang to the dog. She held it in one arm, returned to her chair and asked the boy if he would like to hold the dog himself.

She hadn't always been "Ronnie." She'd changed her given name from *Hiromi* after realizing it was a stumbling block for the children.

The boy jerked his legs out, grunted, rolled over, expanding the process of getting up into a complex ritual of limbs that kicked and joints that poked in alternating gestures of submission and protest. He stood up finally and weaved over to her chair, stopped to lean against the armrest before turning his back to her.

"Here," Ronnie said. "Maybe you'd like to hold Snoopy."

He said nothing but began to push his small backside against her chair in rhythmic, pulselike bumps. He kept on bumping the chair, touching her arm.

"Come around to the front," Ronnie said.

The boy didn't move, and she didn't push. Where he lived, someone was always pushing.

"You talk funny," he said.

Ronnie smiled. Nowadays no one except the children mentioned her accented English. Her *Janglish*, as Frances called it. The boy slid down the side of the chair to the floor, rocking from side to side.

"Well, my arm is getting tired, Kevin. Would you like to hold Snoopy for me?"

The look he gave her, up over his shoulder, was swift and full of doubt.

"Why don't you just put him back in the box," he said with a logic that flooded the room like light. Ronnie wanted to laugh out loud.

"That's a good idea, or maybe you want to do it for me."

He raised one hand up over his head to receive the toy, never once turning toward her. Ronnie placed the Snoopy doll in his hand. Kevin didn't look at the toy but held it stiffly above his head, then flung it across the room toward the box.

Ronnie wanted to bring living animals for the children to hold. A Snoopy toy wouldn't do for a child like Kevin. He needed soft, living fur and animal patience. She mentioned this to Frances, her supervisor and friend, but cautious Frances only pinched her eyebrows together.

"Is it safe?" Frances asked. "Where will you get them?"

From the Animal Haven, Ronnie explained. They will loan out their best: a golden retriever, a placid old cat, and a silky gray and white rabbit.

She would have liked to tell Frances about her happy Japanese childhood, filled with animals and insects. But she was learning that in America it wasn't always useful to admit you'd had a happy childhood. She reminded herself to mention Kevin when she wrote her father this evening. For some reason Father had taken an interest in this rough, wild boy, even though they lived seven thousand miles apart and would never meet.

By the time they reached the East Bottoms in the early evening, the rain had turned to a heavy mist. James opened the trunk and took out the little shopping cart and dog food while Salvador walked over to the warehouse gate, calling King's name. Ronnie found it a strange neighborhood. The homes and warehouses shared their narrow boundaries with railroad tracks. The houses were old and in need of paint, their occupants white, yet the most amazing gardens bloomed here. Ronnie wasn't looking at the chrysanthemums today. She was looking for King, who lived in a large wood crate, attached to the crate by a ten-foot chain.

She knew James didn't like to come here. If the owner of this yard were here, he would yell at James and call him "nigger." King, with his twenty feet of living space, was surrounded by his own waste, which his owner didn't often bother to clean up. So Ronnie did. Salvador was especially fond of King. He believed the dog had a sense of humor in spite of his circumstances.

Sal climbed the fence easily and opened the gate, which was never properly locked but held shut by an elaborate twist of rusting wire. No one in this neighborhood would trust the police enough to call them. Ronnie wheeled in the food while Sal rubbed the big dog's ears and called him Chico, speaking to him in Spanish. James stood watch just inside the gate. Ronnie knew he felt better when they went over to the east side of town.

King had no water. King never had water. "Water weakens bones," said Mr. Wiezenski. Ronnie exhorted him, offered to pay him one dollar every week if he would just keep the old chipped bowl full of water and leave it for King.

"You a little busybody, you know that?" he said. "Where you from anyway?"

She preferred to visit King when she knew Mr. Wiezenski wasn't there, and since he'd never installed an alarm, Sal could safely climb the fence and open the gate. She'd learned about King, as she'd learned about all the other dogs, from complaints sent to the Animal Haven. When she was a student of twenty and newly arrived in the city, she'd volunteered at the Haven. She'd filled up many lonely hours cleaning cages, brushing coats, playing with cats, and walking dogs. The animals didn't mind if she spoke to them in Japanese.

King's crate was large and sturdy as a doghouse. It met the minimum city requirements. Mr. Wiezenski didn't beat his dog. He simply ignored him, hoping this neglect would make the animal fierce. Ronnie asked him how King could protect the yard if he were always tied up. She suggested King might be a better guard dog if he was turned loose at night, and Salvador stopped by one evening to check. The dog was still chained to his crate.

They gave him water and food and brushed his coat, and Ronnie hugged him. King licked their hands, then sat down as they prepared to leave. When she glanced over her shoulder, she saw King watching them, and she was struck by the wonder she so often felt when she realized animals didn't feel sorry for themselves.

The heavens were full of animal angels, of souls released from pain, some waiting to become men. Every day her convictions were renewed: she'd been entrusted with a special task, and her parents had let her leave home, nineteen years ago, so she might fulfill her trust.

They had come to visit her once before Mother died. Ronnie had given her parents her bedroom while she slept on the couch. Mother had wanted to accompany her everywhere, especially the clinic. And without a word of English, she had delighted the children by making them origami cranes and boxes and crabs. (The children had especially liked it when Mother wore her kimono.) The day before her parents returned home, Mother bought her the little shopping cart—"For the dogs, Himi-chan."

James drove them onto Chestnut Trafficway to the Avenue, down the Avenue to the Paseo, turning east at Twelfth. They'd come to visit Scout and Bear and Rambo, all large male dogs of indeterminate breed, chosen for their size and imagined ferocity. James was more relaxed behind the wheel now. In these neighborhoods he didn't feel disadvantaged. He was a tall young man, lean and very black, with a long serious face accented by thick glasses. Ronnie believed if James had been born differently, he might have become a doctor, not a practical nurse. She was struck by his seriousness, his dignity, and devotion to his church. She seldom heard him complain.

"Tell Salvador how you got started in this work," James said, but it was he who liked to hear the story of her life, she knew.

"Yes, tell us," said Salvador, his accent heavier than her own. "How come you wanna do this after you spend all day with those crazy *niños?*"

He meant the children referred to the hospital, the ones like Kevin, whom Ronnie worked with and counseled. She'd been a psychiatric social worker for nearly sixteen years. Frances called their work pediatric psychology, or "pedi-shrink" for laughs. But Ronnie had come to think of her young patients as the children hiding from God.

Ronnie leaned toward the two young men in the front seats. It amazed her still that James and Salvador, both from the hospital, agreed to help her with the dogs, especially since their own jobs offered them so little satisfaction. (It was a double blessing, because James preferred to drive.) She was so grateful she didn't wish to upset this gift of help by asking why.

"Come on, Ronnie. Tell Sal," James repeated.

"Have you ever heard the American Indian story about dogs and men?" she asked Sal, who shook his head. "They say when the gods chose to separate the world of men from the world of animals, they opened the earth along a great chasm. Before the chasm grew too wide, Dog jumped across it to cast his fate with Man, forever." She smiled at Sal and leaned into the depths of the back seat.

"I believe small children and dogs are much alike," she went on. "When you get up in the morning, they're happy to see you, as long as you love them. But if you beat them or shout, their hearts sink down, and they duck their heads when they see you come."

Ronnie took out a piece of paper and wrote the word *dog* on a small pad she carried with her. "Look," she said and showed Sal the word. "What is this word backward?"

He printed each letter painstakingly and said, "God."

"What a funny language!" She laughed.

"Tell Sal how you came here," James piped up.

And so she began again the story she was sure James had heard at least three other times. To Ronnie it wasn't an exceptional story. "That's because you're living it," James told her.

"I was the youngest child of four, the third daughter who did well in all her tests. My parents were very kind. They let me leave Japan because I'd won a Fulbright scholarship and because I was the youngest. So I came here to study English and who knows what else. You see, my oldest sister and older brother have all the responsibility." Ronnie laughed, feeling self-conscious that she'd talked too much.

Her last trip home was five years ago when her mother died. Nowadays she felt no urge to return. Yes, it was the expense, and she allowed this reason to take precedence over all the others, which were nearer the truth. Who would take over for a month or six weeks? How could she ask James and Salvador to step in? And how could she remove herself for more than two weeks at a time from children who suffered so much upheaval?

But Himi-chan, she could hear her sisters chiding, *you have no one to look after you. And no one that you look after.*

She had her friends, she would tell them. So many friends, at work and after work, too.

But friends are not family, they would say, the final argument, meant to bring her down.

"We have a big family, don't we," she said to Sal. "Four children. Big for Japan, anyway. But my father is a Buddhist priest. They often have big families."

"Four kids! That's not big," said James. "Shoot, there're seven of us. How many you got, Sal?"

Salvador laughed. "I forget to count!"

As Salvador talked, Ronnie watched his round, animated face. She wondered if all Mexicans were so cheerful and ready to help. He had kind eyes, and the fact he was nearly as short as she was made her trust him immediately. All she really knew about him was for the last year he'd worked in housekeeping on the same floor where she treated the children, and he and James had become friends. She was happy for this. Frances once told her Blacks and Mexicans had little use for each other.

What she did remember clearly was the moment James began to take an interest in the dogs. It was the day after Ronnie had offered to care for the moribund dog of an old, half-blind black man who ran a scrap metal yard.

"You a meddlin' fool!" the old man had told her. "This' private property. You got no business with me or my dog."

She told him it was likely the dog would die without help.

"No, ma'am. He ain't gonna die. My Rascal ain't gonna die. He just sick in all this terrible heat."

"I can help," she said.

She bent over to lift the animal's head, to look into its eyes, when the old man brought his cane down across her shoulders, startling himself as much as Ronnie. Ronnie gasped in pain, and the old man gasped in surprise.

"Everybody want to take somethun' from the black man," he said, his voice shaking with fear and rage. "Now here come this Vietnamee girl and she want to take away my very own dog. Now, you git! Don't need no do-gooders here!" He raised the cane again, but his arm shook and the cane hung there useless. Ronnie got to her feet and stepped back. She looked into the man's fog-colored eyes and wished she could take his pain away.

She walked out of the scrap metal yard, pulling her cart, and he yelled after her. "Tell me, girl. Would you help a man dying in the street?"

The next day at the hospital her neck and arm felt stiff. When she saw him in the hall outside her room, she asked James if he wouldn't mind pulling open a cabinet door for her, since she didn't seem to have any strength. He saw the bruise, and when he asked her what had happened, she told him.

"You got no business going over there alone!" he said with great noise and indignation. "You need a body guard. I'll come. Now, tell me again. What is it you do?"

That night, in the long slow hour before bed, she thought about the Kyoto home of her childhood, the large drafty wooden house with its slate gray tiled roof surrounded by ferns and rhododendrons and azaleas, evergreens, plum trees, maples, and cherries. In the nearby temple, where her father served as its principal priest, there was a quiet rock garden in front of the east verandah. Here visitors to the temple took tea and contemplated the ancient rocks in their frosty jackets of moss. Ronnie—Hiromi then—found tree frogs in the gardens of both the temple and her home. She and her sisters and brother chased cicadas and dragonflies and beetles.

The space under the family verandah attracted stray cats, and Hiromi left them tiny bowls of water and rice. Then there were Mother's beloved dogs: Shiro (Whitey) and Momotaro (Peach Boy, Brother's favorite) and the large brown animal with the plumed tail called Benkei (Ronnie's favorite), named for the legendary warrior monk. When they died Mother mourned the dogs, keeping a small shrine for them in the kitchen. Not even Father laughed.

Ronnie took a sheet from her writing folder—a pale blue rice paper, a gift from home. She filled her pen with the blue-black ink and thought of her father as though she were reciting an invocation . . . *amida nembutsu, namu amida butsu*. Each evening note was carefully saved, placed in an envelope with the notes of previous days, and sent out once a week. She placed her pen on the paper, resurrecting her Japanese. At least the *hiragana* and *katakana* were still accessible. The old Chinese *kanji* was disappearing. Her skill wasn't so much fading, she thought, as petrified. She used the language so seldom and wondered if this weren't the reason for the daily letter: the only remaining way to cherish one part of who she was. She seldom spoke Japanese anymore.

Dear Father,

Fumiko tells me you are feeling poorly. I'm so sorry. I pray for you every night, and I think of you every day. Perhaps the evening walk, at your age and in a Kyoto winter, is not good for your health.

You mustn't worry that I have become a one hundred percent American. (Fumi-chan thinks I have. She thinks I'm hopeless!) No fear of that. Every day I am reminded of my difference.

No, I don't keep a pet. It wouldn't be fair. I live alone in a two bedroom apartment, as you know, and I'm seldom home, although sometimes I nurse the sick ones. Like a foster mother.

Do you remember the winter night that Benkei-kun slept in the kitchen? You were so horrified to find him inside the house. "Doesn't this dog have his own house?" you demanded of Mother. "Yes," she said. "But it is too small and too cold on a night like this. Just for the night, Oto-san." You protested, threw up your hands and left the house for your evening walk. When you returned Benkei was still in the kitchen, on a rug. Mother had prepared you a hot bath. You said nothing but let Mother scrub your back until you were the color of a boiled prawn.

Your daughter, Hiromi

"Do they beat children in Mexico?" Ronnie asked Salvador while thinking of her young clients to the Children's Room.

"They beat them everywhere," he said. He was returning a stack of towels to the storeroom.

"Does that mean you were beaten?"

"No, I wasn't beaten. Not with a stick or a whip. But my mother, sometimes she—¿cómo se dice?" He pantomimed a hand spanking a bottom.

Ronnie searched back through her thirty-nine years. She didn't remember anyone laying a hand on her, not even the fiercest of her teachers, and never ever Mother.

She asked James while he was taking a break, joking with the women at the nurses' station.

"I misbehaved," he told her. "My mama, she spanked and she spanked. Maybe it did me some good."

Ronnie stared at him and smiled sadly. "It never does," she said.

The boy named Raymond, sitting on Ronnie's left, was always pulling his head down between his shoulders like a turtle. He drew pictures of frightful armored trucks and men covered with metal scales. She asked him what he would do if he had a pet. A dog, say. Would he draw her a picture of the dog he would like to have? He drew a figure covered with plates; not even the eyes appeared. Beside it was a tall, round dog, plated like an armadillo, with spikes around his neck. Ronnie asked him if this was Raymond and his dog. He nodded. She pointed to the spikes.

"Are these comfortable for the dog?" she asked.

He assured her they were.

"What do they do?" she asked, pointing.

He considered this a moment. He was an earnest little boy, blessed with imagination and made serious by too many blows.

"It saves the dog from bad people," he said.

Raymond spoke often of bad people.

Kevin, meanwhile, was making the sound of crashing breakers, of smashing cars and accidents. He was prolific with his noise-making, and so authentic that, once, not seeing him in the room, Ronnie rushed to a window, thinking she'd heard a collision in the parking lot outside. Kevin took a black crayon from the box and scribbled harsh lines over the surface of the paper. Raymond had taken his paper and stretched full-length across the playroom floor. He too had taken a black crayon, and a green one, coloring in the turrets, balconies, gates, and crenellations of a complex, top-heavy fort.

"Who lives here?" she asked Raymond.

"My soldiers," he said.

There was one last child in the first-grade group, a girl so wispy and blond that she reminded Ronnie of a dandelion gone to seed. Ronnie leaned forward and whispered to this child, afraid the rush of air from her lungs would blow the girl apart.

The girl didn't move and kept her hands hidden under the table. Ronnie picked blue and yellow crayons from the box and offered them to the girl, who stared at them a moment before taking them. The little girl was new to the Children's Room, and Ronnie watched her carefully. For a second she was painfully reminded of the dog named Rambo, a Rottweiler-mix, protector of an automobile junkyard, chained inside an old car, and catatonic from neglect.

Ronnie spoke in a lilting feminine voice, a dove coo, a vestige of

Japan, deliberately preserved for the sake of the children, and the dogs.

The dandelion girl held the bright crayons so tightly her knuckles lost their color. Ronnie reached out and covered the child's stiff white hand with her own. She came around the table and sat beside the girl, took a sheet of paper for herself, and began drawing pictures of rabbits: white ones with pink eyes, a gray and white one like Peter from Animal Haven, black ones, and then, for fun, a purple bunny with orange ears and tail. The boys laughed, but the dandelion girl looked at Ronnie, puzzled, and started to cry. Ronnie pulled the child onto her lap and continued drawing white and brown and pink-eared rabbits, talking to the girl, talking, talking with her dove coo voice, until the child picked up a pink crayon and drew a perfect circle on Ronnie's paper and meticulously filled it in.

When she arrived home, Ronnie went immediately to the spare bedroom. The shades were always drawn, and the space was intimate and small. Without turning on the overhead light, she went to the far wall and opened what appeared to be a cabinet but was in fact an altar. She took a matchbook and lit a stick of incense and a candle and began to say her prayers, *amida nembutsu . . . namu amida butsu*. She liked sitting in the dark. When it was dark, she thought more clearly about the three panels of her life—clinic, dogs, and home.

By the time James and Salvador picked her up for their early evening rounds, she felt calm and ready to begin again.

"Where to first?" James asked.

"King. We haven't been there in four days."

"No, a week," Salvador reminded them.

They drove in silence. Tuesday was always a tired day, for the young men as well as for Ronnie. She'd come to think of Tuesday as the most difficult and joyless day of the week.

Twilight was all they had by the time they reached Wiezenski's warehouse, but Ronnie, who liked to plan ahead, had shoved a large flashlight into the deep pocket of her poncho as she left the apartment. Salvador was already over the fence before she and James had the dog food and cart out of the trunk. When they reached the gate, it was still closed.

"Sal! Hey, man, the gate," James called, but there was no answer at first. Ronnie reached awkwardly through the mesh and began to untwist the wires herself.

"Salvador?" James called, louder this time.

They heard feet clicking rapidly over the cement yard, and then they saw Salvador emerge from the gloaming.

"He's sick," Sal said and untangled the wire. "Come."

He moved away from them until they lost him in the dark. They followed the sound of his feet, in the direction of King's crate. By the time they reached it, Sal was stooped in front of it. The big dog lay inside and wouldn't come out.

"King . . . hey, Chico," Sal said in a soft voice and pushed the big dog's eyelid open. Ronnie shone the light down into the animal's face and examined the opened eye.

"Well, he's alive." She handed the flashlight to Sal, bent down, lay a hand on the animal's chest and felt the faint thump of its heart, the feeble pulse at his throat.

"He's dying, isn't he?" James said.

Sal quickly removed King's collar and released it from the chain, which he flung to the ground with disgust. Ronnie took the red collar from Sal's hand and put it in her pocket. Sal took hold of the big dog under its front legs and around its chest and slowly, gently, lifted and pulled him out of the box.

"He's heavy," Sal said. "Maybe we get him to the car."

Sal was small and James so tall that the two men staggered until they had the weight distributed between them. Ronnie ran ahead and opened the gate. They put the dog in the back with its head in Sal's lap.

"Where to?" James asked while Sal murmured to King in Spanish.

Ronnie instructed James to drive to the emergency vet she'd met at the Haven and with whom she'd made an unorthodox agreement.

"How come you don't get yourself a dog?" James asked Sal over his shoulder.

"Same reason as Ronnie," Sal said, and Ronnie wondered if he meant that, like herself, he couldn't bear to lose an animal of his own.

When they reached the vet's and had carried King inside, Ronnie told the two men to go home. Who knew how long she'd be? Salvador said he wanted to stay but had no transportation. James insisted Sal come with him now, and for this Ronnie was grateful.

"Parvo," the vet told her. There was a veritable epidemic this year. "Doesn't look good," he said, and now she regretted Sal wasn't here.

She stayed throughout the tests for fluid buildup in the lungs and probable kidney failure.

"There's too much damage here," the vet said finally. "It's only a matter of time. We ought to put him down. Your dog?"

"No," she said. "But I'll stay."

"It won't take long."

She began to compose the words she would use to tell Mr. Wiezenski about his dog and her trespassing. As the vet filled the hypodermic, she rested her hand on King's head and kept it there, stroking the dog's long muzzle and murmuring in his ear.

At home she sat in the dark and cried silently. Still she didn't feel emptied. She turned on the desk light, took a sheet of the rice paper, and filled her fountain pen.

Dear Father,
    It was a chilly day, and overcast. Wet leaves stuck to
    the pavement everywhere, leaving their print like a

shadow. When I got home, I wanted to run up the back steps and hide in my apartment. I even wanted to crawl into bed and dream of Mother bringing hot milk and rice crackers and little pieces of fruit to cheer me up. But I went on my rounds instead—with my friends James and Salvador.

Do you remember how Mother always thought her dogs were little bodhisattvas, serving out their time helping men? I don't think Man has done a good job of honoring such trust . . . Please take good care of yourself. It's cold here now, and I know how cold it will be in Kyoto.

Your daughter, Hiromi

In the morning Ronnie arrived at the hospital later than usual. Through the plate-glass door she could see Salvador leaning against the nurses' desk, talking with his girlfriend, Lucy. They looked up as she came through the entrance, and stared. It took her a moment to realize she was still wearing her tinted driving glasses. Sal took a step toward her when she approached the nurses' station. Ronnie reached into her pocket for King's red collar.

"For you," she said and handed it to Sal.

He looked down at the collar and turned away abruptly, as though something invisible had taken him by the shoulders and whirled him around. He moved with great purpose toward the linen closet at the end of the hall.

Ronnie glanced over at Lucy, at the furrow that divided her face, but Lucy didn't follow him. Wise girl, Ronnie thought. Salvador was lucky.

Ronnie smiled at the girl and walked down the hall to the Children's Room, stopping first to say hello to Frances.

"Are you all right?" Frances asked.

"Yes, of course. Do I look that bad?"

"Just your dark glasses."

"I forgot to change them. I suppose I should," she added. "They might upset the children."

She put her handbag on Frances's desk and exchanged one pair of glasses for another.

"On the other hand," Frances said, "check out the mirror."

Ronnie glanced into the oval mirror hanging on the wall beside the tall file cabinet. Her eyes were swollen, the flesh underneath, dark, reminding her of smudged ink.

"'Six of one, half dozen of the other,'" said Frances.

She looked at herself again and forced a laugh. "I'll go with the baggy eyes. The children probably won't notice."

None of the children had yet arrived, and Ronnie was glad for the few minutes alone. She checked the toy box, tidied up the low shelves with the different sized and colored paper and crayons and poster paints. She fluffed the large cushions and pushed each small chair under the small table so the room felt neat and restful.

One by one they came. Kevin burst though the door, accompanied by a soundtrack of explosions. Raymond wandered in, holding the stuffed lion he carried everywhere, smiled, and said, "Good morning, Miss Ronnie," sitting down at the table, where he would wait patiently for the crayons and paper he adored.

Kevin stopped careening through the room long enough to ask gruffly why she had a boy's name. Ronnie explained that her real name, Hiromi, was difficult for people to remember. Kevin said it was a funny-sounding name anyway, and she smiled to herself, pleased the boy was in such a talkative mood.

This left the dandelion girl, who arrived twenty minutes later than the boys and stood outside the playroom door, waiting to be invited in.

"Hello, Amy," Ronnie said, beckoning her over to the table.

"I want to draw," Raymond said.

"Good. Let's all draw."

Ronnie encouraged the children to go to the shelf and choose their favorite paper and crayons. Ronnie took Amy by the hand and escorted her over, soothing her, telling her it was all right to pick whatever she wished. There was a long, unbearable pause before the child, who would not release Ronnie's hand, took one pink crayon. Ronnie grabbed several sheets of white paper and a tin can of crayons and brought them and the girl to the drawing table. All but Kevin sat down. Kevin had constructed a fort of pillows, and muffled machine-gun noises could be heard from inside his structure. Ronnie decided to ignore him.

The others sat close by her. Raymond needed no prompting but began to draw his elaborate castles, filled with armies and armaments. Today, Ronnie was heartened to see, Raymond added brown to his customary black and green pictures. The dandelion girl waited.

Ronnie was suddenly filled with the need to draw. From the moment she'd gotten up, she'd been haunted by a strange and urgent feeling. While she drank her morning coffee, images had filled her head, building up while she drove to work and talked to Frances and welcomed the children for the day. Only now, sitting at the children's table with its paper and colors did Ronnie understand what she must do. With no ideas and nothing planned, she picked up a royal blue crayon. Her fingers danced over the white surface of the paper. When she'd finished, she saw she'd drawn a likeness of King with wings like those of Pegasus. Her fingers were moving on their own, and another dog, a poodle with a smiling face, flew over a shimmering sun. A boy who looked like Kevin, wearing Kevin's striped jersey, emerged from the paper, resting his head on his hand while he lay sidewise on a blue cloud.

Ronnie realized the room was unnaturally quiet; the children on either side of her were watching her paper closely. How quickly her

fingers flew, picking up and putting down new colors. She felt something around her neck and realized Kevin, who never let her touch him,
was draped over her shoulders. He pointed to the boy resting on a cloud
and, recognizing himself, laughed. Amy picked up blue and yellow
crayons and begin filling her paper with soft, bunchy shapes.

Ronnie's drawing moved on, unfolding like a scroll, to a second page
and then a third, a triptych of fleecy gold and pastel clouds, of smiling
children climbing over suns and moons and stars and steeples. A flock
of winged puppies soared with them among the sunbeamed clouds,
while an airborne collie chased a startled pigeon. Then a woman
dressed in a kimono appeared, caressing a large brown dog with a
plumed tail. Ronnie couldn't stop. The pictures surged out of her as
though she were a bridge.

Raymond leaned over to her and pulled her sleeve. She looked down
into his bright, dazed face, and for a moment, she thought his smile
might crack her heart.

"Miss Ronnie?" he asked. "Are you drawing heaven?"

It was her turn to feel amazed. She looked over the triptych carefully
and nodded, giving him a hug. Without hesitation, Raymond reached
over and took a new sheet of paper and a blue crayon and began to draw.

"I thought so," he said in triumph.

THE JUICE-SELLER'S BIRD

⟨⟨⟨⟩⟩⟩

The child has been with us since she was very young. No one, not even the girl, can be certain of her age. Whenever she asks, we pretend it's unimportant. "What does age matter? You are old enough." The sisters smile, gently teasing that the time will come, the joyous time, when she will take her vows. But she does not smile or say anything at all.

We are used to considerable traffic: peddlers, grocers, clergy, mendicants, and paupers. We lead a quiet life, our numbers varying from eight to ten, but we are always found. The sisters respond with the kindness of their calling, but the household staff is brisk, as if they feel empowered to protect us from ourselves. Mexico City is a needy place, and I was utterly daunted when I first arrived—a sheltered novice from a northern prairie. Over the years I came to consider it my only home, so much so that even my native English skills have declined. And still the city swells.

I was in my study on the day she came. I heard the muffled knock, easily ignored when one is busy with the endless correspondence that sustains the charitable life. Our old char María rushed to the door, trusting no one but herself to answer properly. I heard her throaty bark—"¿Qué?"—a sound, to us, as unremarkable as church chimes.

Another, lighter voice joined the discussion, and María's fractious mutter trailed away into the back of the house. The new voice invited someone to come inside. I returned to my writing until I heard a tap.

Sister Magdalena was standing in the open doorway. So young and yet so just. I'd come to think of her as our peacemaker. She turned back into the dark passageway and said, "Come," bringing a child into the room.

I saw nothing unusual about this girl. She appeared to be four or five, dressed in the torn and cast-off garment one grows used to seeing. Her limbs were thin, legs scabbed and gray from ancient dirt. Magdalena pulled back the coarse black hair that hung like a curtain across her forehead, and I knew then how this child had traveled: utterly safe and undisturbed. It wasn't a face one cared to look at. Her nose was flat, and one eye bulged, sightless, at an angle. But the child was clutching a remarkably clean blanket.

"Tell the Reverend Mother what you told me," Magdalena said.

"Please. We've come a long way. There's no one left for us."

How often I've heard these words. Someone else had placed them on her tongue, like the Eucharist wafer, until the words became as holy for the child as the Host itself.

"And where is this place you've come from?" I asked.

She shook her head and stared at the floor. The bundle in her arms moved.

"What are you carrying?" I asked.

"Felicia."

"And who are you, child?"

"I am Concepción."

The baby awoke, hungry and distressed. The girl tightened her grip.

"Perhaps we need to change the little one and give her a bottle," I said. "Can you take care of that, Sister?"

Magdalena reached for the baby, but the girl screamed, "No."

"I must care for her," she said, tears streaking her face.

"We'll bring her back," I said. "But now she needs care and food."

"I'll feed her."

"Take them both," I said.

Concepción clung to the baby, unwilling to sleep anywhere except the nursery, so we put a pallet for her on the floor. Here she stayed, day and night, attending to her sister's every need. On the one occasion we tried separating them, I'd asked Magdalena to feed the infant. I took Concepción by the hand and said, "You must eat with us this evening." The girl hurled herself out of my reach, fingers arched like claws. We didn't try again. We didn't dare, but after several weeks, I instructed Magdalena to bring her to my study.

"We want you to stay with us," I said. "Both you and your sister. But now, child, you must agree to leave the nursery."

She stared at me with that disconcerting eye, then nodded. I was relieved, but not for a moment did I mistake her answer for capitulation. At least we'd achieved a momentary truce, and without protest she took the corner bed in the girls' dormitory room.

We still allowed her to feed Felicia until the baby could feed herself. Concepción's attention seemed to have a beneficial effect, for Felicia was a tranquil baby and soon a trusting child. Her skin was pale, and as she grew, her hair turned deep red. The sisters couldn't pass without running their fingers through those blazing curls.

I reminded the sisters constantly they mustn't pet or spoil the children, but with Felicia they couldn't help themselves. Our sweet mouse Graciela lost her customary meekness defending this new child. When a distant church group sent a box of Christmas toys, Graciela took charge. She wouldn't let the little ones choose until Baby Felicia chose first. The day Felicia first walked, the sisters rushed to tell me and Cook and María the char. When she began to talk, Graciela ecstatically recorded every word in a small, leather-bound book. And so the baby grew from strength to strength, so calm and pretty the other children fought among themselves to be her friend. I marveled at Concepción's restraint. She seldom interfered. There was no need. She was the only one Felicia turned to for help.

My window overlooked the courtyard. Years of reading and writing had weakened my eyes. When my tasks became so wearisome my vision blurred, I rested them by watching the children. Felicia was not yet five when one of the boys dared her to climb the lemon tree. She scrambled up bravely, looked around from a fork in the trunk, and suddenly cried out. From a place beyond my view, Concepción flew across the yard, arms outstretched, as if she moved on wings, not feet. She stood at the foot of the tree, coaxed Felicia down, and then carried her away from the excited group. The other children soon lost interest, chasing each other across the yard. On the verandah, Concepción combed Felicia's tangled hair until the little girl stopped crying and rested her head against her sister.

"How lucky you are," I said to Felicia in my mind.

Children often behave as though they are a pride of lions, cuffing or withdrawing from an imperfect cub until, abandoned, it dies or leaves the pride. In this cruel manner they shunned Concepción, although I sometimes thought it was she who did the shunning. I no longer found it odd that she never played. She'd always preferred helping the sisters, drawn somehow to our quiet, isolated kitchen. Our old cook let her clean the pans or wash rice and beans. I heard Cook's patient voice correcting and teaching and initiating the girl into all her kitchen rites and secrets.

Within a year, however, Cook retired and left. She didn't tell the girl, for reasons I didn't probe: out of kindness, I would like to think, or more likely because she couldn't see her own departure as a loss. The task of telling Concepción fell to me, but I regret to say I didn't tell her. I had been interviewing one dreary applicant after another—our wages were so small—and finally chose the least objectionable candidate.

Old Cook left one night, and a stout new cook with a pinched face stood at the stove when Concepción entered the kitchen the next morning.

Within the week, this new cook had come to my study. The sacks of flour were too heavy, she complained; the kitchen, too small; the children, too noisy. And the child we'd hired to help her was silent and unhelpful. *Manos aguadas.* Such a butterfingers.

"She's not hired," I said. "She's one of ours."

"Is she deaf? Mute?" the woman asked. "Maybe a little off in the head?"

"Of course not. She's only shy."

Regrettably, Cook soon took her pleasure in ordering the girl about. Since my tasks were numerous, I asked Magdalena to supervise but suggested that discretion was the better part of valor. I had no time, and even less desire, to replace another cook.

Sometime later, Cook stormed angrily into my study.

"The kitchen is possessed." she announced. "I reach for sugar and find salt. I drink my coffee but the cup is full of pepper. The other day I was eating my eggs and nearly died—a chili was hidden inside. Yesterday morning, the vegetable knife vanished. All day I had to do without. Just as I'm about to come to you and say enough is enough, the girl finds it. Lucky for us all. I won't be tormented by a ghost. The girl says we should call the bishop and have him drive it out. What do you say, Mother?"

I controlled the urge to smile. How quickly the girl had found a way.

Unpleasant incidents faded into simple daily problems. Nothing extraordinary marred the domestic landscape. The children's days resembled our own: a reassuring circle of prayer, lessons, chores, meals, and play. Appropriately enough, my mind was full of plans to renovate the schoolroom when Magdalena came with a new appeal: Concepción wanted to take lessons. Surely she was old enough, and I chided myself for not thinking of this sooner. Our thoughts of her were so easily eclipsed by more appealing thoughts of her sister, Felicia.

"Let's ask Teresa," I suggested, perfectly aware of Magdalena's hesitation. She'd hoped I'd agree without consulting Teresa. *¡Pobrecita!*—poor dear. So easily unbalanced. Surprises made Teresa irritable. Of all our sisters, she was the least contented. A life of study is what she needed. I gave her what time I could spare, but we were not a contemplative order. We needed her to teach, and our children were her burden.

When Teresa joined us, I repeated Concepción's appeal.

"How can she possibly read?" Teresa said hotly.

"One bad eye does not mean she's blind," said Magdalena. "You must let her try."

I agreed, saying, "She may look unpromising, but I believe you may find her clever. Indeed, you may even find in her the student you've always wanted."

With this appeasement—Teresa was clearly unconvinced—I sent them off and asked Magdalena to find the girl. I had something else to say as well and wished to speak with her alone. Concepción arrived from the kitchen, wrapped in a flour-dusted apron. Thanks to Sister Magdalena, I explained, she would begin the lessons. A tiny smile appeared.

"Now there is one small thing I hope you can do for me."

She looked up, attentive.

"It's necessary, in running a home such as ours, to know as much as possible about our children. Do you understand?"

She nodded seriously.

"You have been with us several years, you and your sister, but we know nothing about you. Unpleasant as it may be, it's necessary for me to ask. I want you to tell me as much as you can about your life before. I can't ask Felicia, because she doesn't know. You have the special task of remembering for her, for both of you."

"I don't remember much," she said hesitantly.

"Of course not. You were very young. But perhaps you can tell me, more or less, where it is you came from."

She shook her head. It was a foolish question. A poor beginning. How would she possibly know?

"Only I will know. But I must know. Let's begin with the people you lived with. The people who sent you."

Her head shot up, eyes wide but guarded. "There was a woman," she began, so softly I could scarcely hear.

"Yes?"

"She wrapped Felicia in a clean blanket. I remember because she washed it the day before. She put two warm tortillas in my pocket. Then she gave me Felicia."

"What did this woman tell you?"

"She told me I must walk straight down the steps to the boulevard."

"Steps?"

"Yes. We lived up high. She said when I reached the boulevard I must turn north. 'Walk along the boulevard,' she said, 'until you reach a statue of a man on a horse.' I still remember the statue, Reverend Mother. It was so tall. The horse's head was pulled back, and its nose and eyes and mouth were wide open, like it was trying to speak."

"And you and Felicia lived alone with this woman?" I asked.

"No. There was a man. He didn't come out when I left."

"Who was he?"

She shook her head. "Just a man."

"Did he speak to you?"

"No, he spoke to the woman, but I wasn't listening. I was watching Felicia. The woman got angry with him and said we couldn't wait and no one would bother me. Then she said to me, 'You must take care of the baby.'"

"But how did you know where to go?"

"She told me. She said that when I reached the statue, I must take the street across from the horse's head. I must walk until I reached a long white building. I would see lemon trees in the courtyard and a tall blue door."

I began to wonder, *Why this urgent need to know? For whose sake did I ask?* As the child spoke, my heart began to pound. The steps. The statue. The boulevard. Our door. I knew exactly where she'd come from, the dense terraced streets that housed a thousand tiny dwellings, fragile in their discarded wood, cardboard, and tin. This child had walked four miles, perhaps five, one mile for each year of life.

Relieved to be finished, I heard my voice quaver. "Well, then. Is that all?" To my astonishment her face brightened.

"No, I remember the bird. The juice-seller's bird. It was a beautiful green and yellow. I used to stand by its pole and watch it, but I felt sorry for it."

"*You* felt sorry for it?"

"Yes, because it couldn't fly. It had a chain around its foot."

"And this woman?" I said, emboldened by her confession. "Your mother?"

The child stared at me a moment, expressionless, then dropped her gaze and whispered, "She was very pretty."

Even those in the committed life can only pray that when we are called upon to serve, the occasion will not exceed our means. But this was not to be.

Concepción and I were in the pantry when the first wall fell. The earth floor rose and rippled as though we were standing on snakes. Sacks of rice and flour pitched forward; strings of peppers quivered. I grabbed her shoulder as a shelf of pickled tomatoes danced to the edge and fell. "Get down." I pulled her to the corner and covered her with my body. The sound of breaking jars rose about the dull thunder of falling walls, and when it stopped, we were covered with thick, red juice. "Blood," she cried.

"It's not you, child." I pointed to the jars. A dreadful hush followed, and then we heard the screams.

Dust hung everywhere, blotting out the light. The pantry door was shut so hard against us, we both had to push until the door gave way.

"Stay here," I said, but she followed right behind.

We stepped through a corridor now filled with chunks of wall and ceiling plaster. In the kitchen, pans and dishes lay helter-skelter. We picked our way through, following the screams. Graciela appeared at the door, one hand clutching her crucifix so tightly her fingers bled.

"Where are the children?"

"Everywhere," she whispered.

I grabbed the girl's sleeve to keep her with me. When we reached the dining room, we heard the terrified cries. Concepción pulled free, scrambled toward the usually sun-lit yard, and choked.

Stepping through what once had been a door, we saw scraps of color through a dust scrim. "Felicia," she called, but every child answered. They were bunched up throughout the courtyard, some partially covered with dirt and tile. Quicker than I, she picked up the closest child, wiped the face before moving on, calmly telling each one she touched, "Wait for Reverend Mother." Two lay still, a tattered dress and T-shirt beneath rubble.

The sisters rushed out, habits smudged, hems unraveled, moving across the yard like wind-scattered leaves.

"Concepción," a small voice cried. The girl ran to Felicia, scooped her up, smoothed the dirt from the red hair, then cried out, "Oh, Mother, no!" I looked down and saw Felicia's shattered feet.

Sirens wailed above the cries for help. Smoke rose, mingled with dust. Narrow seams broke out along the floor, wide seams along the standing walls, as if a stooping, underground giant had stood up and dropped the city from his shoulders.

I sent Magdalena for a doctor and another sister to find the roster in my office. In the melee I, who always knew the children's names on sight, was afraid one was missing. Gratefully, none were missing; all were accounted for, including the two most hurt by the debris. Concepción ran to ask Cook to fill the water jars, but Cook was gone and there was no water. Not far off a glorious fountain rose up from a vast hole in the street, and then stopped.

Magdalena was gone for hours. When she returned, she looked ill. No one could come, she said. The streets, the clinic. Everywhere we looked we saw ashes and craters, like the moon.

All night we heard men calling out. Torchlight poked through our creviced walls while candles inside sent our grotesque shadows dancing. Tirelessly, the sisters swept up debris, moved beds strewn with plaster away from walls. The girls' room was the most badly damaged, the corner beds crushed.

Rest was impossible, and we worked two feverish days without stopping. When at last I did sleep, a fearful vision woke me: I'd dreamed of a bird with huge white wings that dropped across the dwelling as we slept, enclosing us until we smothered.

For days we lived with the strange flickering lights, the lack of heat and water. Everyone moved like ghosts, afraid one heavy step would cause a landslide. Sisters went out every morning, searching the pocked streets for whatever produce they could find. At the end of the fourth day, the two severely wounded children were dead.

"Others have lost more," I told the sisters, as though this could possibly console them. I wrapped the small bodies myself and took them away in the night. That evening, when the children said their prayers, Graciela told them to pray for Raul and Lucinda. And so we did, giving thanks in our hearts we were not the ones.

After several days, Cook, who had fled the earthquake in terror, returned subdued. She had no other place to go.

Broken into bits, the stricken city didn't take much notice of our losses. We were only a scratch among its wounds. Still, I sent for help each day. When a nurse finally came, she made her visit brief. I heard her tell the sisters she could do little more than they had done already: crudely setting bones, cleaning flesh, restoring spirits.

"You're lucky," she said briskly, closing her depleted bag. "But the poor mayor's lovely home. And the bishop. He can't even say mass inside the cathedral."

"Then tell him to come to us," Magdalena said to her. "We invite him to say the mass here. For all the city's missing children."

The startled nurse looked at Magdalena's ashen face and wisely chose not to reply.

Of all the children, Concepción worked the hardest. Watchful and swift, she dove on scraps she found in the street, pounced on anything we might use or sell. If she had been older, I thought unhappily, she might even have sold herself. She spent hours with the wounded children, washing torn and broken limbs, changing bandages for towels. Each day she boiled and scrubbed the linen, for it had to be used again and again. I took her hands out of the washtub one afternoon and held them tight.

"You're working too hard," I said. "You're still a child. Please don't forget so soon."

Before pulling her hands away, she looked at me with eyes that had never seen a childhood. In my many years, I'd learned to recognize the urgent gestures—the misplaced laugh or cry, the dangerous glance, the footstep that's too hard or soft, the hands that won't be touched.

"There's something else, isn't there?" I said to her.

Her face was a silent plea.

"Come, child. Tell me."

"In the night, Mother. Something terrible happened. I woke up and it was there."

"What happened?"

She touched her face. "I feel other eyes using mine." She touched her heart. "It's not mine either. This new one is too hot and fast."

"It's only the earthquake. We all feel strange."

"No. There's something in there . . . living inside."

Day and night I appealed to the diocese, the bishop, churches near and far, until letters cluttered my desk. I hardly rested, hardly felt the need, relying on the sisters to maintain our routines. During those weeks I seldom left my office except for meals and prayers. At last, in one day's mail I received encouraging news and summoned the sisters: the American ambassador's wife had taken an interest in the children, and the bishop had recommended she include us in her tour.

They talked excitedly, voices rising, falling, disbelieving. Someone moved outside the door, and I saw Concepción dart away.

The news seemed to be a source of worry, not consolation. We'd been cut off so long, they felt suspicious of sudden help. I couldn't let their apprehensions disturb the house, so I took on a hopeful posture, a forced and unnatural optimism, as a defense against their doubts. During the week, several sisters came in private. I listened and soothed and deliberately dismissed their fears. Even Cook came.

"It's the girl," Cook hissed, leaning across my desk, her face inches from my own. "She's too secretive. She runs and hides. Won't even speak to me. And she has the evil eye."

"Why do you worry so much about her?" I asked impatiently. "These are troubling times for everyone. And the girl is not at fault." For an alarming moment I saw Cook's fleshy limbs devoured by carrion crows, her eyes plucked out. I dismissed her quickly, counseling myself it was the product of insufficient sleep. But the frightening image lingered.

I thought it wise to renew my rounds and, when I did, discovered Graciela had converted the verandah to a clinic. Tidy, clean, immeasurably sad. The first time I visited, I found Concepción tending Felicia.

"She comes every day," Graciela said. "She tells Felicia help is coming soon."

I was glad someone else's faith was sturdier than my own. I watched Concepción sitting on the edge of the porch. She carefully guided Felicia onto her back and held the thin legs firm, the shrouded feet sticking out in front, while Felicia clung to her sister's neck like a newborn monkey. Slowly, Concepción stood and began to walk the circumference of the courtyard.

"She walks her every day to help her sleep," said Graciela. "They hardly sleep, you know."

The bishop wrote at last, sending a courier to inform me the ambassador's wife would visit sometime the following day. I heard my own voice, jubilant above the others, but the next morning the atmosphere had turned solemn. The sisters barely spoke above a whisper, except for Magdalena, who could be heard roundly scolding Cook in the kitchen. A crowd had been gathering outside all morning, and at two o'clock I went to the kitchen to alert Cook, telling Magdalena and Concepción to come with me.

Large black cars blocked the street. Men gestured grandly and gave each other sharp, important commands while women in pastel dresses and white hats fanned themselves against the heat. The crowd parted for one last car, and behind me Magdalena drew her breath.

Our priest, Father Olivar, emerged first. After a deliberate pause, during which the crowd pressed excitedly toward the car, the bishop stepped out, and I went forward to kiss his hands. A man in sunglasses opened the back door for a tall, gold-haired woman, her suit as pink as the lining of a shell.

Nuns and children stood in facing rows like a boulevard of linden trees. The man in dark glasses scanned us quickly, turned, and scanned the crowd. Graciela appeared unexpectedly in the doorway, holding

Felicia, whose red hair rose up around her head in a radiant copper halo.

"This is one of our children," I explained. "She was playing in the courtyard where two of our children perished. Little Felicia was lucky, but you see, madam? Her feet?"

The ambassador's wife reached for Felicia and took her gently, as a mother would. My own heart lightened. I invited the dignitaries inside, where it was cooler.

Nuns and children followed in a tight knot as we toured the rooms, out to the courtyard with its lingering scars, back to the dining room where Cook had laid a table with cakes, fresh fruit, juice, and wine for the fathers. The kitchen door opened a crack, and Cook hissed at Concepción. Reluctantly the girl went to help. Inside, I heard flatware clatter and Cook mutter, "Clumsy." A moment later Concepción darted out to the dining room and arranged forks across the linen tablecloth.

Later, I led the visitors to the verandah while the children, laughing, swooped down over the remaining fruit and cakes. Graciela had artfully arranged the injured children on mats, small chairs, and improvised beds. It weighed on me heavily that we'd felt so compelled to put them on display. The bishop approved, however, and began a long account of our sufferings, which both pleased and vexed me. Not once had he come to visit. Just as our illustrious guest was seeing our bruises for the first time, so was he.

"We would even welcome wheelchairs," he exclaimed, as if he thought these were a fair exchange for legs.

Magdalena ushered the other children to the courtyard. As they passed, the bishop leaned toward me and announced in a highly audible whisper, "There is even a possibility of finding homes."

I couldn't look at him, couldn't answer, for out of the corner of my eye I saw Concepción behind our chairs. The guests rose, and Graciela thrust Felicia into my arms. How pale she looked. I hugged her, and she accepted this without a word or a smile. On our way out, Concepción tugged my habit.

"I'll hold her, Mother, if she's too heavy."

I thanked her and said I was fine. Behind me I heard the bishop laugh heartily. "¡Qué chiquita! How could she carry anyone?"

The lips of the ambassador's wife flickered in an odd smile. "How sweet," she said, but I saw her shrink from Concepción. The girl saw, too.

I prefer to think it was only my anxiety that made me neglect to tell them she was Felicia's sister. Instead, we said our farewells, passing Felicia around like a doll. At the entrance, the bishop stopped to bless the crowd, his elegant arms stretched out over the bowed heads—over shopkeepers and onlookers and men desperate for work, over the glistening ladies who had come to be seen, the sisters on their knees, our children dressed in smocks. And as he prayed, I couldn't suppress the furtive hope he might stumble before he reached his limousine.

The weeks that followed proved more fitful than the weeks that came before. I waited impatiently for each day's mail, only to be disappointed. I heard nothing. No progress. Not even a polite decline. So, I thought, disconsolate, we are to live suspended while the brokers of mercy consult their hearts.

When the letter did arrive, it contained plans, destinations, flight arrangements, and money. After the evening meal, I made the announcement: the seven children wounded in the quake would be sent to a special hospital, in *el norte*. When I read Felicia's name, Concepción leaped up ecstatically, as if sprung from a box.

It was difficult getting the children to bed. Youthful energy, pent up so long, filled the dwelling like a river flooding land. It was dark when I finally made my rounds. Far off a dog barked frantically, then stopped, while inside a solitary cricket chirped. Graciela was asleep on the verandah, where she slept every night, guarding her fragile brood. I thought I was the only one awake until I heard a murmur. I followed the voice, stepping back against the dark wall to avoid being seen. Concepción sat on the verandah, her short legs dangling over the edge, holding the motionless Felicia in her lap.

"We'll be going on a long trip," she whispered. "Remember the lady in pink? She'll fix you up, you'll see. And won't it be fun, leaving Cook."

All night I tossed and turned, unable to sleep. The next morning, determined to speak with the girl, I went to the kitchen and found her singing.

"What's gotten into you, magpie?" Cook grumbled.

Concepción laughed, and I lost the will to speak.

Even Magdalena, who was sitting beside me at breakfast, noticed the change in the girl. "See? Even Concepción is pleased, Mother."

After the meal, fortified and determined, I asked Magdalena to join me in the kitchen.

"It's good to see you so happy," I told Concepción.

"I'm happy for Felicia. I'm happy we'll be going up to the children's hospital."

"Hah!" Cook cackled. "They're not taking you, silly. Prayer couldn't cure what ails you."

Magdalena burst out, "You should be ashamed!"

I took Concepción's hand and led her out of the kitchen and into the dark, quiet hallway. Magdalena followed.

"I'm going too, aren't I," she said. It wasn't a question.

We walked to my study. I closed the door and sat down behind my desk.

"Why would you be going, child? You aren't hurt."

"I know, but Felicia's my sister. She'll need me."

During the silence that followed, I took off my glasses, cleaned, and adjusted them, but they were useless to me now.

"I'm sure Felicia needs you," I said. "But we need you too. None of the sisters are going either."

I bade her come closer. She inched forward and stopped at the edge of my desk. I beckoned until she came around to where I sat. Perhaps Felicia needed her here, I said. To be here when she returned. I took hold of her shoulders, and her lips trembled. For the first time in years, she wept. I held her close and then asked if today she would like to join Sister Magdalena on her rounds.

She pulled away, shaking her head fiercely, and said, "Felicia won't come back, will she?"

The girl scarcely spoke, not even, apparently, to Felicia. Her visits continued, her ministrations unchanged, except for the impenetrable silence. She patiently brushed her sister's hair, strand by fiery strand, massaged her needle-thin legs, rewrapped the broken feet. When the day came, she dressed Felicia in a white smock she'd cleaned and ironed herself.

The bishop sent his limousine and a nurse. I joined the household, who were waiting outside. Magdalena led the remaining children in a farewell song, but Concepción stood apart. The nurse carried one child while sisters carried others, and Graciela appeared last, holding Felicia. They approached, and Magdalena put her hands on Concepción's shoulders.

As they passed, I heard a bird's piercing shriek. Felicia looked back over Sister Graciela's shoulder and screamed, "Concepción," until cries hung in the air like voices from the quake.

Suddenly, Concepción tore loose, back arched, arms spread wide. My vision blurred, for I thought I saw a fluttering of enormous pale wings and the girl rising off the ground in flight. Magdalena grabbed her, plucked her out of the air, and ran indoors, where I followed. She held on with all her strength until suddenly the girl went limp, as if something heavy inside had fallen to the floor of her body. Sister cradled her and rocked until the shrieks turned to sobs. Over and over I said, "Can you hear me, child? Can you hear my voice?"

Her hooded eyes peered out as though we were standing at the back of a cave. I spoke on and on, hoping to draw her back.

"Felicia was chosen because her need was great. But you have been chosen, too. Do you understand?"

The sobs died out.

"We want you here with us," I said softly. "Soon you will become one of us. One day you'll understand," I whispered. "I promise."

She looked at me in such a way I knew the voice and face I'd thought were mine belonged only to a stranger. What was left to say? Each of my sixty years became a stone, resting on my heart.

I took her hand, led her behind my desk, and lifted her up into my chair. There she sat, swollen with sorrow, her fresh smock drenched, her feet unable to reach the floor.

GIRLS LIKE US

'd been feeling poorly from the moment I got up. I sent the boys outside to play on the deck their daddy had built, while I tried to make
peace with my body. Summer was in full swing, for the children any-
ways, but in southern California I've learned it's mostly summer year
round. I looked out the bathroom window in time to see Timmy, my
second boy, hitting Mikey, my third, with a whiffle bat. I yanked that
window up, lickety-split.

"You know the rules," I yelled. "No hitting, no punching, no biting,
and no tears. You mind me, hear?"

I put my arms around my stomach and closed my eyes. Over at the
Post a doctor no older than myself had run the tests and told me what
I already suspected—and Bud, away from home for months.

Navy life teaches a mother to be tough and eagle-eyed. The men are
gone so much, we women try to swell up large enough to fill their place.
If you'd asked me ten years go whether I could organize four sons, I'd
have told you *no,* straight out.

I pulled the window up again. "Jason, honey. Pull that stroller back
away from the edge."

I watched them a moment longer, playing on that big redwood deck.
Jason, my oldest, watches over the baby and tries to make the others

mind. Only Timmy doesn't mind. All four boys are as different as they can be, and except for Jason, they all look just like Bud. I was nineteen when we married; Bud was twenty-two. The boys came rolling out like pinballs, one every eighteen months.

I thought Bud was some catch. Light-haired, blue-eyed, perfect teeth in a yard-wide smile that showed them to advantage. He hasn't gotten the least bit bulky in the nine years we've been married. Somewhere along the line, though, I realized it wasn't Bud I'd seen, but the smile, the gold braid and snappy hat and spotless white gloves.

We both grew up just north of where the farmland of Missouri rolls down into the Ozarks, the closest water from rivers dug out by the Army Corps of Engineers. I used to wonder if growing up landlocked made him want to go to sea. I know I was glad to leave. He'd come back, wearing his dress whites, and escorted a girl I knew to our senior prom. That uniform turned heads. I steered my date over to Bud and his date, batting my eyes and making jokes until it might have been considered rude if the men didn't ask each other's partner for a dance. As soon as Bud took me in his arms and I felt the linen of his uniform, I got him to dance me close to the band. We lost our dates in the crowd.

Two days later Bud invited me to go down to Springfield for dinner and a show. Springfield isn't San Diego, and dinner meant pizza, Country Kitchen, KFC, Shakey's Steaks, or one catfish smorgasbord. The next day he took me bass fishing at Pomme de Terre, but we didn't waste much time casting our lines into the lake. He only had a short leave, and a few days after that he shipped out from somewhere back east. He wrote me letters once a week, and I kept every one.

I don't recommend military life. The separations are too hard, and so is living here and there. Still, Bud's been steady, never drunk much, and never laid a hand on me or any of the boys. He has a sense of humor that still makes me laugh. Even if he never changed a diaper, he liked to hold the children when they were babies. He takes a keener interest as soon as the boy can talk. So I thought our marriage was solid until some months ago when we somehow ran aground. Funny, how people can bump along, lost in dinners and diapers, strollers and decks, never once talking about what really matters or what they dream of ten years down the line. One day it's there. An empty space. A feeling you have that what you want and what he wants no longer overlap.

I imagined those stories in the paper about so and so and his *estranged* wife. I thought maybe I was about to become *estranged*. I wondered if the boys would become *estranged* children, or whether it was only something between adults. In the long months when he was away, with no one to talk to but children and girlfriends—wives like me, raising kids and mowing lawns—I'd learned to economize on words.

"No more kids," I told him one day. "I'm twenty-nine years old and all wore down. I'm going in and get my tubes tied." I couldn't imagine why he was so upset.

"But I thought you wanted a girl," he said.

"How many more boys could we afford to have first? Don't you think enough's enough?"

He didn't think. He stormed out of the house, leaving me confused. I asked my friend Arleen, who lived just a few houses down. She allowed as how the men didn't expect you to have opinions, except about whether to buy the pork chops or the beef. She said her Jerry was just the same. You could be the drill sergeant while he was away—in fact it was encouraged: "You boys pick up those toys now, hear?"—but you better shape yourself into the girl he married the moment he gets back home.

"I forget myself," I told her.

"So do I," she said.

Later that week, I went out to window-shop, off the base to those upscale stores circling the harbor. A little pick-me-up I took once in a great while. I liked to check out the styles to see if I could sew them at home, even if it's the accessories that usually catch my eye: belts, socks, scarves, pins and earrings, and hats. Arleen says you can always tell a girl with class. "She knows how to accessorize." I was walking slowly along the sidewalk, gazing at the mannequins, when I saw Bud, sitting in the front window of a fancy bar with four of his Navy buddies. Each one of those jerks had an arm around some girl.

I stood stock still in front of the plate glass and stared, clutching my little faux alligator handbag he'd given me for Christmas. One of his friends nudged him. Bud glanced out the window to see me standing on the sidewalk, giving him the finger.

When he came home, he accused me of spying before I could get a word in edgewise. I told him I didn't need to spy. If he was going to play around in broad daylight, maybe I'd do the same. He slammed his hand against the refrigerator and stormed out of the kitchen, the second time in a week. I was glad to see him go.

"Any man who loses his temper," I called after him, "especially when he's in the wrong, isn't fit company to keep."

I wished I'd minded my tongue. I could hear my older sisters, chattering inside my head. *Speak in haste, little Sis, and you'll repent in leisure.*

Bud didn't stay for supper, and later that week he informed me he was scheduled for a tour of duty.

"Then maybe it's time I called a lawyer," I said, steam boiling up inside.

"You do that," he said. "Let me know what you decide when I get back."

"I just want to know one thing, Bud. Is this all because I told you I didn't want any more kids?"

He didn't answer me at first, even when I told him I hadn't done anything permanent, that it was just a thought traveling through my head.

"Don't go off half-cocked," he said.

I made a tart reply, and that's when he got real huffy and left for the night. I told the boys at dinner their father had things to do.

"He's pissed off, isn't he?" said Jason.

"Don't use such language at my table," I said. "And yes. You're right. He is."

"So how come you're always chasing him away?"

Tears came into my eyes. I couldn't help myself.

"Honey, your father's a grown man. He'll go where he wants when he wants. Nobody has to do any chasing."

The night before he left, Bud asked if I was going to come up and help him pack. I'd always helped before, organizing the bags, lining up the toiletries while we talked of this and that, filling each other up with news as if we thought it could last for months. It used to make us feel together, but this time I felt too far apart. I told him no, I'd be in the kitchen with the dishes. My words took him by surprise. He stood in the dining room staring at me, so I turned and walked away. I don't remember ever feeling so resentful. I didn't want to be in the same room, biting my tongue, playing nice, while I dreaded the long months ahead. In the morning he drove down to the pier with Arleen's husband, alone.

Arleen came over later, and we spent the afternoon moping on the deck. I told her I was actually glad to see him go. "Why, honey," she said, "that doesn't sound like you." I wanted to tell her about the space I'd felt opening up between us, but I couldn't find the words. Besides, I didn't want to make her feel any worse than I knew she already did. We had the summer ahead of us and seven kids to organize. I didn't say any more, and the two of us got down to brass tacks. My two oldest enrolled in summer school and Little League; our babies spent two mornings at the Methodist Mother's Day out; Arleen's two girls and Mikey went to Day Camp at the Y. Arleen and I lived in our cars.

The men had been gone three weeks, the children busy for two, when Arleen's brother Ron showed up, enjoying his own extended leave. A

Marine Corps captain, Ron had decided to travel the country, visiting family, which isn't the way I'd have spent my leave. I hadn't realized how close Arleen was to all her family. I wasn't close to mine.

Maybe that comes from being the youngest in a big farm family. An afterthought. An accident, turned into the family joke. My folks were almost elderly by the time I came of age, so I had designs on leaving Missouri before I reached my teens. I didn't intend to spend my life feeding chickens, canning beans, putting up pickles, cooking ten-course meals for summer boys who'd come to help bale hay. I looked at my much older sisters in their plain farm dresses, flour dusting their sturdy arms while they pounded dough against a board and added two cups of sugar to every pie. *Uh-uh,* I thought. *Not the life for me.*

"You're soft, little Sis," they'd scold whenever they came to see the folks and saw me reading a magazine instead of scrubbing the linoleum floor. They were righteous women, God-fearing, proud of their chores, even proud of the weight they'd put on as if it dignified their bones. "You're spoiled, but you'll learn," they said, shaking their heads when I told them I was leaving Missouri for good. "Remember, Sandy. In this life there are no free rides."

As far as I was concerned California was paradise, and Bud was my ticket to a whole new life.

Ron was younger than Arleen, jolly as a Santa and just as barrel-chested. Like Arleen, he was short, with the same dark hair and eyes, a striking family resemblance when you saw them side by side. He'd already visited his parents and brothers in New Jersey, the other sister in Detroit. By the time he reached San Diego he was ready to stay awhile. Lonesome for our husbands, we couldn't believe our luck. I was making homemade ice cream on the deck when Arleen first brought him over. He shook my hand, then reached over and gave me a peck on the cheek.

"Any good friend of Arleen's is a friend of mine," he said. "Now let me do that."

He took hold of the handle and began to crank up the ice cream, the children standing around to watch. He looked up, counted five eager little heads and two more in strollers, and said, "We'll have to do something about this." The next day he went out and leased a van. The day after that he and Arleen's crowd arrived to take us all up to Disneyland. A few days later we went down to Sea World, and then one afternoon the following week it was a trip to the zoo. When Arleen phoned to ask if we'd all come have a picnic on the beach, I had that hamper packed and the boys ready long before the van pulled up.

Arleen and I took the babies, spread the beach towels, and stretched out under the umbrella. Ron lined up the five older children and played a relay game in and out of the waves. Then he had them all building a long fort in the sand, the littlest ones running in and out with buckets of water to help the bigger ones build. Not once did we girls have to referee a squabble. We sat there watching, relaxed, enjoying the sound of water lapping on the beach.

At first our two fatherless families ate the evening meal together, with Ron sitting at the head, until the noise and trouble got to be too much. Arleen and I were constantly hopping up to tend a crying child, clean a spill, or deal out discipline. The children were in a constant brawl over who got Uncle Ron to himself. I'd never seen that much competition over one man's attention. So we divided him up between us during the rest of his month-long stay. I got him for suppers on Tuesdays and Sundays, and Arleen got him the rest of the time. Every Wednesday afternoon and all day Saturdays we piled the kids in the van and traveled up and down the coast.

All the while, Arleen and I competed for Ron, but in entirely different ways. She wanted him to change the car oil and fix the back screen, while I started to dress up. You get so hungry for attention when your husband's out on tour, you can act real silly when anyone looks your way. I took out my short skirts, bought some makeup in a shade called

Venetian Nights, and wore it every day. I had my hair styled and got a pair of pumpkin-colored sling-back pumps. I told myself I'd earned them, since I hadn't bought myself new shoes in over a year. I half expected my son Jason to look at me with his father's eyes and say something unkind, but Jason had his eyes focused on "Uncle Ron."

Whenever Ron came over for dinner, Jason glued himself to Ron's side. I knew who the boy needed—and needed him right now. So I watched Ron with my sons, watched him real close. You'd think a Marine Corps captain might be rough on boys, but Ron was like a Christmas uncle, laden down with gifts. He played Hearts with the kids, and Go Fish and Parcheesi and marbles. He helped Jason put together a balsa airplane, played catch with Tim, and tossed the little whiffle ball to Mikey, who was learning how to bat. He even held Baby Leon in his lap. By the time Ron left for the evening, the boys were wound up tighter than ticks.

"Hard to believe you don't have kids," I said one night while serving up peach cobbler. I thought he might have a child or two stashed away from a marriage that hadn't worked out.

"I would've liked kids," he said. "But I never married. Military life is too hard on a wife."

I let my gaze drop down to my plate. I couldn't imagine Bud ever saying such a thing. I thought I was going to cry.

"I still might consider it," he said. "After I retire. I'll only be forty-five. Get myself a pretty young wife and have some boys like yours. What d'ya say, lads?" He grinned down the table. Jason snickered. Ron reached over and ruffled his hair. If the boys hadn't been there, it might've been me he touched.

On the last Sunday Ron came to eat, I felt a catch in my throat. Jason was so upset, he clung to Ron. I put the little boys to bed while Ron read Jason a story. I let him tuck the boy in while I went back downstairs. A half-hour later he came down to help me clean up in the kitchen. That's when he put his arms around my waist.

The house was quiet, the boys asleep. No one made a sound. We tip-toed up to the master bedroom and lay down in my queen-sized bed. I wanted him to stay the night, but he was gone when I woke up at 2:00. We'd already agreed he wouldn't come back to say good-bye, since he was leaving Arleen's early in the morning.

Jason moped all day and wouldn't eat his lunch. I was a little sad, but at the same time I felt satisfied and relieved. It didn't upset me like I thought it would when Tim and Mikey asked where Uncle Ron had gone. Arleen and her kids came over in the evening, her face long and melancholy. *My little brother,* she kept repeating. *He turned out all right.*

"He sure got back late, though," she said, staring at me. "What'd you guys do?

"Backgammon," I lied. "And I lost seven bucks."

Before long I was suffering the fiercest morning sickness and found myself, once more, sitting in the clinic.

I could have passed it off as Bud's. I'd have to juggle with the dates, and I knew girls who did. Still, I had this feeling whoever it was inside would end up with Ron's brown eyes, when Bud and I had blue. Besides, more urgent things were pressing on my mind: I didn't have the strength or courage to raise another child. Even now I lay awake at night wondering where the money would come from if Jason wanted to go to college or if the little boys had problems with their teeth. Some days I felt so down, I'd talk to my reflection in the dressing table mir-ror. "See what happens to girls like you for loving a man's dress whites?"

It was mid-August and Arleen was on my deck with her three kids. Four of the children were playing on the grass, jumping in and out of a large plastic pool. Except for the toddlers, they'd soon be in school, and we could hardly wait.

"Are you putting on weight?" she asked.

"You could say that."

She stared at me, and I stared out at the play pool full of kids.

"I'm pregnant," I said finally.

"Why, honey, that's wonderful. I guess."

"Guess again." I couldn't look her in the eye.

"Uh-oh," she said. "I hear you."

"I sure hope you do." I finally turned and looked at her, my face all twisted up. "I can't afford another. And I don't have the strength."

Tears stung my eyes. Arleen scooted her lawn chair over to mine and put her arms around me while I sobbed. Her older girl, who'd been playing with the babies, came over and stood right in front.

"Mama?" she said. "Is Sandy all right?"

"Of course she is, honey. She just misses Bud, like you miss your daddy."

I wished it were that simple.

"I got to have a plan," I said before I realized just how much she'd have to know.

"What d'ya mean?" she asked.

I wiped my eyes and blew my nose and told the first of many fibs. A friend of Bud's had stopped by, I said. *In my loneliness . . . a weak moment . . . I sincerely believe it's his . . . There's no way I can keep it.* She was staring at me with her round dark eyes that reminded me of Ron's.

"I'm not going to get rid of it either, not the way you think."

That night after everyone was in bed, I lay in the dark, wide-awake, and tried to organize my thoughts. I didn't know why I'd told Arleen what I did; it just popped out of my mouth. Maybe it had something to do with Ron not having any boys and how good he'd been to mine. I tried to invent what Ron would say if I told him I was carrying his child. *Wow, Sandy. My kid? I think that's great.*

But of course it wasn't great. It was one big mess. It wouldn't take a rocket scientist to figure out I didn't love Arleen's brother. For a month Ron had made us feel like queens, and that was what I loved.

All I could really imagine was Bud's outraged surprise. Could I fake it and tell him it was his? I didn't think I was strong enough to carry a lie of that size, and I had no intention of hurting or leaving my boys. Even the thought made me shiver. Was there any other choice?

People only think the umbilical cord links the mother with her child. They forget just how much that cord ties parents together, too. Like it or not, I already had four cords tying me to Bud.

I remembered as a child, how each February I'd help Mama plant seeds in little starter boxes back in the laundry room. We'd line the cups with newspaper and fill each one with dirt. Every day I'd peek into the small warm room, hoping to see lettuce, pepper, and tomato shoots reaching for the light.

The agency was located in a pretty Victorian house, out near the Mission. You wouldn't know it was anything but a private home. The woman I talked to on the phone sounded like some petty officer working payroll on the post. When I finally met her, she asked questions about my background in a fast, businesslike voice. At one point she asked, "For whose sake are you doing this?" I looked her straight in the eye. I'd been rehearsing. For once I'd planned ahead.

"For all our sakes, but mostly for the child's. Look, I've made up my mind."

She turned from cool to warm, as if I'd waved a wand, and told me to call her Margaret. She explained they had women coming in who weren't ready or sincere. Her job was to weed them out. "To separate the wheat from the chaff," she said, which sounded like my sisters. Legal problems could develop, women suddenly changing their minds, and all the broken hearts.

"So, what's the drill?" I asked.

She smiled at me, but the smile was kind. "I can tell you're a military wife."

Margaret gave me a booklet that explained things and said I could take it home to study. My next visit I could ask her questions. Even after the birth, I'd have a month to change my mind. But when she told me Ron and Bud would both have to sign, I nearly stopped and turned back. I went home depressed. I wanted it all finished and arranged by the time Bud came home.

A few days later, I asked Arleen to take the baby for a couple of hours so I could do some chores. She'd already given me Ron's address when I told her the boys wanted to send their thanks. I went to the kitchen and sat down at my little maple desk, the only piece of furniture I'd taken from the farm. I took out my best writing paper, with the tiny rosebuds in the lower right-hand corner. I sat a moment and then wrote, "Dear Ron," staring down at the empty page. My mind was just as empty, and I was suddenly afraid. How do women give up babies and lift their heads up the next day? I began to cry.

When I looked up finally and saw the time, I told myself to get on with it and finished what I had to say with no fuss or frills. I folded the sheet, enclosed the documents, and sealed it tight. I felt such a heaviness, you'd think I was sending him my life. I had to lay my head down on the desk.

I calculated when he might get the letter and added two more days for good measure. Then I spent one whole day inside the house so I could easily reach the phone. Every day for a week I met the mailman at the door. I wanted to hear Ron's deep warm voice telling me everything would be all right, but he never phoned or wrote. *Act in haste,* I could hear Mama say, *and then repent in leisure.* Three weeks passed before Margaret told me Ron had signed and returned the papers.

I thought I'd feel relieved, but what I felt was sorrow. Did he think so little of me he didn't want to write? I worried maybe my letter had sounded too blunt or businesslike, when what I felt was tender. Maybe he thought I blamed him and wouldn't want to hear from him. Funny thing is, I didn't blame anyone at all. The need to hear his voice some-times drove me crazy. I don't know how I found the strength not to pick up the phone. My dreams at night were only making me feel more con-fused. Bud turned into Ron and Ron into Bud, blending into one another or a whole new man. They even wore each other's uniforms.

Margaret thought it best to wait until Bud came home, then I could fully explain. Plenty of time for him to sign, she said. "He'll be home soon, won't he?" I thought those papers would burn a hole in my maple desk.

The following Monday Margaret said, "Now we begin the most chal-lenging part." I thought it was all a challenge. She got up and went to a cabinet, unlocked it, and took out a large album with a blue and pink satin cover, each inside page protected by a clear plastic sheet.

"These are the Couples looking for a child."

Every time she used that word I saw capital letters. The Duke, the President, the Princess, the Couple.

She opened it to the beginning. On the right-hand page were photos of a husband and wife and their first names. On the left-hand page was a little history of their lives and jobs and photos of a house. No address-es or cities mentioned. My head sank to my chest. I couldn't touch the book. She came around the desk and said, "Let's spread it out on that table over there." She put her arm around me and squeezed.

"That's a tall order," I said.

"Yes, but at least it's your order. Here. Take your time."

I got that feeling I sometimes get that everyone, except me, is mod-ern and up-to-date.

She picked the book up off her desk and carried it over to the table where we could sit side by side, looking at the pictures of the Couples and their homes, reading the story of their lives. After the first few pages, it wasn't so hard. I started to get the hang of it, started to look for certain things. Bit by bit, I began to swell with hope: this kid could grow up with millionaires or carpenters, and I'd be the one to choose. I started to look for coloring. My hair was sandy, like my name. So was Bud's. I was tall and thin when I wasn't pregnant, with fair skin and eyes a sort of blue. But Ron was black-haired and brown-eyed, not tall, and thick around the chest.

"Remember," Margaret said. "The baby has as much chance of looking like you as the father. Most women come in here with their heads full of confused pictures of the father. And they forget about themselves."

"That's why girls like us end up here," I blurted out. "We got confused over the fathers."

I looked at those pictures every day for a week, but Margaret didn't seem to think I was taking too much time. I kept coming back to one couple. They were both tall, with gray-blue eyes. His hair was light brown and hers, a bottle blond. He was a teacher of some sort, and she was a nurse. I liked their smiles and the way they wrote about themselves, their pretty ranch-style house with the gold hills behind. The house looked to be on an acre of land. Why, the kid could have a horse.

"Why didn't you have the sonogram? Arleen asked. We were sipping lemonade on the deck.

"Because I don't want to know until it comes."

"It might be nice for the couple if they knew."

"It's not for them to ask."

Arleen shrugged. I was sorry I'd snapped. Even the kids knew how tetchy I'd become. I guess I was afraid she'd say the very thing I didn't want to hear. I watched Arleen closely these days, but I guess Ron hadn't said a word. By now I was over three months gone, and our husbands would be home in a week.

Jason and Timmy helped me decorate the house. We put up balloons and streamers and made a huge sign with poster paints that read,

"Welcome Home, Dad!" and hung it over the door. I baked a three-layer cake, fried up some chicken the way Bud liked, and bought a pretty maternity nightgown. When it was time, I got the kids in the station wagon while Arleen put hers in the Olds, and we caravanned down to the pier.

It was still warm, and I wore a shapeless sundress. Jason took charge of Leon in his stroller while I took the middle boys by the hand. I watched Arleen with her two daughters and felt such a longing in my heart. I held back, far away from the crowds. I was tired of all the hoopla the Navy expected from its wives, tired of the loose talk about the importance of family life. We women all knew who was expected to keep our families intact. I planted myself near the back exit while Arleen pushed ahead with her kids.

"Aren't we going up, too?" Jason asked.

"You go ahead with Leon if you like, honey, but I don't feel comfortable up there."

Jason nodded and stayed where he was, by my side. Timmy and Mikey, pulling and jumping, were more than I could handle. Jason turned on them like he was nineteen, not nine, and said, "You want Dad to see you acting like idiots? You're Navy, remember?"

Four-year-old Mikey put his arms around my hips and started to cry.

"That's just great," said Jason, exasperated.

"Hush now," I said and stroked Mikey's hair. "You'll get the baby started."

When the men began to disembark, the band began to play. In no time pandemonium broke loose, and all the screaming wives drowned the music out. It was like we'd been put on a gigantic stage, and now we girls had to play our parts. My stomach pitched and rolled, like I was the one aboard ship. Never had I hated a homecoming so much. Then Jason jumped up and shouted, "Dad! Over here!" We were rushing into one another, the boys hanging off Bud as if he were a tree.

When Bud finally broke loose and grabbed me, he felt the hard belly, pushed me back gently, and held me at arm's length.

"What's this?" he said with a smile.

I looked him straight in the eye. "We'll talk about it later."

Bud held Leon in his lap the whole time we ate dinner, and afterward when we sat out on the deck. Arleen's family came over later for coffee and dessert. The men sat beaming in their chairs, a couple of Old King Coles, with their pipes and bowls and kids. If things had worked out differently, I might have enjoyed the sight. It was pitch dark when we got the boys to bed, all of them wound up and cranky with fatigue. Afterward, Bud and I went back out on the deck and looked up at the sky.

"I guess you didn't have your tubes tied," Bud said and laughed.

"I didn't have the chance. But there's something else I need to say."

I was glad it was dark so he couldn't see my face. I sat completely still and looked up at the night. I told myself to make a wish on each and every star. Then I began to talk. By the time I finished saying it, Bud was deadly quiet while I held my breath. The stillness was so enormous it made me want to shout. Finally, he got up and went indoors, letting the screen door slam.

The next morning at breakfast, Bud spoke to the boys but not a word to me. I got the children off to school with the usual noise and fuss, then put Leon in his romper chair to play. Bud turned on me then and said, "Why didn't you just have it taken out?"

"Is that the answer?" I snapped back. "Out of sight, out of mind? You look me straight in the eye and tell me you've never had another woman, then I'll do the same."

He couldn't look at me but stared beyond me, his jaw clenched, his mouth pulled down.

"Look at me, Bud, and say it."

He got up slowly and went back up to bed. I took Leon with me and drove down to the PX to buy groceries. I must have traveled every aisle at least a dozen times, making up my mind. Leon had fallen asleep in his baby seat by the time I left the store. When I returned, I could see Bud through the kitchen window, sitting on the deck in his shorts and T-shirt, drinking coffee. I put Leon down for his nap and went out to join him.

"Hi," I said and stroked his neck. "What's up?"

He looked at me, I guess. He was wearing sunglasses, and I couldn't see his eyes. I sat down carefully in the chaise lounge next to him, reached over and took his hand. I was glad he didn't pull away.

"We've got a nice family with four boys who love you dearly. Why mess things up? On top of everything else, I don't have the strength. This one's taken more out of me than all the others combined."

"What if it's a girl?" he said, leaning toward me.

I stared at him in disbelief. After all I'd told him, why did he need to hurt me in this way? I wanted to reach out and snatch those glasses off his face. I wanted to see for myself what was written in those eyes. *Act in haste,* I told myself and took a few deep breaths instead.

"Why are you asking me now?" I kept my voice low. "You may find this hard to believe, Bud, but your question's out of line."

He considered this a while, sitting ramrod still. His silence was becoming almost more than I could bear. I thought one angry outburst might have cleared the air until I realized it wasn't anger he was wrestling with, but feelings he'd never had before.

"It's the chance I take," I said quickly. "Under the circumstances, I thought you'd want it this way."

We sat without saying a word, Bud sipping his coffee, me sipping my ice tea. And a Couple I'd never met was waiting somewhere, surrounded by golden hills. The palms riffled in the breeze. The jade hedge along the garden border had never looked so full and green. I leaned toward him and said, "I'm trying so hard to do the right thing."

"How soon do you have to know?" he asked.

"There's this couple who want to adopt, you see? The sooner the better, I think."

He stood up, as if he'd aged a hundred years, and walked to the edge
of the deck. For the longest time he stood there gazing westward, as if
he thought he might catch a glimpse of the ocean from our little house
or hear the breakers pounding on the beach. Then he sighed. I don't
believe I'd ever heard a sound so lonesome.

"Okay, Sandy," he said at last. "Show me what I have to do."

The tears caught me by surprise. I thought I'd never stop. He got up
quickly and took me in his arms and led me upstairs to bed.

When Margaret told me I could meet the Couple, my heart started
to pound. I didn't have to, she said, but it might put my mind to rest.
The day of our appointment, I couldn't fix my hair the way I wanted.
I tried on three different outfits, and not one of them looked right. Bud
said I was acting as nervous as a whore in church. I told him I didn't
appreciate the remark.

"You shouldn't take everything so personal," he said, which was easy
for him to say, since he wasn't going to come.

I arrived at the agency feeling large and untidy, but when Margaret
saw me, she said, "Why, Sandy, you look lovely!" I wondered what it
was she saw or what it was I'd missed. She took me into the interview
room, sat me down, left again, and came back in with two cups of herb
tea. I'd brought some pictures of our family and showed them to her.
She thought the Couple—Halden and Tess—would enjoy them too,
but I wasn't so sure. I felt awkward, like someone lost in a strange town.
Margaret heard voices in the reception area and went out to see. I heard
her greet people, and then the door opened wide.

I thought I should stand up, but my ankles were swollen. When she
brought them in, the first thing I noticed was their height. *Baby,* I

thought, *you better be tall like me!* They were so much older, too, in more ways than one. *Mature,* that's what Arleen would have said. I looked at the wife's light hair and realized I'd been wrong. She was a natural blond.

Only after they sat down did I notice their faces, bright and eager and afraid.

Halden, the husband, folded his hands, and I noticed they were shaking slightly, while his wife kept her hands out of sight. Once they started asking questions, I began to patter on. My talking didn't seem to bother them. In fact, it seemed to put everyone at ease. They looked at the family picture, admired my boys, and finally, solemnly, asked me the Big Question: *Why?* I told them why: I knew it wasn't Bud's.

"My husband and I were a little estranged before he shipped out last," I said. "I don't want anything to stand in the way of our reconciliation."

I felt proud of myself for using two words I seldom used, and both in the same breath. Hal, the husband, kept talking about how difficult this must be for me, which only made me feel self-conscious.

"You've got to do what you got to do," I said and quickly showed them a picture of Timmy in his Pony League baseball uniform.

We were together for over an hour. When Margaret finally showed them out, I felt sad to see them go.

This was a baby with a mind of its own. When the due date arrived, I felt like I had weeks to go. Still, I told Bud to be ready any time. I'd made pies and casseroles and put them in the freezer, changed the beds, and laundered all the clothes. I'd have to launder clothes several more times before the time was ripe.

During the waiting period, Bud and I decided we couldn't keep the boys in the dark, at least not the older ones. On a rainy spring day while the little boys were napping, we asked Jason and Timmy to come into the living room. I sat down on the sofa, one boy on either side, while

Bud took the La-Z-Boy rocker. I asked Jason if he knew why I was going to the hospital, and he said he reckoned he did: I was going to have a baby.

"That's right, but this baby is different," I said. "Kind of special."

When Jason asked me how, I had to stop a moment and think. All the words I'd planned to use flew right out the window. For a while all I could hear was the rain tapping against the panes. I told him that this baby didn't belong to us. He gave me a puzzled look. All the while I kept hoping Bud would step in and help, but he didn't offer one word.

"This baby's not ours," I said. "It's only borrowing your mom. This baby has a home with another mom and dad. So what I wanted to tell you boys, because you're grown up enough to understand, is when your Daddy brings me back I'll be coming home alone."

"That's good," Timmy said. "I don't want any more brothers."

Bud and I laughed, but Jason didn't say a word. His serious eyes never left my face.

"Are you going to be all right?" he asked, and I said of course I was.

"You sure you're coming back?"

Tears sprung into my eyes and choked off my words. I dropped clumsily to my knees in front of Jason. I took both his hands in mine and rested them on my swollen belly.

"Of course she is," Bud spoke up. "I'll be bringing Mom home myself."

Two more weeks passed before I felt the first contraction. Bud drove me over to the hospital and walked me up to Obstetrics, holding my overnight case. Once I'd been eased into the wheelchair, he said, "I won't come until you ask me to. Phone whenever you can now, hear?" He leaned over and kissed me on the top of my head, which made me laugh out loud.

"What's so funny?" he asked.

"You kissed me the way you kiss the boys."

"What's wrong with that?" He sounded all defensive.

"Nothing. I kinda liked it." I grabbed his hand and held it tight against my cheek. When the nurse came back and asked if he wanted to stay, he shook his head, kissed me again, and left. I don't believe I'd ever missed him so much.

Margaret came in while I was being prepped. I told her I wanted that baby in my room until Tess and Halden picked it up.

"We don't do that, Sandy. It's not a good idea."

I fixed on her a heavy look. "I want to see that baby or I might just change my mind . . ."

Margaret gazed at me for the longest time. "But, why? You're only asking for more pain."

"Maybe. And maybe not. I'm a mother, remember? I need to count the fingers and toes."

She looked down at her shoes, then back up and said, "Okay. I'll see what I can do."

I was in labor for four more hours before they took me to Delivery. When it was over and done with, I asked, what is it? A little girl, they said.

"Put her on my chest."

I waited and watched while they bathed and cleaned her, heard the crying subside. My eyes were weary, and then I felt her warmth against my skin.

Never have I seen such a head of hair—so full and shiny and black! None of the boys had been so blessed. As soon as I came out of delivery, Margaret was there and whispered, "Tess and Hal will come whenever you're ready."

"The sooner the better," I said.

When they arrived, I was holding the baby, gently pulling a baby comb through her amazing bangs.

They both stared at her, dazed, smiling, wide-eyed.

"We're having a bad hair day," I said and put the baby comb down.

Suddenly they were both in tears. We fell into a huddle, the baby safe inside, three grown up people, sobbing to beat the band. Then out came the Polaroid, the Minolta, and the minicam. I couldn't help but laugh. I held the baby up to Tess, who took her and held her as if she were a cloud. I could hear shutters whir. Then Hal took the baby, and Tess snapped some pictures. I asked and they gave me a Polaroid of Tess and the baby, then they took one with the baby and me. They didn't seem to mind.

At one point I had to get up and use the toilet, so I excused myself and left them with the baby nestled in Hal's arms. I was closing the door when I heard him whisper to his wife, "You know, we're the luckiest people alive." I knew then what some people meant when they talked about a broken heart. I stayed in there a full fifteen minutes, my face buried in a towel, not knowing if I'd ever be able to come out. When I finally did, I put on my sensible Navy smile.

Because I'd had some complications, the doctors wanted to keep an eye on me and the baby as well. So we'd be together for another couple of days. Margaret was worried and kept running in and out, asking, "Is there anything you need, dear?"

When Hal and Tess came back the next day, I asked them what they were going to name her. "Elizabeth Jane," Tess said. I said the name over and over to myself.

"That's pretty," I said and meant it, although *old-fashioned* is what I thought. I was partial to the sounds of *Ashley* and *Tiffany* and *Melissa*. "Is it a family name?" I asked.

"No. We liked it because it's what the mayor of Casterbridge named his daughter." She explained, and I said I'd never read the book.

"I hope she was good to her parents."

"Yes, she was," Tess said. "To all of them . . . very good."

They visited the next day, too, while the baby and I gained strength. I asked if I might have a picture on her birthdays, if they thought that would be all right. They'd send the photos to the agency, and Margaret would send them on to me. On the fourth day I phoned Bud, and Tess and Hal took Elizabeth Jane home to the ranch house in the hills.

I was quiet in the car when Bud drove me home. He didn't interrupt my thoughts or ask me how I felt. I was grateful for his silence. I was trying to decide what I'd tell the child if she ever came and asked.

Bud's been treating me real careful, like someone made of glass. I told him everything I could remember about what went on with Tess and Hal. I feel so much better when I talk. Bud must have worked on the boys pretty hard because they haven't said a word. Only Mikey asked once how come I was so thin. Because of the complications, I was told to spend a week in bed. The boys bring me breakfast every morning— orange juice and coffee, cantaloupe or honeydew, English muffins and marmalade, or a sweet roll sometimes. And there is always a hibiscus from the garden on the tray. Jason and Timmy look so proud when they lay that tray across my lap.

THE MISSING DAY

B efore the warm air from the Inland Sea could reach the mountains above the harbor, it had turned to fog. Here it settled, along a railroad track, where two women waited alone. Early as it was, they would have to wait ten minutes more before the Kobe express arrived. One of them was small, even by Japanese standards, and barely visible as she waited at the far end of the elevated platform.

The other woman was large, even by Western standards, supported on long narrow feet, which the local men found hilarious, particularly when they were drunk. Her bosom jutted out like shelf and became an encumbrance during the rush hour. Heads bumped against the shelf, sometimes with glee, until she had learned to travel before or after the crowds. And so she was waiting now, at 6:57 in the morning, on long legs that supported a high torso, legs that tapered into thin ankles that also startled the natives. Then those outrageous feet.

On the day she could not remember, Elizabeth Burns had arrived early, knowing she would have to wait alone on the wet platform. As she waited, she noticed the other figure at the other end. It was early for a child to be taking a train, but there was no accounting for local customs. Children were always on the move—to tutors and piano lessons and track events—in a steady, omnivorous rush to excel. The only curious thing, to her, was that this child was traveling alone. Slowly she began to walk toward the child. Within a few yards she realized she was looking at a woman, not a girl, and stopped.

Every month Elizabeth traveled to Kyoto with the club to visit the flea market at Toji. She got up early to prepare coffee and tea for the family, then walking down to the train. She usually met several of the women in Osaka, and together they caught an express to Kyoto. Elizabeth looked forward to these trips.

Wives of foreign businessmen had created the club, but others were free to join as long as they could afford the fees. Hers was a limited membership, allowing her access to the library and cultural events but not to the swimming pool or spa. The additional fee was prohibitive for a teacher's wife and, as far as Elizabeth was concerned, unnecessary. She didn't care much for the central location of the pool, designed, so it seemed, for bathers who enjoyed being on display. Truckers honked from the nearby thoroughfare. She didn't own an attractive suit and couldn't afford a new one, even if she found one her size, which was unlikely. Not to mention the competitive cluster around the dressing room mirror. Women brought large terrycloth towels covered with jungle cats or blue seagulls while others unfolded canvas chairs. On any sunny day in August the deck was full of homesick clubwomen, oiling their thighs and arms and backs until, thoroughly basted, they stretched out, turning over and over throughout the day.

Elizabeth did join the women for the monthly trip to Kyoto. Her husband was usually teaching, and the girls were in school. When the trip fell on a weekend, she placed her older daughter, Susan, in charge and enjoyed the day away from home.

Many of the women were strangers to her, wives of cola and farm implement executives, women who entertained a great deal and lamented the high price of beef. Elizabeth didn't share their grievances or their expense accounts, but she liked the company. Perhaps it was the barrage of English she appreciated most. For some time now she had been hearing her own words narrow in on themselves the more they were used among the same few people. Occasionally she thought she was losing her mind.

The same syllables ran around an endless and familiar track in her brain, encouraging the same worn-out thoughts. Once a month, at least, she could listen to the complaints of other women, their voices rushing at her in fresh patterns. They were not women who burdened themselves with the local patois. They wouldn't be here that long. When their complaints grew dull, she listened to the sturdy words instead and to the texture of their voices.

On the day that had been forgotten, she left home at 6:30, too early for anyone but the cat, which stretched and scratched the floor when she came downstairs. She wrote her husband a note and propped it against the ceramic coffee pot, reminding him to enforce a few chores for the children, which he would not do. The chores would be done haphazardly at the last possible moment, and John would do them all. Elizabeth left the note anyway. The kettle was now full of water, only waiting for one of the girls to light the gas. Out of reflex, she checked the milk to make sure it wasn't sour.

The morning was still wet when she walked out of the house. The temperature had dropped during the night, leaving a slight chill in the air. Refreshing, she thought, a break in the locked-in summer heat. Conflicting scents rose sharply through the mist: flowering shrubs and bus exhaust, fresh bread and burnt cooking oil.

The station was empty except for one ticket-taker and a newspaper vendor behind a kiosk. The walk had taken less than fifteen minutes and left her feeling vigorous. Downhill, she reminded herself. She bought her ticket from a machine and then an English-language newspaper from the kiosk. The solitary attendant punched the ticket, and she walked down to the train. She immediately noticed the fog lingering along the narrow tracks. Not that it was cooler here, really. It was cooler at home, in the hills. She walked slowly to the front of the platform and checked her watch, then turned around at the far end and began to walk the length of it, one foot placed in front of the other like a child measuring off a room. No one was watching, so she continued marking off the platform until she noticed the figure at the other end.

Sheets of fog thinned and mixed and split again. In between she noticed that the small woman at the other end was fussing with her shoes. In fact, Elizabeth thought she saw her take the shoes off entirely, cleaning them in quick movements with a white handkerchief. She had grown used to tight body movements. They were experts here. The country was too small for large gestures, too congested for large bodies, not to mention bosoms. The handkerchief flitted over the shoes again like a condensed and ghostly square of fog. Elizabeth watched the small hands fold the cloth as rapidly and efficiently as they would count change at the local market. With each compact move, Elizabeth felt large once more. Strange, that on a deserted platform Fate would contrive in miniature a domestic ritual she witnessed every day. She resented it and always had, the way she resented tidy, birdlike women who knew how to keep their limbs tucked in.

The other woman was putting her shoes down side by side, inches from the edge. She unfolded the handkerchief again and placed it, too, on the damp concrete, just beside the shoes, then bent down, both knees resting on the cloth. The woman drew her feet up under her bottom, toes bent against the pavement, which elevated her off the platform slightly and allowed her hem to remain dry.

Elizabeth wondered if perhaps this was some religious behavior she knew nothing about, like counting beads. The woman looked young— perhaps not so young. Elizabeth had no skill at guessing ages, and the fog made guessing harder. She only knew that none of it—shoes, hand-kerchief, and fog—made any sense.

For her own peace of mind, she decided at first the woman was about to wrap up the chunky shoes and replace them with comfortable san-dals. Instead of putting the shoes on the handkerchief and wrapping them up, which would have fit nicely into Elizabeth's script, the small woman knelt on the cloth. Elizabeth held her breath. With the woman on her knees, she noticed with alarm how close the large cloth was to the edge of the platform. Another few inches and she could fall off, down the four feet to the tracks below. Elizabeth knew the mist was simply not thick enough to conceal the tracks, and a sick, gaseous bub-ble rose to her throat.

To settle both her stomach and her fear, Elizabeth conjured up a story: the woman was a novice required to humble herself under pecu-liar circumstances. Yet Buddhist nuns, not to mention Catholics, did not wear stylish elevated shoes; and if the woman were ill, surely she wouldn't be kneeling. Elizabeth had never found kneeling conducive to well-being, although here it was often preferred. In that case, let her stay. But why so close to the edge?

She was watching with such intensity that she didn't hear the train whistle. If she had decided to take the next train, she would have been spared all this, the fog would have burned off, and no one would have dared kneel on the platform in their bare feet. She continued to stare until the kneeling woman began to sway back and forth, the movement from her waist growing deeper and deeper.

When the whistle blew again, Elizabeth jumped. The train grew vis-ible at last, curving slowly into the station. Elizabeth could not take her eyes off the swaying body, and moved closer. The other woman in no way acknowledged the sound of the train. Instead, she leaned over the edge of the platform until, in horrific slow motion, she began to fall head first toward the tracks below.

Elizabeth lunged forward. She grabbed the woman by the hips and dragged her back. In pulling her backward Elizabeth also pulled her to her feet, holding her there until the train had come to a full stop. The small woman covered her face with her hands. Once the train had stopped, Elizabeth released her and wondered in fury why there was no platform official today. Why? When the conductor blew the warning whistle, the woman grabbed her shoes and handkerchief and ran in bare feet through the open door of the train. Within seconds the doors closed behind her with a pneumatic hiss. She stood facing inward, head lowered, while a handful of passengers went on reading their papers or sleeping undisturbed.

Elizabeth stared at the back of the other woman's head in disbelief. Why hadn't she turned around to look? Elizabeth had not seen any more of her face than a slice of profile, and now the train was inching away from her toward Osaka. All she could do was watch it go, since she had forgotten it was her train, too.

What was she doing here? She felt suddenly fragmented from herself. The air was clammy, and she shivered. And wherever it was she was going, it could wait. Dazed, she walked away from the tracks, up the stairs to the exit, and gave her unused ticket to the attendant. He gazed at her and said something she couldn't grasp—his voice sounded like wind in a tunnel. Instead she looked at him with such full eyes he simply let her pass through with an impatient flick of his hand. Plate-glass and mirrored windows in the station shops reflected her blank, staring face. Yet all she could see, however incomplete, was the bowed head of the other woman, waiting for the train.

She crossed the street. Stores were still closed, as if time had stopped. Like an animal following the scents of a familiar trail, she moved instinctively up the hilly street, toward home. The composition of her mind was grainy, as if bits of memory the size of sand had filled it up. She didn't even smell the gardenias that were now in profuse bloom. As she turned into the residential street and up the steps to the house, she was only aware of being out of breath. She stopped on the steps for a moment and gazed out over a sea of gardenias toward the distant harbor. Haze blocked the view, and she felt the airless heat of summer settling in.

Catching her breath, she retreated indoors. The cat tried to rub against her legs but was brushed aside and jumped back in surprise. She heard someone in the kitchen, and Susan appeared to see who it was.

"Mom? Are you back already?"

She stared at her daughter for a full minute before crossing briskly to the kitchen sink. Taking a cloth from the drawer, she moistened it under the tap and pressed it against her face. Susan followed her into the kitchen and stood in the doorway, waiting.

"Mother?"

"Bring me a cup of tea in a few minutes, would you dear? I'm going up to change." She passed her daughter again and went upstairs while the cat, Elizabeth's pet, watched from a safe distance.

"What do you make of that?" the girl asked the cat.

Her husband was in the shower. She could hear the water running and was relieved she didn't have to say anything yet. By the closed door she assumed her younger daughter, Libby, was still asleep. Inside her own room, she removed her dress and stockings. Her shoes had already been left in the entry, a concession to local custom even though the house had been Westernized long ago with hardwood floors. She left her clothes where she dropped them and put on her light, summer robe. Lying down on the unmade bed, she closed her eyes and wished she'd brought the damp cloth with her.

Her eyes were still closed when John opened the bedroom door. He saw the clothes on the floor and then his wife in her *yukata* lying on the bed, hands folded over her stomach like a corpse.

"For crying out loud, Elizabeth. Are you all right?" He came over to sit beside her on the bed and took one of her warm hands in his.

"When did you get back?" he asked finally.

"Splitting headache. Must be the humidity. I just couldn't stand it."

She wished he would leave. Instead he continued holding her hand, which was growing hotter in his. She didn't feel she had the right to pull it away. She lost track of how long they sat like this as he waited for her to explain.

"John," she said at last, since something, anything, was expected. "You'll think I'm silly, but do you believe if you save a life, you'll inherit its burdens? People here believe that, don't they? That's why they never help."

"The heat has finally gotten to you," he joked. She opened her eyes and forced herself to smile. "What can I get for you?" he asked.

"Not a thing. Susan's bringing up some tea. You run along, dear," and she dismissed him as she would their children. He kissed her forehead and went. He met Susan coming up the stairs, beseeching him with questioning eyes, but he only shrugged.

"Beats me," he said over his shoulder, annoyed she wouldn't tell him anything, his annoyance making him feel small.

John struggled into his shoes, left the house, and was met by the thick, sweet smell of gardenias. It was then he noticed the haze over the harbor, the heaviness. The day would only get worse. Not much air was stirring, and Elizabeth's flushed and sickly face came to mind.

When her daughter came in, Elizabeth pretended to be asleep, hoping Susan would simply leave the tea and go. The girl whispered repeatedly until she answered. She knew Susan wanted just a word, a smile, but at the moment she felt unable to give her anything.

"Just put it down, dear. I'll get it in a moment."

"What's the matter, Mother?"

"Nothing, really. A headache. It'll go away."

She was a woman who cherished the company of her children, and now she felt dreadful that she wanted the girl to leave. And so she didn't hear the edge in her own voice, but Susan heard it. The tone was unfamiliar, and the girl didn't like it. Her mother never had headaches, either. She left, telling herself that she would check in again later.

Elizabeth opened her eyes when she heard the door close. She would give herself a few minutes to rest while she sorted out some sensible reason for her fatigue. Instead, she fell asleep as soon as she closed her eyes. Her sleep was so deep and dream-filled, and she was so weighted down in it, she didn't hear her daughter check in regularly, didn't notice the sunlight cross her bed and come in through a different window, or hear her husband return by taxi in the late afternoon.

When she did awaken, it was because of a strange weight pressing down on her diaphragm. She opened her eyes and stared into the dozing face of the cat, which had slipped in during Susan's last visit. The cat sat on her midriff in a hunkered, compact ball, opening its eyes when it felt her stir. She stroked it and then moved it off her stomach to the crook of her arm, but the cat stretched and jumped playfully off the bed. She struggled to sit up and tried to figure out the time of day and the reason she felt so drugged. On the bedside table were a cup and pot of tea. She touched them and found them stone cold and couldn't remember leaving them there. Picking up the tray, she moved sluggishly out of the room toward the stairs.

"Mom?" Libby called from her room. "You're up?"

"Yes, I'm up. You make it sound like such an event." She navigated the stairs carefully and found Susan and John waiting anxiously at the bottom like two firemen holding up a ladder.

"If the two of you could only see your faces! Have I risen from the dead?"

"More or less," Susan answered and took the tray out of her mother's hands, heading into the kitchen. John put his arms around her and asked her how she felt.

"Fine. Fine. I didn't know I was so tired. Must have been building up for weeks. But you two are certainly acting funny." She laughed in a tone he found a bit too brisk.

"What happened?" he asked again.

"Nothing. An attack of heat vapors." She gave a laugh and wished he would stop looking so intense.

Elizabeth flounced into the kitchen to check on Susan, and with that flounce his morning pique returned. How like her, to make light of something that had worried them all so much, and why did she belittle their concern? He would ask her in private, when she didn't feel compelled to swell up larger than life for the benefit of the girls.

Susan had prepared dinner for the family, and it was clear to Elizabeth she wasn't needed right away. John poured them each a glass of wine, and they sat in the living room while Susan finished.

"Do you know what you asked me this morning?" he said.

"No, frankly, I don't," she answered with a snort he supposed was a laugh. The directness of her gaze told him she really had forgotten, but it left him dismayed when she didn't even ask.

"You know, it's not too late for a short trip somewhere."

"I don't know. Planning it would be more trouble than it's worth," she sighed, touching his arm.

"You wouldn't have to do the planning," he said, pulling his arm away.

"Thank you, but we can wait."

"Wait for what?"

"You know."

"No, I don't know. Perhaps for hell to freeze? We could all use a change of scenery. I'm perfectly capable of making the arrangements, you know." He tried to sound humorous but realized he'd only succeeded in sounding loud.

Abruptly, Susan announced dinner, yelling up to Libby, who was still reading in bed.

He didn't think anymore about his wife's behavior until she woke him in the night, thrashing and demanding in her sleep, "Turn around . . . turn around. What are you doing? Please turn around."

Gently, he nudged her awake, and she announced she'd had a peculiar dream, which he didn't doubt. She couldn't remember much now, she said. Everything was too foggy. When they finally drifted back to sleep, she managed to sleep through the night.

For the first time in her life, she suffered a recurring dream. Caught in the middle of it, she thought nothing had ever been so vivid. Nothing. Then someone pulled her away, just as a child is yanked out of the path of a speeding car. Each time Elizabeth woke up, she heard a door slam shut and knew she was left outside once more.

They finally planned vacations, some with the girls and some without, followed by the long-awaited trip home. As their daughters grew older, they took up interests and jobs and men, leaving the older couple to decide how to spend their holidays alone. Resources expanded as the family contracted. Bank accounts grew as shopping lists shrank. John's retirement loomed, and they were besieged with nostalgia that had been nourished by a large collection of slides.

So they chose to indulge their memories—the girls were gone, mothers in their own right now—and to return to the Asia that had been their home, so many years ago. They drew up extravagant lists of every beauty spot they'd ever visited and a few they'd never visited but had heard about from ecstatic friends. As they traveled from place to place, they grew irritated by changes that had tarnished landmarks purified by memory. And the expense. The nerve of the innkeepers! On an angry impulse, they left Japan and traveled south to dusty, once-cheap Taiwan. On to Hong Kong with its fragrant squalor, its well-traveled harbors.

They were mistaken for an English couple, those vestigial colonials who still populated the small island of Victoria, leaving Kowloon to the Cantonese and the Scots. They followed their itinerary to the letter and traveled by taxi to the base of the Peak. Here among the terraced lanes and bougainvillea, they could recall a different suburb, a different harbor view, and forget about the packed-in refugees a short ride across the water. The cable car would take them to the top.

Elizabeth stepped up to buy their tickets and pushed her money across the counter. As she stopped to have their tickets punched, she caught the eye of the ticket-taker. There was something in his narrow but directed gaze that reminded her of another man collecting tickets. A millennium ago? They sat backward, not facing the Peak but the valley, to watch where they had been. Or perhaps to watch where they would go in case the cable broke. As the car climbed over ravines, lifting its occupants above rooftops and hills, it brought the island-dotted sea into view. It was nearly sunset, and the sky was flushed in shades of rose. They had ridden up in silence, each remembering in his or her own way the time they'd traveled here before: when Libby cried for fright going up and Elizabeth cried for beauty coming down. Now she was searching for a different memory, which she suspected had little to do with the cable car or the Peak or even this island, but another one. As they climbed out of the car, she remembered the train she once forgot to climb aboard, remembered the man who thought she'd gone mad because she'd returned her ticket to him unused and couldn't tell him why.

Hand in hand, they followed the walks from one edge of the cliffs to the other until the low sun reflecting off the sea blinded them. Suddenly, Elizabeth turned to her husband, grasping both his arms and looking him in the face.

"John, do you remember the day I saved that poor woman's life and came home all in a daze?"

"No, I don't," he said irritably. "What day are you talking about?"

"Oh, long ago. For some reason it just came to mind."

"You probably read about it in the papers."

"No, it happened. I'll tell you when we go back down. Right now, I simply have to get something cold to drink."

She pulled him in the direction of a restaurant constructed mostly of plate glass. She was sure it wasn't here before but noticed it had a commanding view of a string of green, hunch-backed islands. She had wept once for this view.

They stayed past sundown, until there wasn't any point in staying longer. As the cable began its descent, the light turned grainy. Again, they sat with their backs to the Peak, and she reminded herself to tell John about the woman and the train and the day she'd missed the club trip to Kyoto. In a moment.

They watched the dark enfold them as they reached the lower hills and terraced streets, watched the lights appear. Everywhere lights! A complete galaxy in the harbor, as though each freighter contained a star. In one distant but radiant blink, she thought she saw herself and John retracing routes traveled light-years ago, traveling so far in a long-shared life you might think they had, once and for all, extinguished the moments unshared.

The cable car gave a sickening lurch, and they both gauged the distance of a fall. Again she forgot about the life saved and the day lost, misplaced them completely, as if a door had closed somewhere inside her overlapping memories.

CENTER ZONE

———❦———

N icholas had recently returned from New York when I complained he was spending more time in flight than at rest. I'd be happy to accompany him, even happy to pay my way, but he frowned at my suggestion. I'd end up amusing myself alone, he said. So what? I was used to being on my own. Besides, I'd enjoy a trip to New York. Or Omaha, for that matter, which was another place that took up a good deal of his time.

His reaction puzzled me. I didn't know why he wanted me to remain behind in a city where neither of us had any roots. I knew Nick well enough not to be suspicious of a girl in every port. Nick was private. Perhaps a bit too aloof. I'd been with him long enough to know he was already married to his work.

We'd just moved from one side of Missouri to the other, from St. Louis to Kansas City, where we would stay while he finished a magazine piece that required access to stockyards, the West Bottoms, American Royal cowboys, and locally famous barbecue joints. Contracts for other articles spun out of this assignment, and it appeared we'd be in KC for some time. I'd given up a job to come with him and was feeling the anxiety of dependence.

"Take some classes," Nick said as I complained about this newfound time. "Learn something you've always wanted to learn and never had the chance."

So I did, studying philosophy and Spanish at the Jesuit college within bicycling distance of our house, beginning what felt like a life of premature retirement. I pedaled to my classes, to the library and art museum, and made a few casual friends. Nicholas was usually writing, and when he wasn't, he was in the field or on the phone.

We'd moved on a weekend in early August. Nick had a few contacts in the city, but he hadn't bothered to ask any of them about places to live. So we went to a rental agency that recommended the house on Forest. We took it after one look. It was the nicest place we'd ever rented: a two-story brick and frame home with a big kitchen and sunny breakfast space, three bedrooms upstairs, and a long sun porch at the back that Nick converted into a study. The yard was large, too, fenced and hedged, with a detached garage, where we parked the rusty Toyota. The street was shady, apparently integrated, most of the homes kept up while a few had slid into decline. I would have described the neighborhood as aging, but acceptably middle-class.

On an evening early in October, police sirens screamed in the night, stopping at the home of the woman who lived across the street—a disheveled but friendly woman I'd spoken with only once. Her two sons, half brothers, were fighting, and one was mean-drunk. When I slipped onto the porch to watch, Nick called out from the living room.

"Don't stay out there, Vickie. You don't know if anyone has a gun."

I came indoors and teased him for inventing dangers, for carting his St. Louis mentality to a metropolis half its size. I hadn't thought it important to tell him what our elderly neighbor Ruth had recently told me. "Keep your doors locked, honey. I've lived here since the '50s, and it's not safe here anymore."

The first of December was bitterly cold when I drove Nick to the airport. I planned to wait until the weekend and drive to St. Louis for a visit. I was looking forward to the trip. I'd been missing my old job, so after New Year's I promised myself to look for something part-time.

I went to bed Thursday night a little after 11:00 and read until I felt drowsy enough to fall asleep. In the dead of night a noise woke me. I didn't know the time and couldn't see the clock. I raised my head off the pillow, then propped myself up on my arm. There was no mistaking the sound. Someone was in the house. Without thinking, I called out, "Nick?" I scooted to a sitting position but didn't put on the light. The sounds had stopped, and I had a sudden desperate feeling. I didn't really believe he'd have returned in the middle of the night.

There was a chain lock on the bedroom door, but in the dark I'd forgotten it was there. The sounds started up again. I heard a foot on the bare wood step, heard the next step squeak. I shot out of bed and braced myself in the doorway, one arm on the opened door, the other on the frame. Whoever it was hadn't made it to the landing.

"Nicholas, you might have at least phoned first!"

"Come on down here," a man said. It wasn't Nick. "Bring yourself down here now!" The voice crackled with anger.

I should have closed the door and locked it, but I remembered the phone was in the room across the hall. I slipped into the adjoining bedroom and picked up the receiver. The line was dead. The man yelled out again to come down, and I walked through the dark to the stairs. I had no idea why I did this, although later I would spend months in self-reproach. Without a phone, what good was chain lock on a hollow-core bedroom door?

Clutching the banister, I made my way down the stairs. Light from the street lamp glowed through the landing drapes, but the rest of the house was dark. I got to the bottom step, keeping my eyes on my feet so I wouldn't stumble, when a coat was thrown over my head. I felt the suede of my new winter jacket, just as a gun muzzle was thrust between my shoulder blades.

"Do what I tell you. Get the money out."

My purse had been hanging on the hook beside the jacket, on a rack of ornate wrought-iron hooks that faced the stairs. I had less than five dollars. The man thrust the purse under the coat and told me again to "fetch the money out." He pushed the gun harder into my back.

"I don't have much," I said.

I located the bills, held them out, and felt them pulled from my fingers. A hand gripped my left arm, and I was being walked into the living room. I'd expected anger about so little money, but when he put his left arm around my throat and thrust his right hand under my nightgown, I understood why he didn't care.

I felt myself being jerked around, marched back the way I'd come, the jacket still covering my head. He told me to lie down and pushed me to the dining room floor until I was flat on my back. What I felt next has invaded my sleep and defeated my power to forget. My temperature swiftly dropped. I'd never felt so cold. My mind's eye saw clearly the gun pointed at my head, and one clear sentence framed itself. *So this is how you die.*

There was no shot, no sulfur hanging in the air, no swift transport through death's tunnel to the light at the other end. Instead, I felt the man's weight come down and force itself inside. Suffocating, I drew up my hand and felt coarse hair, a corduroy jacket. I smelled hair oil, sour with age. Swiftly he turned me over and bent down again, whispered words I scarcely heard, got to his feet and ran out the basement door, shouting what sounded like a threat.

I lay there, listening, until I felt certain he had gone. I threw the coat off my head and labored to my feet. The phone had been taken off the hook downstairs, and it struck me with sickening force that whoever it was had been in this house before. I replaced the phone and called the police. Trembling, I next phoned Nicholas in New York and got him out of bed, swiftly telling him what had happened. There was a huge silence before he spoke again. He'd return as soon as possible, he said. I assured him I wouldn't be in the house, if I could help it. Once we'd hung up, I felt as if every cubic inch of air had been extracted from my lungs. For a moment I couldn't breathe. He'd said scarcely a word except, *I'll be home as soon as I can.* I slumped into a dining room chair. I must have turned on every light.

The police arrived in minutes. Five of them, perhaps seven. By the careful way they looked at me, their cautious reserve, I knew they were used to emotion, but no emotion came. I'd turned into a machine: describing, explaining, reading some document, and then signing my name. A young man, as uncomfortable as I was, walked me to his squad car, apologized for the mess, and drove me to St. Luke's. I felt ridiculous in my nightgown and robe and slippers, covered with a coat, and for days I wondered if they thought I'd made it up.

Fluorescent lights leached the emergency room of any wholesome color. I sat awhile and then slowly paced, back and forth, intensely aware of the other people sitting in the room, the pallor of their skin. I waited my turn, since I wasn't about to die. When I was finally brought in and examined, the young intern was coming off an eighteen-hour shift. I didn't have a physician, I told him. Not yet. I was new in town. He offered a medical referral and asked for a card from a nurse wearing a neck-brace like a white sponge doughnut under her chin.

"We don't give out referrals, doctor," she told him briskly and gave him a tight, fast smile.

"This time we do," he snapped, his eyes red-rimmed with fatigue.

The nurse handed him the card without a word, and he handed it to me. I kept wondering why on earth referrals should not be given. I looked at the nurse—attractive, early forties, type-A personality—and felt an immediate loathing, my eyes riveted on the sponge doughnut under her chin. I wondered whether it was a man or a woman who'd tried to wring her neck.

A kindlier nurse encouraged me to wait in the examining room for a detective, who must have arrived soon after, although I couldn't say with any clarity how much time had elapsed. A minute? An hour? Someone entered the room and spoke my name, but what I noticed first was his tie, bright as a Thai monk's saffron robe.

The detective was short, with dark hair and a cast in one brown eye, which made it seem as though he wasn't actually looking at me but looking around the room. I found this immensely comforting. His voice was high and nasal, and he took his time saying what he had to say. Something about his deliberate gait struck me as both serious and chatty. Someone was working my area, he explained, someone who liked to use pillowcases and curtains—and, yes, a coat—to hide his victim's head. Whoever assaulted me was probably a neighbor, had probably watched me ride by every day on my bike. In fact, they had someone in mind.

He spoke, I listened, his displaced and reassuring eye taking in the room, the world, until I felt we were allies and had been since the beginning of time. That rape was like diphtheria—unfortunate but unavoidable in a world where no one was immunized. I leaned into his drawled words as if his voice were a buoy thrown out to save the drowning.

I returned to the house for lack of anywhere else to go. Our neighbor Ruth came over in the early afternoon and asked if I was all right, "after that man insulted you last night." I stared at her. The old woman looked stricken. How could she possibly have known? I'd lost all sense of time, but the event had already reached the newspaper. My name was omitted, but the street and block were printed for all to see, and I felt violated again.

I canceled my trip to St. Louis. I was in no shape to drive. I sat in the living room, amid the comings and goings of crime scene investigators dusting for prints, combing the house for clues. I was dozing fitfully on the couch when Nick walked in at 3:00.

"Glad you could make it," I snapped and promptly burst into tears.

Telling got harder, not easier, while a single thought burrowed into my mind: There hadn't been a gun at all, only a coat hanger, now lying on the floor in the hall, the very hanger that had held my winter jacket before the man threw it over my head. When I finished with the facts and moved on to speculation, Nick gave me a funny look. There was a flare to his nostrils, a hardening around the eyes that made me feel utterly dejected, as if he were outraged not at the rapist but at me. The look on his face launched an armada of unwelcome thoughts. *Should I have resisted? Should I have put up a fight?*

I hadn't wanted to spend one more night in the house, but as Nick pointed out, it really couldn't be helped. We combed the classifieds, made a few calls and visits, and quickly located a third-floor apartment where I felt reasonably safe, and we moved three days later. The apartment cost the same as the house but was a fraction of the size. No sun porch. No garage or garden. Only numerous dead-bolt locks.

I had to have something to do, even over Nick's mild objections— "Don't rush into anything, Vick." Since I wasn't particularly fussy, it took me no time to find a part-time job with a concerned citizens' group, a creatively messy office run by cheery ex-priests and motherly ex-nuns and volunteers of retirement age. I was grateful for the convivial traffic moving in and out and found myself too busy phoning and typing to pick like a dog on the bone of my private thoughts. Between 8:00 and 1:00, four days a week, I didn't feel tormented, and Nick went on with his work.

I didn't realize it at first, only perceived it after I'd been working for a while, but we'd been tiptoeing around each other, as if contact might leave a bruise. I'd meant to bring it up but couldn't find the words. In the evening Nick started getting up from the dinner table and retreating into the tiny second bedroom where he wrote. Once I asked him what was on his mind. Why the rush? "Just this deadline, Vickie. That's all."

So I washed the dishes alone and explored the edges of my anger. The next time that preoccupied look came over him and he was moving his chair back, preparing his retreat, I flew into him. "Talk to me," I screamed into his face. "How dare you turn your back?"

Enraged, I ran into the kitchen, opened the refrigerator, grabbed a can of beer and hurled it across the room, then another can and another. After the first can hit the wall, he leaped up and followed. Still ranting, I collapsed. He picked me up and carried me to the couch, where I cried until the outburst subsided. When it finally passed, I felt drained but free, incapable of pretense. Maybe he ought to leave, I said. At least for a while. "I'm sorry, but being with you I've come to feel like you're the one who's been wronged."

"I think you're imagining things," he said. His voice sounded cool, or perhaps I was only hearing things. But there was no mistaking the change, as though a frayed cord had finally broken.

He called a friend and left the next day, phoning once a day to see how I was getting on. The following week, he unexpectedly returned. His return upset me more than his departure and made a complete muddle in my head. I kept hearing the long, empty space in our conversation when I'd called him in New York, saw his eyes narrow again and again, heard over and over his solemn and distancing words. Where, if anywhere, did I fit into this private man's life? We might as well have been living on different continents. His presence made me anxious, then angry. After a few days I found the courage to ask him to leave for good.

Would I be all right? It made me sad, the way he asked it, concerned but still aloof. Yes, I told him. I'd be fine. Why not? I'd ask for more hours at work. They were desperate for help. When all his things were finally gone, including the scent of his aftershave, I walked from room to room in the silent apartment, feeling the presence of a new and solitary pain.

The "daymares" began before Nick moved and increased with his final departure. I was always trying to nap. The need to sleep grew huge, because it was constantly interrupted. Just before I drifted off, I would jerk awake. I would hear a footfall on a stair step. Where? Outside? On the third-floor landing? Coming up the back? Sleep eluded me, and I was left with the image of a dark figure creeping up the stairs.

When I finally fell asleep at night, Nick came to me in dreams, one night reproachful, repentant the next. I woke up abruptly from these encounters, my face wet with tears. Exhausted, all I did was sleep, as soon as I got home, until I imagined myself sleeping away my life. I began to see myself as a person without any life at all.

I found myself one Saturday sitting in the third row of a small auditorium filling out a theatrical resume with two dozen other hopefuls. I'd read the announcement in the paper: "Local Theater Group Plans Auditions for *Winter's Tale*." I hadn't acted or worked backstage since I was in college, ten years before. When asked what part I was planning to read, I said, "Any one at all."

"Try Paulina, dear," the director said in a large, emphatic voice. The woman herself was large and emphatic, dressed in a tie-dyed caftan, draped with bangles and beads. She had spread herself and her papers over a writing board that covered two auditorium seats.

"You've got a lovely mezzo. Perfect for Paulina. We need a soprano for Hermione."

Amused, I reached the stage and took a script, wondering if she intended us to sing our parts.

"Eddie. Frank. James." The woman trilled the names as if there was nothing in this world so delightful, so important, as heading an amateur troupe. "Read for us, will you, darlings? Act II, Scene three. Where Paulina enters. Eddie, go ahead with Antigonus, and James, you take the lords and servants. Frank, you're Leontes. All right, dear. Vickie, is it? Begin any time."

The man reading Antigonus came and stood beside me. He seemed about my age, thirty-something, but who could tell? We were probably the same height, but for some reason I felt as if I were gazing down at him from a great distance. Then he winked. Winked. I was sure of it. I had one of those fitful moments when you can't decide whether to be offended or laugh out loud.

Sunday evening the woman named Gwen phoned to say what a marvelous job I'd done, but, alas, she'd given the part of Paulina to someone whose work she knew better. Was I new in town? Would I be willing to come "on board" as an understudy? Would I please, oh please, consider running props? I said yes. I wanted something, anything at all.

I arrived the first night of rehearsals to discover that Gwen's stage manager was in charge of the crew. I didn't remember his name but remembered his face from auditions, the man playing Antigonus. The one who winked. Before the first crew meeting he came up and said in a fake Irish accent, "Well, Vickie McBride. You should've got Paulina, ya know. You're a natural. Sound just like a school marm." He grinned and stuck a cigarette behind his ear.

"I *was*," I said, "once upon a time."

"So, what are you doing now?" he asked, and I told him.

"And you?" I asked.

"I'm a cop. Center zone. You know where that is?"

A chill rippled my scalp. Had he been one of the men who came to the house that night? Did he remember me?

"How do you have time to do this?" I asked finally.

"I've got enough years on to work days. Get off before rush hour, so I don't work much overtime."

I'd never exchanged many words with a policeman, except the detective in the hospital. Before that, they'd been faceless men we used to call "the fuzz" and joked about from a distance. I'd never had a serious ticket, never caused an accident. A pristine life, until a few months ago. I wanted to ask him what it was like to be a cop, but what I really felt was disbelief. I asked him his name instead.

"Eddie," he said.

Eddie. A name I'd never liked. A name that sounded like wood being chopped. I must have given him a funny look, because he cocked his head and said, "Eddie as in Edgar. Not Edward or Edmund. *Edgar.* Like Gloucester's son. The madman on the moor."

I smiled, but he didn't smile back.

"*Lear*'s one of my favorite plays. I studied theater and thought about an acting career, but after three years of abject poverty—*ppffftt!*" He shot his arm in the air like a rocket, and then shrugged. "But that was a long time ago. Anyway, I prefer something a little more steady."

How was being a cop any steadier? I would have liked to ask, but couldn't. Being a cop struck me as infinitely less secure.

"Would you rather act or stage manage?" I asked instead, wondering if he was as disappointed as I had been.

"Six of one, half dozen of the other. You get more attention if you act. You have more power if you stage manage." He sounded as if it didn't matter. "I've worked with Gwen before. She asked me to be her stage manager, so I said yes."

"So you weren't auditioning?"

"No. Just helping out. But that doesn't mean I agree with all her choices." He gave me his sudden smile and went off to talk to someone else.

I began to watch him when I wasn't busy with my props. I felt like a kid who couldn't take her eyes off the object of an adolescent crush. He was so different from the men I was used to. Certainly different from Nicholas. He moved quickly, with purpose, from light booth to stage to wings, giving every task a definitive shape. He bantered constantly and made us laugh, which made me like him all the more. I might have believed this was the whole picture until the evening Gwen was too busy on stage to witness the arrival of the pompous young man playing Florizel, late for rehearsal the third night in a row. Florizel had scarcely entered the auditorium when Eddie came down on him like a duck on a June bug, so direct and hard I felt my pulse speed up.

"Once more, asshole, and you're gone!" Eddie yelled. "Hear me? Finished! I know a dozen actors who'd be happy to take your place!" His finger pointed at the younger man's nose.

Then Eddie turned and ran up to the light booth while the speechless Florizel moved down the aisle at a fast clip, the edges of his ears deep red, a look of consternation on his face. For an instant I imagined Eddie in uniform, fierce and businesslike, a picture I found so reassuring that for an instant I felt ashamed. I was suddenly glad to be a member of the crew, where his loyalty seemed more reliable. For several hours each evening, several evenings a week, I felt oddly safe.

During a break in rehearsal on a different night, I found Eddie looking over a handful of cassette tapes.

"For the show?" I asked.

"Nah. Just for me." He handed me the lot. Five tapes of Celtic music, at least three of them by the Chieftains.

"Do you like Irish music?" he asked.

"I don't know anything about it."

"I'll play you some one day."

I don't know why I said what I did next. I'm sure I meant it as a compliment, a desire to share something, anything, after he'd offered to share his tapes.

"You don't seem typical," I said. "I mean, for a cop."

Eddie gazed at me. "So? What's typical?"

I heard myself laugh with embarrassment. "I don't know."

"But I do. You expect us to have nothing but crime on our minds. Never have a life. Too much TV, Miss Vickie."

I was tired of feeling humbled. I lifted my chin and stared him down.

"And is this a life?" I made a circle with my hand, to the milling actors and crew members in torn denim, the clutter of partially constructed sets.

"It can be. Why not? You're here, aren't you?"

"But I'm not sure it's my life."

He nodded and looked away. "Where would you rather be?"

I shrugged. I didn't have an answer.

"Well, I'll tell you what I know," he said. "I'd rather be *here* than a lot of other places, including out drinking with a bunch of cops. I don't want to hang around talking about my job once the job is done, and I don't want to listen to a bunch of rookies brag. My line of work is just like your line of work and every other line of work—you gotta kiss a lotta ass to make it up through the ranks. Or you can forget about all that. Live your life, do what you want. I go to movies. I go to the gym. I listen to music, do a little acting, some stage managing, have fun helping out my theater friends. See what I'm saying?"

Gwen caught a cold and let us out early one Friday evening so she could go home and rest. Eddie was prepared to step in, but Gwen wasn't one to delegate. Eddie asked if I was in the mood for Celtic music. I said yes, and he invited me over to his place.

"I'm a very safe guy. Won't jump you or nothing."

He rented a studio apartment about two miles from where I lived. I made a note of the fact that his place was located on a dangerously accessible ground floor. A much-patched quilt covered a double bed. Several days of dishes stood neatly stacked in the sink. Hieronymus Bosch posters of Heaven and Hell were pinned to the wall, along with two theatrical posters announcing university productions of *Macbeth* and *A View from the Bridge.* He had a long, green, vinyl-upholstered couch and matching armchair, a coffee table cluttered with magazines and books and overflowing ashtrays, a small kitchen table and two chrome chairs, plus a large color television. The place looked masculine and bereft. I wondered if he'd ever been married. I glanced at the library books on the coffee table to see what he was reading. Espionage novels and biographies, mostly.

I saw his gun on the bedside table and felt myself go cold. He must have seen me staring at it and gave me a look while I tried to make a joke. "Do you always keep it lying around like that?"

"Sorry. I just take it for granted."

He picked it up and disappeared into a large adjoining walk-in closet. I heard a drawer open and close. He invited me to sit down and went over to make coffee. On a low bookcase stood a small stereo and tape player, a shelf of records, a box of tapes.

"May I look?"

"Sure. Go ahead. I like to go out on paydays and buy something new."

I flipped through the albums and tapes. What a curious collection. Rock. Country. Classical. Folk. I thought ruefully about my own carefully guided musical taste. I doubted I would have found Celtic music on my own, or the Eurythmics for that matter.

"What is it about Celtic music you like?" I asked.

He set two mugs of coffee on the table.

"It takes me away from everything," he said. "Makes me feel like

I'm living in a completely different world. I like that. Don't you?"

He went over and put in a tape.

"It's the combination of instruments that gets to you," he said. "Two different kinds of pipes, Irish harps, then that tin whistle and flute, some fiddles and something they call a tiompan drum. Here. Listen to this one."

As the tape played, he leaned into the music—eerie laments and lullabies and fighting songs. He asked if I was getting bored. I wasn't. A jig came on. Eddie hopped into the middle of the small room and began to dance. He was so different from the dark, contemplative, six-foot Nicholas. Eddie's hair was reddish brown, his eyes gray. He stopped dancing, embarrassed, as if he'd just discovered I was there, but I was delighted to watch him do the jig. Some of the songs were so joyful I could see why you'd want to leap to your feet. Others were sad, filled with haunting bagpipes and drum rolls that made me imagine musicians leading a procession to the gallows or the grave. I told him this and he nodded. "It gets to you sometimes."

"One more," he said. "My favorite. It's called 'The Rowan Tree.' I don't know whether is Scottish or Irish. I looked it up once, *rowan tree*. It's like a mountain ash, but I can't remember its significance anymore. Thought it might be a hanging tree, or the tree where you bury your beloved." He paused a moment, looking at me.

"I heard a guy say once, 'It takes a bleeding Irishman to play the pipes.'" He laughed, but I didn't get the joke.

He stopped talking, started the track, and I listened with him. When the song was over, haunted by the sound of the pipes, I was overcome by a hollow feeling deep inside my stomach. Tears stood in my eyes.

"Here now, what's this?" he said. "Give us a hug."

Everything that had happened to me came pouring out in a flood. We talked on and on, until after midnight. When I thought I should leave, he followed me home in his car and walked me to my door.

"We must live in the same 'zone,'" I said. We'd driven maybe a mile and a half west and a little south.

"Yep. The same one I work. I'll see you Sunday night," he said, meaning our next rehearsal, and gave my hand a squeeze.

There would be no moist advances, no frantic rush to bed, and I felt the most wonderful relief. I leaned over and kissed him on the cheek. He smiled and thanked me and closed my door. I stood still, just inside and heard him humming down the stairs. When I finally went to bed, I slept straight through the night.

By the time we began dress rehearsals, the day- and nightmares had returned. I woke up at 3:00 in the morning, convinced I'd heard windows pried open, a key in the lock. Always I heard the footsteps, just inside my door, and the angry voice, "Bring yourself down here now!" I was losing sleep. The flesh around my eyes looked inky and pinched. The kindly people at work asked if I was feeling well, and I usually answered, "A little insomnia, that's all."

At the theater Eddie noticed and asked if I was all right. I laughed nervously, told him I was having this little problem with auditory hallucinations. Wasn't that the term?

"You know what it sounds like to me?" he began.

Before he could explain, Gwen bellowed from the back row of the auditorium, and Eddie shot me an exasperated look, whispering, "We're about to witness the downside of community theater." Gwen flew down the aisle and onto the stage, shrieking something to a lighting technician about the gel on a downstage light, swept furiously through the wings where we stood, back down the stairs, and into the auditorium. I glanced at Eddie. He was doubled up with laughter.

"'Exit,'" he said. "'Pursued by a bear.'"

We looked out onstage to a knot of woebegone actors—badly cast, misdirected, and painfully under-rehearsed. From the back of the auditorium Gwen harangued them in full throat, but no amount of yelling could help them now. I went to my props table and did a second quick inventory of shepherd staffs and May baskets. Eddie left for the light booth, muttering, "Let's get this turkey on the road."

Everyone stayed to strike the set after the final Sunday matinee. A sense of loss crept over me. I was taking a ridiculously long time removing a screw from a flat when Eddie came up and offered to do it for me. I handed him the screwdriver, stood back and watched, feeling mournful and dull.

"Can I give you a call next week?" he asked.

Such a simple question. Such power to save. I'd hoped he would ask and was too old-fashioned to do it myself. We'd been busy with the play, and there hadn't been much time. I suddenly felt like giggling. Did people over thirty still go out on dates? The following Friday I was waiting for him downstairs when he drove up at 6:00. As he was parking, I bounded like a puppy out to the car.

"I would've come upstairs and got you, you know," he said.

"I know, but I couldn't wait."

To your amazement your life goes on, shaped by the most ordinary and incongruous events. You meet new people, go to movies, and marry someone kind. You discover you now possess an unwanted power: you can create a disturbance by simply mentioning your husband is a cop. Eyes widen. Smiles crack. By measuring these reactions you become adept at distinguishing a snob from a mensch. And everyone, it turns out, has a police story to share. So you learn not to mention it, at least not in the company of strangers. You add it to the other secret in your life. Sometimes you hide, instead, behind a flippant remark. *So Patty Hearst married a cop? Makes perfect sense to me.* You flinch at the friend who tells you, in the most casual of conversations, how her sister was raped in the pines behind the museum. But still you do not talk. It sounds too sensational, somehow. Whenever the opportunity presents itself, a small voice warns, *Don't tell.*

It comes back to me in hidden form. A remembered voice, a footstep, a prickling in the scalp. I might be chopping vegetables or stooped over the bathroom sink. I feel my blood run cold and my breath turn shallow, as if to make a noise ensures a certain death. I become a fawn frozen in long grass. *If only I'd locked the bedroom door . . .* But safety is a cunning thing, as elusive as sound and light.

I don't know how Eddie knows, but generally he does. It happened the other night, just as I was starting dinner, even though it's been many months since the incident took place. I was listening to a news story that seemed too lurid for NPR. I shut it off, feeling the cold sea inside me pitch and heave. I lost track of how long I stood there. It was a sultry evening, the beginning of September.

He came into the kitchen, embraced me, and said, "Why don't we go out to Tío's instead."

We left the house and drove to the restaurant where we ate in relative silence. I felt a little better after the meal and the margarita, and he said, with a smile, wouldn't it be fun if he gave me one of his special city cop tours. He made a U-turn from where we were parked and took us straight downtown. We drove along Twelfth St. to Charlotte, turning west on Fourteenth, and right again on Holmes.

"Roll down your window," he said.

Puzzled, I looked at him. He grinned and shut off the air-conditioner, lowering his window all the way. Damp evening air seeped rapidly into the car.

"Listen." He stopped the car near old St. Mary's Episcopal Church. Behind the building, in the patchy light of a parking lot, we saw a man with a tall gold scepter facing a group of musicians standing in neat rows, each one holding a drum or a bagpipe or a flute. Among them were several women in soft summer dresses and two tall boys in shorts.

Eddie got out and ran around to my side, opening the door. We leaned against the car and waited. The leader held up the scepter and spoke a few words to his band. The drums rolled in a stately tattoo. The bagpipes wheezed, taking in air. The leader turned regally toward the street, facing the same direction as his musicians. Then the pipes began in earnest, the song familiar. They marched slowly in their loose summer clothes, under the gaze of the mercury lamps, marching in imperfect unison. Before the pavement reached the privet hedge, the leader turned them around. The music grew muffled as the corps marched away from us to the other side of the church.

Eddie gestured for me to get back in the car, and we drove around the block to Thirteenth and parked in the far left-hand lane. What was usually a busy one-way street leading to state and federal office buildings was quiet as a graveyard at night. Eddie got out and I followed.

Once again the leader lifted his scepter and ran around from rear to front. The drums tapped out the tempo, the pipes wailed, the musicians moved their sandaled and Niked feet up and down to the rhythm of the lament. They marched together—men, women, and boys—moving with solemn, unhurried grace. I recognized the song. The sound faded as the musicians turned away and again disappeared behind the brick of St. Mary's. Church spires and bagpipes rose up against the institutional drabness of the street, and I was strangely transported. The band turned around as the drums rolled. I felt a chill, but not from fear, and for a while nothing mattered but the keening of the pipes.

SECRETS: THREE SHORT STORIES

SNOW

Mukashi mukashi. Long, long ago . . . She first heard these words from Grandmother when Grandmother told her stories, and then from Mother before Mother died, but after that the stories stopped. When Yukiko was old enough, she read the fairy tales to herself in her small, dim room. But the story words made her think of Mother, and she would quickly close the book, cover her head with her quilt, and weep. Father had no time for stories, and the new mother had no time either except to tell her—if she was bad and cried—that her curly hair proved she wasn't pure Japanese.

So many Russians in Sapporo once, Stepmother said and touched the girl's wavy hair, clucking her tongue. *Or maybe some problem in an earlier life. Maybe a curse.*

She wanted to ask Father about this curse, but he came home late, after she'd gone to bed. On Sundays, when he was home, Stepmother never left them alone together.

Yukiko began to stay away from the house. She went to soda shops after school with her friends, and to the movies. When she graduated from high school, she took a job as a receptionist in the big electronics company where the Americans worked. She came home late and only to use her bed, bowing to Father if he were there, and to Stepmother.

Yukiko was never cross or disagreeable, and so they left her alone. Father didn't seem to notice anyway if she was there or not. Yukiko thought he looked tired and old.

She met Gerald when he visited the office where she worked. He'd come to attend a meeting, and she'd had to struggle with her high school English to understand him. He spoke only a few words of Japanese, but he was studying, he said. She asked if he would like to exchange English lessons for Japanese. His smile was the brightest thing on his face. Everything else about him seemed insubstantial and pale: hair, lashes, eyes, skin. She thought the Sapporo winter might give his face some color.

He told Yukiko she should call him Jerry. Whenever she said his name, he laughed and said *jelly* is what you put on toast in the morning. Still, she had made him laugh, and that in itself was a kind of miracle. She was delighted to discover such a gift. She couldn't remember if she'd ever made Mother or Grandmother laugh. From the age of eight, all she could remember was the gloom of the old house, the tired father, and the anxious, whispering stepmother.

Jerry became her home. Jerry told her about his home in the town called Eudora, spoke to her of his parents and younger sister, the quiet, wooded hills of eastern Kansas.

Is it cold? she asked.

Sometimes, he said.

Is there snow?

Yes.

Enough to ski?

Sometimes.

I would miss the cold and snow, she told him.

We have some of both, he said.

And mountains? Do you have those?

No, he told her. There are no mountains in Kansas.

Father and Stepmother gave them a farewell dinner in an expensive restaurant, but the marriage would take place in America. Her father had no objection. She was sure her departure would cause barely a ripple in their lives. They gave her a show of tears at the airport, but she thought they were relieved to see her go. Jerry wore a red rose in his lapel, and they asked her about it, in rapid Hokkaido dialect. *So odd, this red flower on the coat.*

It's worn in celebration, she told them.

Celebration of what?

Of our marriage . . . and his return home.

Ah, yes.

He wore the red rose for the entire flight from Sapporo to Tokyo, from Tokyo to Anchorage, to Seattle, and on to Kansas City, where his parents and sister waited, waving small U.S. flags. They hugged Jerry and kissed his cheeks. They turned and hugged Yukiko, to her astonishment, as if they'd known her all her life. They gave her one of the little flags, which she kept and keeps still.

They drove for an hour, from the airport to Eudora. She was amazed by its smallness. Like a hamlet clinging to a hillside, except the houses were mostly new. Beside the one-story house his mother called "a ranch," the family was building a similar house, for Jerry and his bride. It would be ready in two, perhaps three months, they told her. And the car? Do you see it in the drive? The red Chevrolet? That was for Jerry and Yukiko, too. Jerry hugged his mother and shook his father's hand, and Yukiko, learning quickly, hugged his mother, too. This new mother smelled of apples and freshly ironed laundry, with skin as fair as Jerry's.

When they had been in Eudora a week, Jerry and his parents talked about a dog. Wouldn't he and Yukiko like a dog? She had never had a pet, and the thought of a puppy made her feel as delighted as a child. They read the newspaper ads on Sunday and later in the afternoon drove to a nearby town to pick out the small white poodle. Yuki, she named it, not for herself but because it was the word for snow and reminded her of Sapporo. Soon everyone in the household was calling the puppy Yuki-chan, Little Miss Snow.

Every day except Saturday and Sunday the workmen came to finish the new house. Every day Jerry drove into the city to his work. He explained to her once what he did, but all she retained was the fact that he worked with computers. She followed Jerry's mother around, helping, listening to her English, and repeating everything to herself. The wedding would take place soon, after the new house was completed.

Sometimes the family would sit around the dining room table in the evening to discuss the wedding. They would ask her questions she found difficult to answer. Would she like a wedding gown or would she prefer a dress? What food would she prefer for the wedding dinner? When she said *fish,* they all laughed. She was pleased to have made them laugh—the sound of their laughter wasn't spiteful or unkind—but she didn't understand why. Jerry carefully explained. His mother thought something with shrimp might be nice, but Yukiko didn't care much for shrimp, although she didn't say so, and told them in her broken English that Mother should decide what was best for a wedding in Kansas. Silently, each member of the family congratulated Jerry on his good fortune.

Yukiko and Jerry had been in Eudora six weeks when he decided they should take a drive to see the countryside west of town. Perhaps they'd go into Lawrence. Wouldn't she enjoy seeing the university Jerry had attended? Besides, it was a pretty town. She wanted to take Yuki-chan, too. She made so few requests Jerry was eager to please her. Of course Yuki could come along. If they decided to eat lunch somewhere, the dog could remain in the car.

It was overcast when they left and unusually cold for April. Before they had gone far, it began to snow, a wet snow that turned to gritty rain and back to snow again. Jerry was disappointed, but Yukiko held the dog in her lap and gazed, delighted, out the window.

I like the rain and snow, she told him. Water gives the earth a beautiful color. Don't you remember the snow in Hokkaido? And how beautiful the hillsides were in spring?

He turned his head to look at her and admire her profile. At that moment a passing truck skidded across the wet pavement and into their lane. Yukiko gasped. Jerry swerved the car right and then left, but the truck blocked all escape like a colossal metal wall. The red Chevrolet spun around once and crashed into its side.

Yukiko awoke to find herself in a bed, her head and hands bandaged, one eye patched. Slowly she understood her surroundings and realized Jerry's mother and father were sitting on either side of her. Mother had tears in her eyes and placed her hand across Yukiko's. Father, hat in hand, leaned forward with his arms on his thighs, his head hanging, staring at the floor. Something stronger than gravity was pulling him down.

We want you to live with us anyway, Mother was saying. For as long as you want. Forever, if you like.

What could this mean? she wondered. How is Yuki-chan? she asked.

I'm sorry, dear, but she's gone too.

Gone? Too? What was the meaning of this word *gone*? And why *too*? She didn't have the strength to ask. They left her to rest, returning the next day and the next, until, with an empty heart, she understood. The doctors removed her eye patch, watched her walk stiffly up the corridor and back again, then decreed she had gathered sufficient strength and was free to go. Mother and Father drove her back to the quiet, empty house.

It was a Thursday. Men were working on the second home, now nearly completed, and the ring of a hammer rose and hung in the air. For a startling moment she could see Jerry clearly—what astonishing pale hair and skin he had—and tears rose in her throat. It was as if he had simply melted away with the snow.

What will you do with the house now? she asked Jerry's father. He shook his head, looked away, and said he guessed they'd sell it.

Mother moved slowly through the house as she did her chores. Yukiko remembered how Mother had once laughed and was sorry the sound was gone from the house. What could she do for Mother?

Yukiko asked if she would like to try on one of the kimonos she had brought with her from Sapporo. Mother was a small woman and would easily fit into one. They went into Yukiko's room. From the bottom of her trunk she removed a carefully folded rectangle of brocaded cloth, folded undergarments, fabric belts, and a stiff formal obi. Slowly, methodically, Yukiko placed each garment around Jerry's mother, trying to explain its function in her inadequate English.

I'm so sorry you and Jerry weren't at least married, Mother said. Well, it doesn't matter, and she gave her head a weak but defiant toss. I'll always think of you as a daughter.

Yukiko went quickly around behind Mother so she couldn't see her eyes, and busied herself adjusting the obi. At last she led the older woman to the full-length mirror so she could see herself. She looked lovely, Yukiko thought, even if the kimono pattern was too youthful. But Mother only said she felt hobbled, like an old horse.

Yes, Yukiko agreed. You have to learn a new way to walk. It was like learning everything you thought you knew, everything, all over again.

SOAP

Marva Schotts used the last wedge of yellow laundry soap cleaning her six children's clothes. She was rubbing Gerard's overalls up and down the washboard when the soap broke apart. Marva searched the gray water, but the pieces had melted and vanished.

It was the middle of July, and there was no money left to buy laundry soap, or anything else for that matter. Marva had been feeding her children beans with bacon fat and pokeweed for three days straight.

Marva, who weighed one hundred three pounds and never more than one hundred fifteen during any of her pregnancies, stood up and felt the full weight of her thirty-three years. She went inside the house, took the silver dollar from her underwear drawer and kept it tight in her hand so she'd know where it was. She didn't bother to close the drawer but turned and walked back through the bedroom with its three double beds and three broken dressers, back through the front room with its dulled yellow linoleum, down the splintered and unpainted porch steps.

None of her children noticed when she walked by, slow as a sleep-walker, out to the road thirty yards off. None but six-year-old Gerard. She touched Gerard's soft hair as she passed, and he said to her back, "Where you goin', Ma?"

If she heard him, she didn't show it but kept walking down the weedy drive until she reached the blacktop county road. She turned left and never looked back. Gerard didn't say anything until bedtime, when one of the others asked, "Where's Ma?"

"I seen her go," he said and pointed. "Down the road."

None of the older ones bothered to wipe his runny nose or even to notice him. He sat in the dust of the yard, facing the road so they wouldn't see him cry.

Marva walked for four miles, accepting a lift from an old man in a bro-ken-down pickup, a young man in a broken-down Pontiac, a middle-aged truck driver with bad eyes and bad intentions who thought he'd shave off some miles by taking the Franklin County road, bypassing Interstate 35. His right hand ended up on her knee no matter how far she moved toward the passenger door, until she was clinging to the handle.

She left the truck driver at a Stuckey's when he stopped to let her buy a soft drink with her silver dollar. She didn't buy the drink but hid in the bathroom two hours. When she finally came out, he'd gone. She wandered out to the highway, not knowing where she was or where she wanted to be. A different man in a semi watched her pacing back and forth on the grassy strip beside the curb.

"You waitin' for someone, lady?" he yelled over the growling truck.

Marva looked up, distrustful, and pushed her long, fawn-brown hair away from her face. She wished there'd been just a bit more of that laundry soap left so she could've washed her hair that week. But the man had good eyes.

"Cat gotcher tongue?" he asked, not smiling. "I'm goin' as far as Wichita. You can come or not. Suit yourself."

"I'll come," Marva said and ran around to the passenger side. He didn't try to help her up into the cab, and for that she was grateful. "I'm goin' to Wichita too. Thank you kindly."

The next day, when Heber Schotts walked through the yard on his way home, the children parted like a plowed field row. Heber was sober but hungover and hungry. June, the oldest girl, was in the kitchen cooking beans and rice for the younger children. She heard Heber's step and her heart stopped. Age fifteen, she knew the feel of her father's hand, both hard and soft.

"Where's your ma?" he asked.

"Don't know," June whispered. "Gerard saw her walking to the road. That's all."

He picked up a kitchen chair and brought it down like a club against the floor. "You fibbin', girl?"

"No, sir," she said and braced herself against the stove. "Ask Gerard."

Heber had seen the wash bucket in the front yard but hadn't paid it any mind. He walked back outside and stood on the top step of the porch.

"Gerard. Come here, boy."

The child hung his head and inched his way toward the porch.

"You saw your ma?"

"Yes, sir. She was doin' our clothes. She stopped and went inside, come back out, and walked down the road."

"None of you stopped her?"

"No, sir. I thought she was goin' to the store."

"What're you talking 'bout, boy? Closest store's two mile."

"She walked it sometimes," the little boy said with a sniffle. "I walked it with her once."

Heber didn't notice the boy's dirty face or that the child stared continually out toward the road. Gerard would stare out at empty roads for the rest of his life. Sometimes in the night he would wake, even as a grown man, with her name caught in his throat.

In the morning the children dressed silently for school. June found one loaf of white bread her mother had overlooked, way back in the cupboard, and cut off the little bit of mold. She put a wedge of lard between two slices and wrapped each sandwich in brown paper she carefully cut from a grocery bag. The five younger children went to school with a sandwich. June went without. When they walked down to catch the bus, their father was still asleep on the front porch sofa.

A boy teased Gerard about his lunch, and Gerard kicked him in the shin. In the staff room teachers of the other Schotts children remarked coincidentally about the lard sandwiches, then went to see the principal.

At a recent luncheon with her sorority sisters, Carolyn Evans, married one year, talked about how meaningful she found her work. One of the sisters, the pretty one who'd married a dentist and never had to work, made a joke about "rubes on parade." Carolyn had never heard the phrase before, and it stung her to the core. When the Schotts children stepped off the school bus after school, Carolyn, in a dark blue dress, was waiting.

She followed them up to the house and asked if their parents were home. June thought the woman smiled too much. And her voice kept lifting into the air as if she were interested in them, when June was sure she wasn't.

"And who looks after you?" the young woman said in her flyaway bird voice.

"I do," June said and stared her in the eye. Flustered, the woman looked away.

"We're doin' just fine," June said and made her voice as hard as she knew how and put her hands on her hips.

"Where's your mother?" the woman asked.

"Visiting *her* mother," June lied.

"And your father?"

"Working. I'm in charge."

The woman said she wanted to ask about the sandwiches.

"It's all we got," June said. "The county won't give us no more."

Before leaving, Carolyn talked with each sullen child. When she returned to her office, she carefully typed out her report, carried it into her supervisor's office, and promptly burst into tears.

"I'm so sorry," she said in a quivering voice. "I'm trying to get pregnant, and I just can't take the stress."

The older woman consoled Carolyn in a reassuring voice and then told her to go home. Once she was gone the supervisor sighed, convinced the young woman, like all the others, would be gone by the end of the month.

Marva saw a sign near the highway where the trucker dropped her off. HELP WANTED, it said. Right there in the window of a big motel with pretty red doors and cream stucco walls. She slipped into the restroom of a nearby service station. She tried using a small black comb she'd found on the truck seat, but it broke in two when she pulled it through her matted hair. She saw a tiny bar of soap then, right there on the sink. Marva grabbed it, pulled off the paper, stuck her head under the faucet, and scrubbed, drying her hair on paper towels. She tucked her shirttail into her slacks, took off her smelly socks and threw them into the trash, washing her feet with the pure white bar.

When she finished, she wrapped the small bar in a paper towel and put it in her pocket beside the two pieces of comb. She took a deep breath, left the restroom, and walked slowly across the parking lot to the motel.

"You mean, you got no place to stay?" said the woman named Gert, the one teaching Marva how to be a maid.

Marva said she was going to stay with a friend, but her friend wasn't in the phone book anymore. Marva looked the woman in the eye when she said this. She didn't know anyone in Wichita.

"Junior can fix you up in one of the rooms here, or you can come on home with me till you get settled. I got a one bedroom, but I also got a hide-a-bed." She sounded proud.

Marva liked Gert's eyes and her big hearty laugh. Gert liked the fact Marva was quiet as a mouse. Gert didn't ask questions, gave Marva storage space in the hall closet, and loaned Marva some underwear, even if it was too large. The first night at Gert's she took a long bath and rubbed sweet-smelling soap over every inch of skin.

With her first paycheck, Marva bought two sets of underwear, a skirt, blouse, and four bars of soap, each a different brand and color. Gert once opened the hall closet to put in fresh towels and called out, "Hey, roommate. You afraid of a little dirt?"

Marva smiled. She liked Gert's teasing. When she finally moved into her own small place, where the hall closet was hers alone, Marva filled one whole shelf with Camay, Dial, Lava, Jergens, Ivory, and Dove. Every night when she came home from the motel, she opened the pantry doors, smiling back at the towers of canned tuna and vegetables and soup. She went to the clothes closet next and admired the few simple garments hanging there.

Saving the best for last, she would go to the hall closet with its two towels and two matching washcloths and an extra set of sheets. She would reach into the soap shelf and stroke the brightly packaged bars, counting every one, while the memory of Gerard's soft hair faded slowly from her hand.

GOOD NIGHT, MR. JOHNSON

I thought the dog belonged to the man ringing the Salvation Army bell outside the Piggly Wiggly. The dog had laid itself down at the foot of the collection bucket with its head up, watching the door. A big, longhaired animal—caramel brown and white, with a bit of black along the nose and eyes and tail. It had a broad, trusting face.

I began my work at 10:00 as usual, an hour before closing, and worked straight through the night. I stacked shelves and freezers, cleaned up broken glass or corn meal that'd busted out of the bag. I saw the dog once while I mopped up front. He was sitting right outside the plate-glass door, staring in.

I got me a nice three-room apartment, overlooking a little park, but they don't allow no pets. Bedroom, living room, eat-in kitchen. It's all I need, since I work at night, sleep in the day, and watch a little TV in between. I used to visit my Nana and Auntie, who raised me, but they both passed on. Nowadays I visit my niece instead.

Now, I like helping Miz Davis. She has one of the apartments downstairs. I reckon she's my age, but I have a hard time telling age with white folks. She's a big woman, with weak knees and bad circulation that makes her legs swell up like stumps. I been helping her carry in her groceries and laundry for the five years I've lived here.

When I first moved in, I thought she'd move out, seeing as I was the first black man in the building. It was that look in her eye told me she thought I was just lying in wait for a chance to climb in her bedroom window and insult her. Took two years and lots of helping with the groceries before that look left her eyes.

"Why, you're awful nice for a colored man," she told me once. The way she said it was so sincere I had to laugh out loud—once I got upstairs. Miz Davis is just doing the best she can, and I got too much gray in my hair to make her nervous anymore.

I saw the big dog the next night I come to work. Same spot, too, right up where the bell ringer had been collecting. *Now, ain't that a shame,* I told myself. *And the weather turnin' cold.* I went inside to my locker, hung up my coat, and changed my shoes for work boots. I saw Mr. Jarman, the manager, and asked him then and there. "Whose dog?"

"What dog?"

"Big brown and white one. Out front. Seen it yesterday too."

"Oh, yeah. Henry told me about it. Asked if he should save it some bones. I said, 'Hell, no! We'll never get rid of it then.'"

Henry's one of our butchers. Henry'd give scraps to birds.

"It's getting cold," I said.

"Don't fret on it, Johnson," he answered. "That dog'll be gone by morning. You can count on it."

He said it like getting rid of a dog was something to brag on. Trouble with these city folks is they only know concrete, and scared of anything on four feet. Folks here see a dog coming toward them, they wanna cross the street. First word out of their mouths is, "That dog bite?" Down at Nana's farm we had dogs galore. Yard dogs, house dogs, hunting dogs, Nana loved 'em all. Why, you couldn't cross her gallery without tripping over some hound, fast asleep. Henry's the only one around here with any feeling for natural life.

It was still dark when I left the store at 7:00. The dog wasn't out front. I peeked out by the dumpsters on my way home, but I didn't see him there. I figured Jarman was right, and he'd gone. Then I caught sight of a brown and white tail, poking out of a big box.

Every day Henry came to work, I asked him, "Seen that dog?"

"And it's a crying shame!" Henry said. "Now I ask you, Johnson, what kind of people would drop a full-grown dog at the supermarket and drive off? Hateful, if you ask me."

"You been feedin' it, Henry?" I asked and smiled.

"Me?" His eyes grew wide behind those thick, smudged glasses.

"I was hopin' someone would. Ten days 'fore Christmas, and it don't seem right to let it starve."

Henry leaned toward me and whispered. "I give it scraps."

"Why don't you take it home with you?" I asked. "You got kids, don'tcha?"

"Got a dog, too. And a missus who'd file for divorce." He shook his head and walked off in an unsteady line toward the walk-in freezer.

Each day that passed, Mr. Jarman got angrier. He kept finding excuses to go 'round to the back. I asked him if he wasn't waiting for a special Christmas delivery. I couldn't help myself.

"No, Johnson," he said, all huffy. "I'm not waiting for a Christmas delivery. It's that damn dog. I'll bet good money Henry's feeding it."

"Don't nobody need to feed it, sir. I'd say this was a good enough place for any stray to stick around."

"I don't want a mutt hanging around the store, scaring the customers. It's our busiest season."

On Christmas Eve, Mr. Jarmon came to work just as I was fixing to leave.

"I called animal control," he said.

"Whatever for?" I asked. I was tired and for a moment I'd forgot about the dog.

"They'll take that dog away."

I went back to my locker, changed into my shoes and overcoat. When I came back out, the animal control truck was there. Mr. Jarmon was talking to a salt and pepper team, both real young men. I looked close at the black one. He was the one holding the noose. Jarmon led them around to the back. Something made me follow along behind.

The dog caught sight of us and backed up, eyes scared, tail tucked down. It got itself caught next to a brick wall, with no way out. "Get him, Cox!" the white boy said. The black boy poked out the stick and noose. The dog pulled away. The white boy yanked the noose out of the other one's hand and tried himself. He missed too, hitting the dog hard on the neck. The dog yelped in pain. I didn't want to see no more. I walked up to Mr. Jarmon.

"If you give me a ride home, sir, I'll take the dog."

"Whaddya say, Johnson?" He stared at me. "You want that miserable thing?"

"That's what I'm saying. I seen him the first day he was here. He wasn't so miserable-looking then."

Jarmon called the two men off. I went inside and got Henry to give me a bone and a length of rope. I found the dog soon enough, crouched behind a box. When I lured him out, I wondered how the both of us were gonna fit in my three rooms.

Mr. Jarmon came around with his car, looking uneasy. The dog still had hold of his bone, and I had hold of the rope. I said, "We'll get in back. I got a hold on and he's not fussing anymore. He's not mean, just lonesome."

Jarmon nodded and we drove on up the Avenue to Hardesty, then up St. John to the apartment building.

"That where you live, Johnson?"

"Yes, sir, it is."

"You're close to a park," he said, like I didn't know it. "The dog'll like the park."

Miz Davis opened her door when she heard me coming in the front, talking to that hound. It was cold in the hall, and she had her arms wrapped around her body. The dog wagged its tail.

"You won't tell?" I said first off.

She looked down hard at the animal and then leaned up toward me. For a moment her eyes got round and bright. "To tell you the truth, I keep a little cat. You won't tell on me either, will you?"

We both laughed.

"You doin' anything special tomorrow?" she asked.

"I'll be over at my niece's," I said. "And you?"

"I'm expecting a call from my son, you know. The army boy."

"You have a nice Christmas, Miz Davis," I said and headed upstairs with the dog.

I laid out a blanket for it on the bedroom floor. Didn't know what else to do. I hadn't been asleep an hour when I woke up and found the dog laying across my feet. I lifted my head and stared at it for a moment. I wasn't sure I liked having an animal on my bed. But I was too tired to care. Next time I woke, he'd crawled up a foot or two. I fell asleep this time thinking about what folks used to say about a one, two, or three dog night.

I was having a dream when I felt something lapping at my hand. I looked down and saw his head across my chest, his brown eyes watching over me. I scratched behind his ears till his eyes dropped shut. If he'd been Miz Davis's cat, he'd have purred.

"Good night, Mr. Dog," I said and rubbed its head.

I swan that out of the dark I heard a sweet, soft voice answer me back, *Good night, Mr. Johnson.*

WHEN LUZ SINGS HER SOLO

———— ✺ ————

D arius's wife had locked herself in the bathroom again, crooning a
bolero. She had a passionate voice, deep and smoky, and her song
moved him to tears. He would have liked to tell her but couldn't,
so long as she believed he was one cause of her sorrow. What Darius
believed was this: she was hiding in the bathroom to mourn her losses,
and that was something he understood.

"Qué lejos estas, qué vacia nuestra casa," she sang. How far you are,
how empty is our house.

"Luz, please," he called out. "Let's deal with this together."

She stopped, waited, then hurled her words at the door. "And who is
this arrogant person who believes he knows my heart?" The song
resumed. *"No me queda más que el amargo dolor . . . Cuándo volverá la
esperanza?"* Nothing more remains but bitter pain . . . When will hope
return?

The first time she'd locked him out, he was an inexperienced husband. What could he possibly do? He pleaded, but the more he did, the
more theatrical her tears became. When she started to sing, he stopped
pleading and listened. The song was beautiful—it was always the same
song—and he intuited the meaning without understanding a word.
When she'd finished, he was crouched on the floor outside while she sat

on the floor inside, only the door blocking his reach. "That was beautiful, Luz. A beautiful Colombian song."

"My song, Darius. MINE. I wrote it. A *latina* song for *latina* grief."

She pronounced it the Spanish way. Pure vowels. Soft consonants.

"And what is my wife doing, singing such a sad song?"

"Oh, Darius." (He heard a sniffle.) "How can I expect a Persian to understand?"

He left the bedroom, walked into the dining room and cleared the dinner dishes off the table, filled the kitchen sink with soap and water, and sponged the countertops. Her lyrics filled the apartment.

He had no difficulty figuring out the cause of her distress. Only two weeks before they'd received news that his adolescent brother might join them here. Not that Luz objected to Jonathan. On the contrary, she was a wellspring of family feeling, as their telephone bills could attest. Hours of calls to her mother's in Cali. Hours of family sharing without a family touch, from yet another country that endangered its young. The issue wasn't Jonathan at all. In fact, Luz was the one who insisted the boy must leave *his* family home in Tehran. Immediately.

"Listen to your father, Darius. They will turn your little brother into a human minesweeper."

No, the issue was the size of their apartment and her belief she was pregnant.

All this—Jonathan's arrival and their likely parenthood—should be cause for celebration, he thought. For *esperanza*. Not *amargo dolor*. He could understand her dismay, but there was nothing to be done. Before they could own a house, he'd told her firmly only the week before, they must wait a little longer, save a little more. "I want my wife to have a house she can be proud of," he said in all sincerity. "I want her to have the best." She'd given him an admiring look that only increased his resolve.

But such was the burden and ecstasy of his new life that his beloved

Colombian wife had the emotional range and speed of an express elevator: headstrong and imprudent one moment, wise the next. From the beginning, she'd sent his mind and heart racing into territory largely unexplored. And now, one hour after she'd announced Jonathan must escape and live with them, she'd talked herself into this exorbitant frenzy, finally yelling, "Darius, how can you do this to me?"

Worried parents had sent Darius away as well, during the long war with Iraq. He was twenty-three at the time and had nearly completed his dental studies. Too old really to be a boy soldier, but his father was afraid he might still be drafted.

"You have two misfortunes," his father told him. "First, you are too young, and your youth provokes the wrath of elderly clerics. And second, you are both Zoroastrian and Jewish. You must leave, Darius. Your mother and I wish it. There is no future for you here." Within weeks, simultaneously thrilled and grief-stricken, he was dispatched to family members living in Missouri.

Now Jonathan. Age fifteen. The perfect minesweeper. He would come because he must. And so they bought another bed and put it in the spare bedroom no bigger than a broom closet.

They formed a delegation, Jonathan's family-in-America, driving to the airport in caravan: Uncle Bahman first, in his Lincoln town car, accompanied by his wife, Sophia, and their two young daughters; their son next, driving his own Toyota Corolla because he refused to ride with his father.

"I want to live, Papa! Not die on some road in the boondocks!"

Darius brought up the rear in his elderly Honda, with Luz periodically reaching out to give his arm a cautionary touch.

"Slower, Darius. Remember I'm carrying your child. Faster, Darius! That idiot is passing us again!"

He couldn't imagine how long Jonathan had been traveling, since his own memories of the trip were entirely blurred. Nor could he imagine what the boy looked like, even though his mother had sent pictures. In the photos Jonathan reminded him of Uncle Bahman, which meant he would probably grow up to resemble their grandfather. Which meant he might be very tall. Which also meant he might have Bahman's generosity of heart and unfortunate sense of humor. Such were the woolly contents of Darius's head as he parked the car that he didn't at first realize Luz was scolding him.

"Darius, where are you? I've been talking to you for five minutes, but you are gone. GONE."

"Do you think he'll recognize me?" he asked. After all, he hadn't seen his brother since the boy was nine. Or was it eight?

Her voice softened. "You're worried, aren't you?"

"Yes. What do we do with a teenager, Luz?"

She clucked her tongue and touched his arm. "Not to worry. Leave that to me."

And for a moment he felt restored.

The flight had already arrived, thirty minutes early. When they discovered this, all seven Shaloris raced to the gate, shouting instructions to one another, Sophia cursing the airlines in Farsi while Luz cursed them in Spanish.

"Didn't you phone ahead?" Sophia asked Bahman.

"You know I didn't. We've been together all day!"

They couldn't see him at first. He was sitting down, patiently waiting. Then a voice called out, "Darius?" Smiling, the boy stood (unfolded, Darius thought) and leaned over to pick up a small bag. All Darius could think was how tall Jonathan was and how much taller he would eventually become. By this time the family had fallen upon him, and Darius marveled that the boy could breathe.

When they returned to the apartment, Luz ushered Jonathan inside while Darius brought in the boy's two bags. He was an attractive kid,

Darius thought, with an endearing, lopsided smile. His voice had started to change. It rose and fell, squeaked and cracked, dipped and curved.
Bahman's daughters were smitten. In love. As if he were a young film
star, with Sophia already calculating future damage. Never mind, Luz
told him. The novelty would pass. All young girls have crushes on their
male cousins. "They're practicing," she said in a lofty tone. *Practicing
for what?* he wanted to ask but thought better of it. They planned to let
Jonathan rest, then take him to Bahman's for a dinner celebration, but
Jonathan had no apparent need to rest, not even to sit down.

With Luz in the lead and Darius in the rear, they showed the boy his
room. Jonathan was too excited to care and merely smiled at Luz while
he spoke to Darius in Farsi, sharing messages from home. Luz pressed
him for an immediate translation: "What did he say? What does he
think?"

"He thinks it's very nice and modern," he lied, since Jonathan had
said nothing whatsoever about the room except "thank you," and Luz
had heard that.

She showed him his small bathroom with its modern shower stall and
then, taking him by the arm, the kitchen and small patio outside the
back door. Relieved that Luz had taken charge of the boy, Darius stayed
behind and sank into a living room chair. He supposed they'd rise to
the occasion—clearly Luz already had. They would have to learn as they
went along. The last time Darius had seen his brother the boy was so
small, holding a toy while tears hung from his large and tender eyes
because Darius was leaving the family home for the last time. Now here
he was, nearly grown. It was miraculous, and daunting, but his Luz had
taken up this new responsibility like a valuable Dior cape and thrown
it over her shoulders. He couldn't help but smile.

Luz took Jonathan outside, where they remained, surrounded by
her geraniums and orange tree, petunias, begonias, potted tomatoes,
and peppers. "Whatever you need," Darius heard her instructing him.

"Whatever you do not understand, you must come to us." But what did Jonathan understand? Darius suspected his English barely existed. A deceiving wisp of nods and smiles, "yesses" and "thank yous" and "okays." And from his cousin Fahd a quickly learned and well-placed "cool, man!" Darius closed his eyes, gathering strength from the sound of her voice. In a moment she would call for help.

Mitra and little Zee opened the door before Sophia could intercept them. The girls stood blushing and giggling while their cousin complimented them on their home. Fahd called out, and soon everyone had piled up in the entry hall, welcoming Jonathan. Luz was buoyant, her mood light, which was a great relief. Darius had feared the attention falling on Jonathan might set off an attack of attention-withdrawal. Colombians, he'd discovered, did not play supporting roles to anyone. But today Luz was amused to the point of laughter by the giddiness Jonathan had provoked in his little cousins. She was fond of Bahman's children, if not his wife, and now Darius found her carefully watching the little girls. The urge to observe had suppressed her natural urge to perform, and he realized Jonathan had enchanted Luz as well.

Sophia moved with authority into the throng of young people. Expensive amber earrings hung from her ears, a companion brooch nestled at the first button of a deeply plunging beige silk blouse that stopped at the perfect declivity of her handsome breasts. Luz had also noticed the brooch and its strategic location, and drew herself up, flinging back her thick shoulder-length hair. (How many times had Luz scornfully pointed out that Sophia shouldn't imprison her beautiful chestnut hair in "that jelly roll"?) He hoped Jonathan would see Sophia in a maternal light—elegant and soft. His Luz presented a different image, best described as tastefully flamboyant. Between these two women, Jonathan oughtn't to suffer too much the absence of a mother.

Sophia encircled him, leading him to Bahman, and they all trooped into Sophia's white- and gold-brocaded living room. Bouquets of life-like silk flowers filled oversized round vases. Swags of gold and white and navy cloth hung from rods above the windows. Framed squares of Persian cloth and reproductions of ancient pictures decorated the walls; a mosaic vase and box rested on side tables. Luz held her breath. She always did. Although the style and contents differed, the room remind-ed her of her childhood home in Cali, also reminding her, he imagined, that they lived in a modest apartment absolutely lacking in gold. But who needed gold? The way she had decorated their apartment delight-ed him. She'd made a warm nest that he admired, even as he knew it wasn't good enough for Luz. Her envy, her sense of loss awakened each time they visited Bahman and Sophia, and so Darius vigorously pur-sued a policy of reciprocal visits, with Bahman's family spending as much time in their apartment as they spent in Bahman's large home. Only Jonathan's presence eased his wife's discomfort tonight.

After dinner, Luz joined Sophia in the kitchen to clean up, and Fahd retreated to his computer and his chat room, not finding Jonathan suf-ficiently interesting to invite him along. Darius stayed behind to dis-cuss with Bahman the news Jonathan brought, the politics of home and mosque. Meanwhile, the boy sat trapped between Mitra and little Zee on a vast brocaded sofa, scanning the family photograph album. Out of reach, he could make out Luz and Sophia stumbling about in English.

Darius owed everything to Bahman, his father's youngest brother. It was Bahman who arranged for him to finish his dental studies, paid the fees for the state boards, helped him set up the first dental office, and supported his marriage to Luz over Sophia's considerable objection. Not only was he not marrying a good Iranian girl, he was marrying some-one with whom he shared no language at all.

"But they are very well-suited," Bahman had said in Darius's defense, while the three of them had discussed his intentions over coffee.

"Marriage is hard enough!" Sophia answered hotly. "Why make it even harder?"

He reported none of this to Luz. Nor was it true that Luz and he did not share a language. Sophia was merely judging their English by the measuring stick of her own, which was very short indeed. They were all products of the same language school, but Sophia had quit soon after reaching a bare proficiency, while he and Luz and stayed on as long as they could until there didn't seem much point in staying longer. By that time, they'd both found suitable work, he as a dentist, Luz with a travel agent who did Latin American tours. It was Sophia who limped along in her functional English, ignoring Bahman when he nagged her to return to the school.

"What do you have to lose?" he exhorted. "The school's free!"

Darius had a fair idea what Sophia felt she had to lose, and it had everything to do with her heirloom amber brooch, her saffron rice, her love of Persian literature, and the relentlessly broken dream of returning home. He and Bahman and the children had all accepted their new life, but not Sophia. And now, as Luz's pregnancy unfolded, he'd begun to harbor doubts regarding her as well.

Luz's English wasn't much better than his when she had first entered the school. Within a month she moved to the next level and then the next until they found themselves gazing at each other from opposite sides of the same room. She took an interest in everyone, organizing birthday parties, showers, holiday parties, parties, parties, and more parties. If the teacher had been willing, Luz would have had the class singing every day.

He thought she was splendid. Spirited and hardworking and beautiful. She'd come to visit her brothers, blessed with parents who'd looked at the incomprehensible violence around them and sent their children away. Parents like his own, he thought after she'd told him. *We've both been sent away. With love and sorrow.* He became aware of a remarkable new feeling, something grand and larger than himself. He pored through his English dictionary to pin the feeling down. *Fate, futurity, predestination, kismet* (he rather liked this one; it didn't sound English), *chance, doom, fortune,* finally settling on *destiny.* The only melodious word, the only one with the right weight and feeling and tone. This is what they were to each other, he felt sure of it. Before he knew what was happening, he had invited her out for coffee and then to dinner at Bahman's house. If it ever occurred to him she might not feel the same, might not embrace her "destiny" as he had done, he never let the doubt intrude but pursued her quietly and with great care. Sophia knew instantly he was in love and would have launched a campaign to discourage him if Bahman had not intervened. Then Luz's brothers moved away, and she remained because of him.

After Jonathan fell into bed, his first night in America, Darius and Luz sat in the living room and planned.

"He knows this much English." She held up her right hand, measuring a space of an inch between thumb and index finger. "I'm taking him to the school tomorrow."

Darius agreed. In the fall Jonathan would have to go to public school, but for now he could attend the free school where Darius and Luz had first met. But the boy foiled their plans, sleeping eighteen hours until Luz awakened him, afraid he'd be derailed for weeks, awake all night, asleep during the profitable, English-learning hours of the day.

"Circadian disrhythmia," she announced, wagging her finger. "We travel agents know about such things. We will have to deprive him of sleep."

But there was no depriving Jonathan of sleep. For a week his eyes fell shut at breakfast, lunch, and dinner until Luz prodded him awake, gave him coffee and candy and red meat. Toward the end of the second week, she announced, "Enough!" She hurried him to the car and drove him to the school, telling Darius, "Now he'll be too ashamed to sleep."

The strategy apparently worked, and when she picked him up three hours later, he was lively, practicing his new verbs and phrases, full of jokes, depicting his older classmates with deadpan humor.

"He'll be all right," Luz assured him. "They will make him their pet."

Thus began a regimen of English, health care, and shopping, two weeks after the boy's arrival.

"Look at this wardrobe, Darius." Luz threw open Jonathan's tiny closet.

"He could only carry two suitcases, my love."

"But only two pairs of shoes?"

"If a man takes proper care of his shoes," Darius said with conviction, "and those shoes are of high caliber, why would he need more?"

"But they are not of high caliber. Look."

Darius was sure he'd had no more than two pairs when he arrived, perhaps only the pair on his feet, since he'd left home so quickly and with one suitcase, not two. Out of curiosity, he checked his own closet later that day: two pair of good black dress shoes for work; one pair of casual brown suede; one pair of athletic shoes for those increasingly rare occasions when he felt compelled to jog around the block; one pair of once-white "boat shoes" inherited from Bahman; one good pair of leather sandals. He didn't want to think about the contents of Luz's closet. How had this come to pass, that the measure of their affluence was gauged by the quality of their footwear, the contents of a shoe rack? The absurdity of this doubled him up with mirth, and he sat down heavily on the bed and guffawed. Thankfully, no one else was at home.

So Jonathan was led away, as a lamb to slaughter, to Macy's, where Luz flourished her card and bought him a pair of athletic shoes, painted in drunken colors that Darius found grotesque, plus some absurdly priced leather loafers with tassels and narrow toes that surely pinched his feet. Meanwhile, Darius examined and cleaned the boy's teeth, forcing himself not to intrude on her plans for the boy's new wardrobe.

The moment Luz had announced her pregnancy Darius had urged her to reduce her workload. Luz dismissed the suggestion with a toss of hair and a litany of denials, until she found an acceptable way to claim the idea as her own. Pleading two degrees of parenthood—surrogate and forthcoming—Luz announced she would be working only half a day. Carefully concealing any hint of glee, Darius nodded seriously and applauded her wisdom; and for this he was rewarded. She drove him to the dental office, then Jonathan to the language school and later picked him up, made his lunch, and left for her afternoon at the travel agency, stopping for Darius on her way home. He thought it a choppy, even strenuous schedule and was prepared to offer an alternative, but she had taken to the task with fervor. For once she was as needed as Sophia. (Sophia had at first offered to care for Jonathan, but the offer was sufficiently feeble for Luz to insist they would do it instead. "He is Darius's brother, after all." Besides, Luz said, Sophia had far too much to do to add one more person to her life. Sophia agreed, dropping a morsel of gratitude that Luz had feasted on for a week.)

"I'm sure Sophia is more than happy to let you handle Jonathan," he commented later. "And you are more than capable."

"Good. I intend to do it right."

As the summer wore on, the dinner parties escalated at an alarming rate. Sophia would invite them over, and within days Luz was planning her own get-together. He'd told her it wasn't necessary, these competitive dinners. A simple meal would do. Better yet, a family gathering for coffee and dessert. Why add stress to her life? Considering her condition, why not pamper herself?

"I'm enjoying it," she told him more than once. He marveled at this. How could she be? "It's good for Jonathan," she insisted. "He needs as much family life as possible before school starts."

He kept his peace, watching her face grow serious as she examined cookbooks, planned her dinners and what she would buy for Jonathan's first day of school. Perhaps all the activity was good for Jonathan, but what was good for Luz? She was visibly pregnant, and he was growing worried over her pasty complexion.

"Have you talked with Sophia?" he asked, thinking of her pregnancy. Jonathan had gone to the living room to watch television while they lingered over coffee.

"I've talked with my mother."

"But your mother is not here and Sophia is."

"What is it you want her to do for me?" said Luz.

"Whatever you think you need."

"I need my mother."

"I wish we could send for her, but you know we can't afford it."

"I know, Darius," she said, tears welling up. "Just let me dream about it, please."

For the latest gathering they'd arrived at Bahman's at 7:00, eaten heartily, and then dispersed, each according to his custom, throughout the house. Fahd took Jonathan with him to play on the computer, against the wishes of the little girls, who wanted Jonathan to themselves. Bahman pulled out the chessboard and beckoned Darius over. Luz and Sophia, as usual, remained behind to clean up. Jonathan had been with them for two months.

Darius sat hunched over Bahman's chessboard, chin in hand, scarcely contemplating his next move. He wanted Luz to find her way closer to Sophia, a woman of great feeling and not the competitor she imagined. Or perhaps he was overlooking an older, more primitive issue, a deeply embedded myth that two beautiful women, not related by blood, could never peaceably occupy the same space. Connection by marriage didn't count, and only a mother would do.

He stared blankly at the board. Bahman fidgeted in his chair. Conscious of how much time he was taking, Darius moved foolishly.

Bahman exhaled, muttered something about concentration, and made the decisive move.

"Something is on your mind, isn't it?" Bahman said.

"Nothing I'm aware of," Darius evaded and shrugged. "I'm tired, that's all."

Down the hall Fahd and Jonathan were laughing.

"You know, Darius," Bahman said quietly. "We would be happy to take Jonathan." He spread his arms, indicating the spacious room.

"I wish it were that simple. Besides, if you did, it would crush Luz more than you can imagine."

"Of course." Bahman slowly realigned the chess pieces for another match, and waited.

"She's homesick," Darius said finally, in a barely audible voice. "And there is nothing to be done."

Jonathan's school year approached. Forms had to be filled out, telephone calls made and returned, school administrators appeased, inoculations confirmed. If education was mandatory, she asked over breakfast in mid-August, why were so many obstacles thrown in the newcomer's way? Running a carnival would be easier, she announced, and far more amusing than enrolling Jonathan in middle school. She persevered, with unusual restraint. He knew this for a fact. He'd proofread her forms and letters, overheard her conversations. Not one school official encountered a fit of Latin pique. Not one felt the sting of a Colombian put-down although many, he gathered, were deserving.

"I tell you, Darius," she said in exasperation, "nobody knows his ass from his ear!"

As the first week of classes approached, Luz grew preoccupied once more with the state of Jonathan's wardrobe. She consulted sales ads and inexperienced clerks in numerous department stores until the boy took matters into his own hands. At Wards he selected two shirts and two pairs of jeans, announcing, "I like these." The glow-in-the-dark athletic shoes became his daily footwear until Darius insisted they buy him another pair. Anything at all, even another pair of outrageous sneakers. As long as the quality was good. "A man can only take proper care of his shoes," he admonished her, "if he is able to alternate them with another suitable pair." The expensive leather loafers were ignored, except on dinner party evenings, when Luz insisted he wear them. The ridiculous image of Darius's own shoe rack flitted annoyingly through his head.

Meanwhile, Darius observed her declining energy and began to worry. In the mornings, after she dropped Jonathan off at middle school, Luz would return home to bed until it was time for work. He blamed all this on the pregnancy. One would think she'd be happy to have Jonathan occupied for seven hours of each day. Very soon she'd be frantically busy and ought to think of the remaining months as a rest stop before the child arrived. (And mercifully, since Jonathan's arrival, there'd been no mournful solos from behind the bathroom door.) He pointed out the only significant difference in her schedule was she was eating lunch alone. Wasn't everything else the same?

"And very soon, my love," he said, "you won't have to be his chauffeur, either. A bus will pick him up."

Luz burst into tears. "But I like doing it. And why would anyone wish to eat alone?"

"I merely thought you'd enjoy some free time."

"Free? That's not *free*, Darius. That's *empty*."

While Luz dried her tears in the kitchen and busied herself with dinner, he phoned Bahman in desperation. What had he done? Why was she so contrary? And her skin tone, Uncle—really unhealthy! Over the wire Bahman was agreeing. *Yes, yes, I know. I remember. Mustn't blame yourself.* He could picture Bahman perfectly: eyes shut, lips pursed, his head nodding slowly like a medieval sage while propped on a fork of fingers. Darius would have liked to leap into the car and drive over, drink cup after cup of Sophia's perfumed tea, a rock of sugar dissolving in his mouth. He feared that Luz's bravely concealed sorrow was contagious.

"I merely pointed out that transportation would be provided," he told his uncle, keeping his voice low, even though they were speaking Farsi. "She can reclaim her days. She won't have to be a slave to everyone else's schedule. I thought that's what every modern woman wanted?"

"It's a mystery, Darius. A child has been successfully reared, prepared, and released into the world. The mother has accomplished her principal task, but does the mother feel successful? Freed? No, she feels bereft."

How upset Sophia had been each time a child left home for school. Especially little Zee.

"But Jonathan isn't Luz's son," Darius said. "And he's only been with us a few months."

"I don't have the answer. Perhaps when we are all so far from home, we take what we can get."

The long Labor Day weekend grew near. Bahman phoned to suggest they all spend the holiday together. Preferably out-of-doors. Did they think Jonathan might enjoy the zoo? The flash of anger came out of the blue, and he snapped at his uncle: "Jonathan might enjoy the zoo, but I most certainly will not. Besides, Jonathan would do better to stay home and learn to do his homework."

And why, he wondered aloud, would anyone want to join crowds of ill-mannered adults herded by ill-mannered children? Stare at Indian elephants in a fake African savanna? Applaud six sea lions in a tiny pool, performing for their supper? Watch while tattooed humans whooped at dignified apes? The very idea of the zoo infuriated and depressed him.

Then his tongue went limp. He was unable to carry on. It dawned on him then that his concern for Luz had worn him down. In an effort to comfort her and ease her pain—of mind and body—he'd curbed every request and need and expectation of his own. He felt totally flat and empty. Bahman waited for the storm to subside and said finally, "Talk it over with Luz and call me back."

On Labor Day morning, Bahman, Sophia, and the children arrived at their doorstep at 11:00. "At least it's not hot!" Bahman laughed and slapped Darius's back. If this was meant to cheer him up, the gesture was wasted. He'd made his peace with the outing the moment Luz expressed enthusiasm for the plan. Of course they must go, she said. Think of Jonathan. Think of the adventure he'd have. Hanging on Darius's lips was the retort that the zoo was not an adventure he would wish on the most bloodthirsty mullah, but he let it go. If she thought it was a good idea, considering her condition, who was he to object?

Once more in caravan, they drove across town to the zoo: first Bahman, Sophia, and the little girls in the Lincoln; Luz and Jonathan with Darius, in second position; Fahd in his Toyota, bringing up the rear. Neither Luz nor Sophia would allow the boys to ride together. Fahd extended the invitation while they were still organizing themselves in front of the apartment building. The women rose up in unison and spoke: *Absolutely not!*

"Bad enough that a nineteen-year-old drives his own car!" Sophia announced angrily in Farsi. Fahd shrugged and climbed into the Corolla, turning on the radio. Rap music threatened to drown out the conversation until Bahman barked an order. Fahd grudgingly turned the radio down.

"And would you rather hear him complain?" Bahman asked. "Day and night, night and day?"

"I'd rather have him behave like a proper son and not this American hooligan!" Sophia said.

"Our son is not a hooligan! He is a typical American teenager!"

"And this is supposed to console me?"

Sophia had packed a large picnic lunch for later, upsetting Luz, who had come empty-handed.

"But she didn't even phone." Luz said, disconsolate. They strolled behind the others, past a curious emu. "At least I could have brought a cake."

"Why are you letting this bother you? They know you aren't well, and Sophia took matters into her own hands. Enjoy yourself. Let your family provide for you. For once."

"You're my only family here. And Jonathan."

"Then make your boundaries a little wider."

"But I don't feel like one of you. I can't speak in Farsi, and no one speaks Spanish. I feel so much outside."

She leaned against his arm, holding his hand; and her lack of inhibitions took him pleasantly by surprise, as it always did. He squeezed her hand and held it tight.

"I understand, but you're not outside. Think of yourself as a woman with two families. And this is the American half."

"But Darius. *I'm* the American." Then, in a desolate voice, she added, "Except I'm in the wrong hemisphere."

The children bolted ahead of Bahman and Sophia, toward some exhibit around the bend. Fahd walked a few paces behind, not wishing to appear a child but not wishing to be left out. His father and mother walked side by side, without touching, Sophia calling out something to the little girls. Darius gazed down at his wife with her dark hair and luminous black eyes. She could be any nationality, even Iranian, were you to catch only a glimpse of her.

"Tell me," he said and put his arm around her shoulders, "what happened to the Luz who made us sing 'Jingle Bells' in English class? The Luz who made us all learn the Pledge of Allegiance? And that dreadful anthem, 'The Star Spangled Banner'? Where is that Luz now?"

She turned her head away shyly. "Everyone sings 'Jingle Bells,'" she said in a small voice. "Remember the Vietnamese?"

They rounded the bend and noticed the children gathered along a wood fence, beside what appeared to be a hut but was actually a covered stairway. An elephant stood in the shade of the hut while a child stepped gingerly off the platform at the top of the stairs and onto a special seat atop the animal. Bahman and Sophia had already reached the children. Jonathan was grinning and gesturing and saying something to Fahd. Then he moved to one side and spoke to a person in a tiny booth.

"Jonathan wants to have a ride," Fahd said. "Will you let him?"

The family turned as one, awaiting their answer, and Darius looked over at Luz.

"Of course," she said. "If he wants to. What harm is there? See that little girl?"

They looked up as the elephant strode heavily away from the platform. A small and very blond child beamed her pleasure down to anxious parents, who kept pace with the elephant and its trainer, taking pictures and calling to her.

"Of course," Darius said, echoing Luz. "Jonathan has bravely come all this way, alone. Why shouldn't he ride the elephant?"

Jonathan was the only one paying scant attention to the family discussion. He pulled money out of his pocket and handed it to the person in the booth. By the time Darius and Luz had made their permission known, Jonathan had already bounded up the steps and was standing at the top of the platform, waiting his turn. He grinned down at them and waved.

"Hey, man!" Fahd brayed up at him. "You can always change your mind!"

"No way, man!" Jonathan yelled back.

Luz gave a great peal of laughter.

In less than five minutes, the elephant returned. The delighted girl clambered off the animal with noticeable confidence, racing down the stairs and into her parents' arms. Once the platform cleared, Jonathan positioned himself, waited for directions from the trainer, and then climbed awkwardly aboard. The animal waited stoically, flipping its enormous ears. Conflicting emotions swirled back and forth inside Darius. How could people reduce such a splendid animal to a pony ride? Yet look at the boy. For the first time he was seeing his brother full of unabashed fun. The family watched, breathless, as if this were some dangerous voyage instead of a short trundle around a well-worn ring, on a slow and closely watched pachyderm. The animal lumbered away from the platform with the trainer at its side. Jonathan's body rocked forward and back to the rhythm of the animal's gait. Like a cowboy holding on to a horse's reins, he held on to the security rope with one hand and raised his other arm high. He turned toward the family below and waved while an enormous smile spread across his face.

"John Wayne Shalori," Luz said and squeezed Darius's arm.

For the first time in weeks, Darius realized he was laughing.

Sophia's picnic lunch stretched into an early dinner as dish after dish emerged from the hamper. Fahd had brought along a whiffle ball and bat and set about teaching Jonathan the rules of the game. The little girls played badminton, their parents taking turns against them, and Luz finally seemed at ease. Only when they were driving home, as the sky was losing its color, did Darius detect a somber mood.

"You and Sophia had a lot to talk about," he said.

"Yes. I asked her how she'd felt at five months."

"And she reassured you, I hope? You're normal?"

"What's normal, Darius? She said she had strange cravings—I know all about such things."

"Anything else?"

"Nothing important, really. Nothing I feel."

He waited but she'd already let it go, reluctant to tell him or determined not to, but the change in mood was unmistakable. He struck up a conversation with Jonathan, who was dozing off in the back seat. By the time they reached home, her mood draped over her like a black shawl. She didn't wait for him to open the car door but climbed out, moving mechanically up the steps and into the apartment. Jonathan staggered out sleepily and followed Luz up while Darius put away the car. When he finally came indoors, he found her locked inside the bathroom.

Jonathan was slumped on the living room couch, watching television. Canned laughter followed Darius into the bedroom. He closed the door and tapped on the bathroom.

"Go away, please," she said.

"Do you want Jonathan to see you like this?"

"I'm not ashamed."

"Then tell me what I can do."

"There's nothing to do, Darius. Just leave me alone awhile, please."

He drew away from the door and sat down on the bed. Her voice started quietly enough: *"Qué lejos estás, qué vacia nuestra casa."*

The song was a bridge. Why hadn't he been able to see this before? On it she could cross over the bruised places of her life, back to the home and mother she had not seen in years. She was using it to reach him, too, and all this time he'd thought of it only as a wall. Perhaps a different time would come when the song would cease, a time when she would no longer need it. He wondered now if he would miss it.

He waited for her to finish the stanza, and then joined her in the second verse. "Through the walls I hear the empty rooms sighing," he sang. "All that remains is bitter pain."

When she realized he was singing too, her voice wavered. They finished the verse together, and there was a startled silence. Simultaneously, they began the chorus, and her voice grew stronger and more impassioned as they finished.

"Darius?"

He turned and saw Jonathan standing in the bedroom door, looking tousled and confused.

"What are you doing?" the boy said.

"Singing."

"Where's Luz?"

"In the bathroom. She's singing too."

"Why?"

Darius gestured him into the room and motioned for him to sit down beside him on the bed. Luz had reached the chorus, and when that was accomplished he knew she would start in again from the top. He joined her for the finale: "The house of my heart is sad and empty. Oh, when will hope return?"

He stood up, put his arm around Jonathan, and led him out of the bedroom, into his own room. Jonathan sat down on the edge of his bed, shoulders drooping, and Darius sat down beside him.

"What did you do at home," Darius asked, "when you were feeling sad?"

"Not much," Jonathan answered. "I don't remember being sad very often. I guess I'd go to my room. Mother would make treats. Do you remember?"

"I remember her saffron cookies."

"Yes, those were the best. And she'd let you eat a whole plate of them, even if it was supper time."

"Well, this is what Luz does."

"But she's a grown-up."

"Does it make a difference?"

"I've never thought about it." The boy let his head drop wearily between his shoulders, staring at the rainbow-colored sneakers, pulling and flipping the laces. Then he signed. "Darius, will we ever go home, or will we stay here?"

Darius stood up and gazed around the small room—at the poster of a rock star taped to the wall, at the tiny desk cluttered with books, the closet door standing open to reveal the meager contents. He turned back to Jonathan and rested a hand on his head, smoothing the tousled hair. "We'll stay here. Father and Mother want it."

The boy looked at Darius, his eyes searching.

"Luz wants you here. Very much. And so do I. Now get into bed, please."

The boy pulled off his shirt and shorts and wearily eased himself in between the sheets. "I can't tell if the song is sad or not," he said.

"I know. It has a sweet sound, doesn't it? Maybe Luz will teach you the words one day."

Darius turned off the light and started to close the door.

"Leave it open," Jonathan said sleepily. "I want to hear the song."

"Cuándo volverá la esperanza . . . ," she sang.

There was no bitterness in her voice now, only a tired grief. Darius left Jonathan's door ajar and walked into the kitchen, his own heart heavy. Clean, dry dishes from breakfast stood in the dish drainer, where Luz had placed them, and with great care he put them up.

AMNESTY

R osalía Rodriguez first saw them through the window of her ground-floor office: two young men, rather short, crawling out of an old green station wagon. It was 7:30 in the morning, and they were dressed in pajamas.

They'd come for the legalization, Rosie felt sure. Ever since the government passed the amnesty bill, clients had arrived by the scores. They parked in the lot beside the old brick church building, walking quickly to the entrance of what was now the St. Francis Community Center, as if reluctant to expose their lives to the bright light of day. Others took the bus from Kansas City's West Side barrio, a ride, Rosie knew, requiring two transfers. Many of them clutched old utility receipts that might prove their uninterrupted residency, their worth. Few spoke competent English.

The Center couldn't afford to hire anyone else to help with the paper work, even though St. Francis's had been designated a Missouri legalization site. She and Alberto Chavez—the Center's only "Hispanic Services" staff—were left to do it all.

"At least we can do something about the crowds," Al said, organizing chairs along both sides of the hallway and setting up a system, with signs in Spanish, so that clients could be interviewed in the order in which they arrived. He and Rosie would be fair, he said in a bitter voice, even if no one else had ever been. Meanwhile, clients sat wherever they liked, unconcerned with who came first, second, third.

7:45. People filled the hall: men with silent, sunburnt faces; stout women with growing children; even grandmothers. The hall clouded with cigarette smoke while clients sat patiently on Al's folding chairs or simply stood, the line stretching as far back as the unisex restroom.

But these two boys, in the pajamas. (She would always think of them as boys, even though the older one, Jesús, turned out to be twenty-four.) They looked so small and ill equipped, even if this fact had never borne itself in upon them. When Jesús smiled, he opened a mouth of gold and silver that glittered garishly, a parody of wealth. And his hair. He'd bleached it yellow-white, teased the top into spikes while the bottom ends stretched down his neck to his shoulders in another parody of fashion. Rosie wanted to laugh when she first saw him. He looked so cheap. She didn't want to say it, but there it was: Mexican punk rock. And why did he have to smile so much? Like a pimp.

She pushed the thought away, nestled her vast bosom across her desk, and took out a fresh application form, searching without haste for a sharp pencil. Finally, she looked out to the line of applicants waiting in the hall and spoke, her voice deliberately gentle and warm. *A drowning warmth,* Al teased. *La madre,* Rosie preferred to think.

She knew what they said about her in the office. "Ah, Rosie. A heart as big as her behind." A behind, Alberto once informed her, as broad as all outdoors. But Al had said it with affection, not ridicule like the others.

"¿A quién le toca?" She directed her voice toward the hall. She knew who was next—the boy/man with the hair and teeth.

Both brothers approached her desk, Jesús in front with shy Juan, the younger one, a little behind. They were dressed now, looking clean and tidy, in spite of the earrings.

"Where are you staying?" she asked deliberately.

Jesús smiled. Metal flashed and Rosie turned away. They had just left their apartment, he said, and were forced for the time being to stay in the car.

"*Una vez más* . . . the car?" She wanted to slow him down, hear him explain.

He pointed toward her window, to the parking lot outside. "*Sí,* Señora. That car."

She half stood, bracing her large body against the desk, peered dramatically out toward the crowded lot, and nodded, as if she didn't already know and this charade of surprise were required. Carefully, she lowered herself back down. The chair gave a long, penetrating squeak, and Rosie pushed it back, away from her desk, to hush it up.

"And where did you dress? Clean up?"

"In the washroom. Down there." He gestured toward the end of the hall.

Jesús placed a manila folder on the desk. The clasp had broken off; the corners were dented. She turned it over and saw one large, discolored spot, round as a coffee cup or a cookie. Rosie pulled back the flap. A remnant of adhesive tape held the envelope shut but had grown so weak and creased it wouldn't hold anything in much longer. What little there was. Carefully, she inserted her hand and pulled out two electric bills, a water bill, and a single sheet—an employer's letter of reference. The letterhead was embossed: *Ahmad Shah's Fine Oriental Rugs.*

Rosie read quickly. Jesús had worked there, on and off, for the better part of three years. "And before this?" she asked.

"Odd jobs. In Los Angeles . . . Texas . . . Chicago . . ."

"You have receipts? Stubs?"

"No, Señora. They paid me cash."

Of course. And even more would they be paying in cash, to hide the tracks of this undocumented man or that one, who'd come to run the errands, ferry the cloth, pick the corn or beets or cherries. Rosie sighed and absentmindedly turned the envelope up. Jesús quickly reached inside and removed two letter envelopes she'd missed. Nothing but a shell of correspondence. She tried to make out the city of origin. Guadalajara? Guanajuato? The postmarks were incomplete, the ink smudged. The younger one, Juan. When had he come up? Only a date was clear on one envelope. June 6, 1986.

Rosie looked up at him reluctantly, making sure she smiled first, then shook her head. "I'm not sure what we can do for you, but we'll try."

We will try. The carrot of false hope, loaned out from day to day. What else could she tell them? She knew what Al would say: *I will recommend a lawyer. Here, a good fee, not too much. We must have more documents, you see. Something sure,* "positivo." Some would go away forever while others would come back with the stubs of bills a wife had thought to keep. *Now I will see what I can do,* Al would say, with conviction. And so the case would be pursued, filed, the applicant defended by the meager weight of the St. Francis letterhead on an appeal.

She admired Al, the firm way he expressed himself, never leading anyone astray. When she first joined the staff, she'd listened closely while he dealt with his clients—easy enough to do in such close quarters. She thought she'd learned to imitate him. Perhaps she hadn't learned enough.

Rosie glanced out the window. Ghostly pale sycamores ringed the parking lot. In a couple of months their leaves, broad as salad plates, would tan and curl and drift against the low brick fence. Her gaze came to rest on the green station wagon, and she turned back to her desk, making a note on her pad. *No fixed address.*

"Where will you stay tonight?" She looked intently from Jesús to the younger brother, then back to Jesús.

"We're looking," he said.

"I see. There is something else you must do to ensure your appeal."

She took the printed sheet that explained, in English and Spanish, all that must be done to earn amnesty and become legal—the application form, the seventy-five-dollar fee (cheaper than anywhere else, she thought proudly), the one hundred hours of free English and citizenship classes the Center provided. Jesús read the paper while Juan read over his shoulder. When they finished, Rosie pushed herself up from her chair, told them to follow her, and took them upstairs, past the line of sun-burnt applicants, past the Coke machine, up the wide stairs that needed cleaning.

"Stop by my office at noon," she said in Spanish, leaving them at the English school office. She noticed the crowd of students—Vietnamese, Mexican, Chinese, Russian. They stared at Jesús with his bleached and tortured hair, at young Juan and his long earring, the pimp clothes and pimp teeth, the lurid imitation of success. She turned away, not wanting to watch, and walked heavily down the stairs, gripping the handrail.

She felt her abundant weight most painfully on stairs, each step jarring her tiny ankles and feet. Her daughter, Alejandra, said she loved her just as she was, soft as a queen-sized bed. But not Miguel. When he left (fled, she thought, after years of practicing and rehearsing for the final flight), it was with someone untried and untested, free of matrimonial weight. And little Alejandra had cried and cried and said Papa was unkind. "*Malo*, like all men."

Where had the child heard these words? From her? From Grandma? Certainly Rosie had thought it, and said it too, cried out to heaven at the injustice, the foolishness, the vanity of men who chased wisps, pretty faces, smaller waists, chasing after themselves, really, when all they had to do to find what they wanted was to look in the palm of their hand. Little Alejandra was right. *Malo.*

"The line never ends," Al whispered fiercely when she returned to the office. She'd grown used to the way he hid behind sharp words, guard-ing his concern against thieves. So different from her own way. *A soft touch,* Al said. It upset her that he seemed to believe she soiled mercy with her softness. Why did it matter so much what Al thought?

She knew what he was hiding. June the bookkeeper once told her that Al's wife was out of her mind. The wife would lock him out, hoarding the children, keeping them from him. June thought maybe he lived away from home now, but she wasn't sure. He came, he went, he stayed when necessary with his mother in Kansas, then back to his own home in Missouri.

Al had never confided in her, scarcely breathed a word he even had a wife, accepting that Rosie probably knew. He could have told her, she thought sadly. It bothered her more than she cared to admit, being pushed to the margins of his life. She'd have been more than willing to listen. Her own divorce had taken place just before she joined the staff, when she was still too stunned to treat Al with anything but restraint. It seemed incredible now, how much her feelings toward Miguel had colored her first impressions. She mentioned Miguel nowadays, of course, in a joking, unkind way. Perhaps talking about Miguel had made Al hesitant to talk about himself. The thought embarrassed her.

She asked June why Al didn't file for divorce or get custody of the kids. June didn't know, saying, "Maybe he doesn't want them."

Not want your kids? Impossible! But perhaps Al was like Miguel and thought like Miguel: children belonged to the mother. Children need their mother, for there was no one on this earth like your mother—even a crazy one.

"So?" Al looked up from his papers, resting between clients. "How are the punk rock stars?"

Rosie looked up, rolled her eyes, and shrugged. There was scarcely a trace of the immigrant left in Al's carefully styled hair and clothes. He was as far away from the people in the hall as an Anglo was. So was she for that matter, so who was to judge? Still, Al's dark face couldn't hide its history, not like hers had. She gazed at his pressed shirt, the yellow tie, seeing in her mind's eye the sharp, precise crease in the tan trousers hidden under his desk.

"Clothes do not make the man, Alberto."

"De verdad," he said. "But sometimes the clothes can take away what little a man has."

"You should be a teacher. Not a social worker."

"We're not even that," Al said and sighed. "We're just low-paid clerks who happen to be bilingual."

"We are whatever the job requires. So maybe you could talk to the brothers? About their clothes? And the hair?"

"Sure. What're their names?"

"Marrón. Jesús and Juan."

She looked back into the folder to confirm, reading the letter from Ahmad Shah, carefully this time, then the names on the utility receipts. She looked from one to the others. The carpet merchant referred to Jesús as *Javier.* On the receipt from the electric company, his name read *José.* Rosie threw the envelopes down on her desk and cursed in Spanish. Al rose quickly and crossed the narrow room, picking the papers off her desk.

"Which is he? Javier? José? Or Jesús?"

She sighed and looked at her watch.

Al put the envelopes back on her desk and stretched.

"I need to get something to eat. Can I bring you anything?"

She brightened for a moment and then the feeling sank. She'd brought an apple, a hard-boiled egg, four small squares of saltines. The thought of them made her sad. Egg and crackers. She planned to treat herself to a diet soft drink from the machine. Rosie shook her head. "No. Nothing. Thanks."

It was 12:20 when Al left. Rosie could see Jesús and his brother sitting on chairs just outside the door. They talked quietly to each other, unaware that she was watching. How could they be so cheerful? Perhaps it wasn't cheer, only a necessary hope that they propped up with smiles. They could go to one of the shelters, or the City Union Mission. No, not there. She remembered now. Jesús told her his wallet and passport had been pinched at the Mission, along with his watch. She'd phone. The passport might turn up, but the watch and money were gone. The passport had been renewed somewhere in California, and he'd have to return there to get a copy. She felt the deadening weight of their problem settle deep into the very bottom of her stomach. *You take too much inside,* she heard Al say. *Take things only as far as your head or the fingertips that touch the papers. Let it stop there.* She called the boys into the office.

"You'll have to leave Missouri, you know. Back to California."

"Yes," Jesús said. "I thought so."

She watched his face. There was no dismay to speak of, no outlandish smile. No expression at all. She wandered if he understood. "Where to?" she asked. He shrugged. "Where did you get your visa renewed?"

"Los Angeles."

Didn't he care? They should get into their car this very moment, drive the five blocks to Interstate 70 and head due west. She felt impatient now, uncomfortable that she must be the one to spell it out. The feeling passed, leaving only the weight inside. She must be tired. Who had taken it upon herself to remind and remind the staff that the very things that might seem so obvious were as remote as the South Seas to the people waiting in the hall? She'd heard the wild gossip, the belief fed by fear that the INS was waiting for any illegal who came to register for amnesty, that a van stood hidden at the back door, ready to drive them away. When Rosie first told the staff this story, her voice trembled with outrage. *¡Pobrecitos!*—poor dears. Someone standing in the back near the windows had snickered.

No fixed address.

"When will you leave?" she asked Jesús.

"Is a problem," he answered.

"Why?"

He put his right hand inside his trouser pocket and pulled it inside out.

"Yes, I'm sorry. What about your employer?"

"*¿Cómo se dice?* Is finished. No more business."

She nodded and looked down at the application form, scantily filled in.

"He didn't fire you, did he?"

"Oh, no. I was a good worker for Ahmad Shah. He like me."

"And your family? You said you had some family here, I believe."

Something melted around his eyes and mouth. He relaxed, his words gathering speed, talking with affection about the brother in Los Angeles, another—an agricultural worker—in Oregon. The mother and sisters in Chihuahua City. He phoned his mother, you see. Every Sunday. He saved for the phone calls, the stamps, and money orders. Jesús's eyes brightened, the metal teeth appeared and disappeared in flashing accompaniment. The younger brother listened, lost in the narration, a faint smile settling on his mouth. He nodded from time to time as Jesús threw himself into the story, told without a trace of pity, a tale of striving, of opportunities lost and gained.

Rosie felt herself slip deep inside the words, honored to listen, a mother herself. She would be as proud as Jesús's mother to have such a son. A telephone call every Sunday. A good Mexican son.

"I have a room," Rosie said.

"*¿Perdón?*"

"You can stay with me and my daughter. For a short time."

He stared at her. The younger brother was grinning, his eyes suddenly shy.

"You are serious?" Jesús asked.

"Yes, but we must find you some work."

Her words trailed away. What work could he do? Busboy? Salad boy? Roofer? House painter? So few choices. She'd have to ask Al.

"I'll take you there now. You can follow me in your car." She wrote out her address and phone number, in case he got lost. "I'll have to come back, but you can stay. Get some rest. You'll want to come to school in the morning. No?"

"*Sí.*"

"And then someone will help you with a job."

"Maybe is not necessary."

She cocked her head, giving him a puzzled look, and he repeated himself.

"Please wait, Señora. We have something to show you."

Jesús said something to his brother she couldn't hear, and they left the office quickly. Their voices disappeared down the hallway, and for a moment she regretted the offer. She wouldn't tell Al until they'd left town. Al would only tell her she'd completely lost her mind. For a moment she heard his high, authoritative voice, trilling in Spanish, the voice reserved for Rosie. *People are not pets, Rosie. You cannot take them all in, give them a meal, and let them play in the garden. Be careful with that one, Rosie. He's a deadbeat.* She felt a rush of anger. Al underestimated her. The maternal style worked with some people, didn't it?

She sighed, took several Rolaids from the small bottle in her handbag, munching them slowly and with pleasure. What was wrong with him, anyway? Nowadays gloom hung over him from the time he arrived to the time he left. He found fault everywhere, and not just with her: the rest of the staff was insensitive, their clients painfully ignorant. He complained no one in the building knew how to brew a decent pot of coffee, and then scorned the soft drink selection. Last week, he'd jumped all over the janitor for neglecting to sweep their office.

A commotion in the hall distracted her, and she went out to look. A crowd bulged in the doorway of the front office, and she joined it. Jesús stood surrounded by staff: the office manager; June, the bookkeeper; the job finder; a couple of caseworkers; the baby-sitter from downstairs;

teachers from the English school upstairs. A rug lay rolled in a tube at the brothers' feet. The group pressed into the office until there was scarcely room to turn around. Someone pulled a chair out of the way. She peered around heads as Jesús and his brother unrolled the rug.

No one said a word when they stretched the rug out flat. Rosie felt her heart beat faster. June clasped her hands and shook her head in exaggerated amazement, her gesture diluting the beauty of the rug. "Fabulous," June said. "Where on earth did you get it?"

"Where, indeed," someone whispered nearby.

It was Persian, Jesús explained. Rosie looked carefully at the blue background, the blue of expensive china, but not so bright. The blue of a robin's egg? She couldn't put her finger on it. Heads kept blocking her view, but Jesús saw her and caught her eye. *The señora would explain in English, wouldn't she?*

"He wants to sell it," she said. "He got this rug from his employer, who sells rugs. He got it instead of his final wages because the rug man's going out of business."

"Look at the border," voices murmured. "Like a puzzle . . . So blue, and look at the deer figures or is it a camel? A griffin . . . Tight weave . . . S'pose it's a fake?"

"How much do you suppose he wants for it?" June muttered.

"*¿Cuánto cuesta?*" Rose asked him.

"Shah said it's worth maybe eleven thousand dollars, but . . ." He shrugged and smiled the dreadful smile.

"Did he really give it to you?" she asked in Spanish and pushed herself through the group to the front.

"Yes," he answered in English, looking over his audience. "He say to me he no can pay me last time. So he say, 'Here, Jesús. For your good service. Keep or sell.'" Jesús's arms stretched wide. Rosie imagined him gleefully selling tickets at a carnival, his voice too loud.

The group thinned out, moving back to offices and classrooms until only Rosie remained. Jesús deftly rolled the rug back up and motioned to his brother. Juan had been standing away from the crowd near the windows.

"It fits in the trunk," Jesús said as though this was a fact to be proud of.

All of his life fit into his trunk, she thought, and followed them out to the parking lot. Al was just parking and gave her a questioning look as she passed, rolling down his window.

"You missed the rug," she said and walked on to her car. When she drove by, Al was standing beside his car and threw out his arms in a question. Rosie waved at him and drove out of the lot, checking the rearview mirror to be sure Jesús was following.

Her neighborhood was quiet and old, across the state line in Kansas. It was the same neighborhood her mother lived in, three blocks away. The small bungalow had a single attached garage that Miguel had converted into an extra room. The family room. After the remodeling, they had spent most of their time there, using the round table that had made the eat-in kitchen so cramped.

Since Miguel's departure, she'd moved the table back to the kitchen, where she and Alejandra could enjoy its coziness. She decided later it must have been Miguel who made the kitchen seem so small. A tiny TV sat on one end of the counter so her daughter could watch it while Rosie cooked or did laundry or dishes. Nowadays, they seldom turned on the large TV in the family room, seldom went into the room at all, except when relatives came for Sunday dinner. From time to time she wished she had the garage back. She hated scraping snow off the car.

She stood in the center of the spare room, pushing her feet into the large, oval braided rug.

"The sofa opens out into a queen-sized bed," she explained to the brothers. "You'll have to share, I'm afraid."

"No problem," said Jesús.

"Have you eaten?"

"You don't have to worry about us. We can look after ourselves. Juan has a little money. For food." Jesús stretched his arm out in no specific direction.

"I have to get back," Rosie said. "There's meat and cheese and bread in the refrigerator. Chips in the cabinet. If you're hungry, please help yourself."

The boys nodded and thanked her and walked her to the door. When she closed it behind her, she felt a cold draft flow through her heart. Maybe she was completely out of her mind. When she reached the office, she went straight to her desk without looking at Al.

"Where did you take the Lopez boys?" he asked as soon as she sat down.

"The Marrón boys."

"Lopez, Jerez, Marrón. There were so many to choose from."

"I took them out and about." She put her handbag in the bottom desk drawer and shut it noisily with her foot. "They need money, Al. All they had was stolen at the City Union Mission. They're trying to sell a rug. Jesús—the older one—worked for a Persian rug dealer. The man paid him off in merchandise."

"For crying out loud!"

"But you should have seen it. It was beautiful. Of course half the staff thinks it's stolen."

"And you?"

"No. I think he's telling the truth."

"A man who uses three different names?"

"Come on. We see that all the time. I even have a letter from his employer. This rug man. Ahmad somebody." She hated it when he stared at her like that, turning his eyes into two dark probes.

"Wouldn't you just love to take a pair of scissors to his hair," Al said, moving papers in and out of the folders scattered across his desk before adding, "They're very light-skinned, aren't they?"

She caught the tone and glanced up. He was facing the file cabinet. She stared at his profile, saw the Indians of Chiapas in his color and bones, something Al could never change.

"They're from Chihuahua," said Rosie.

"Northerners," Al muttered. "Might as well be Texans."

The afternoon stretched out into a round of useless, flabby chores, of pencils sharpened and documents Xeroxed and filed. At 3:30 she glanced at her watch, straightened what few papers remained on her desk, and took out her purse.

"I'm going home," she said finally.

"So soon?"

"I was here at 7:20." Al, she remembered, had not made it in until almost 9:00.

"The early bird," he teased. "And did you get the worm?"

She looked at his dark, sleepless eyes. "Good-bye, Al."

Rosie parked the car in the drive and sat motionless, afraid to get out. She felt the day settle heavily across her plump shoulders and into the tiny, overworked feet. Little Alejandra would return soon. The girl always stopped at her grandmother's after school, coming home as soon as Rosie phoned. The burdensome day lifted when she thought about her mother and daughter together in the house of her childhood, its windowsills lined with African violets, aloes, and the Christmas cactus that always bloomed on Christmas. When she remembered the Marrón brothers, her shoulders sagged. Mother always said she should learn to think before she spoke.

When she opened the front door, she could hear the television in the family room, the volume low. She left her handbag on the small chest by the door and glanced at herself in the oval mirror. There was a smudge on her glasses, but the mirror was spotless. Startled, Rosie examined it closely and glanced into the living room. The afghan on the sofa was perfectly aligned along the back. The coffee table had been dusted, magazines straightened. She walked slowly into the kitchen. The linoleum gleamed up at her, the countertops and appliances shone. The vinyl tablecloth covering the small round table had been wiped clean, breakfast dishes cleared away, her one violet watered. She stood in the center of the kitchen, afraid she might cry.

Slowly, she moved back through the living room, down the narrow hall between the two small bedrooms and poked her head into the bathroom. The fixtures had been scrubbed, even the shower curtain. In the bedrooms, the beds were made, the carpet vacuumed, her slippers side by side in front of the bed. Nothing personal had been touched but left exactly where she or Alejandra had tossed it. Rosie crept closer to the family room and stood silently in the doorway. The two young men sat side by side on the sofa, watching a game show. She cleared her throat.

"*Buenas tardes,*" she said. Their heads turned and they stood up quickly. "I wasn't gone that long, was I?" Rosie extended her arms wide, taking in the newly cleaned house.

Jesús beamed. "Two people can work hard," he said.

"I can see." She wanted to thank them, but the words got stuck. She shook her head instead. "You didn't have to."

"Our pleasure," Jesús mumbled. "We did not hang up your things. We didn't think you'd like that."

She laughed loudly and Jesús's face brightened.

"I'll make us all something to eat," she said.

She returned to the kitchen and phoned her mother to send Alejandra home. Ten minutes later the front opened and shut with a familiar bang, and Alejandra called out, "I'm home."

"In here, Andrita."

The television in the family room went silent. As her daughter entered the kitchen, Rosie raised a finger to her lips and whispered.

"We have company."

"Who?"

"Come. I'll introduce you."

She took her daughter's hand and led her into the family room. The brothers were standing side by side, shoulders back, and Rosie nearly laughed. They'd caught Juan tucking in his shirttail, and both looked as though they were prepared for a military inspection. What would Alejandra make of their hair and their startlingly blue eyes?

"Andrita, this is Jesús and his brother Juan. They will be with us for a couple of days."

The little girl became bashful and turned away, hugging Rosie's side.

"Who are they?" she whispered.

"Visitors . . . from work."

Jesús immediately stepped forward and bowed, inviting her to join them.

"Here, Alejandra," he said. "Sit here. Please."

He escorted her to the sofa, still talking.

"How old are you?"

"Eight and a half," she whispered.

"No!" he exclaimed. "I thought you were at least nine!"

The girl smiled.

"You have a wonderful mother, did you know that?" he continued. "Our mother lives far away, but our sisters live near her. You know what, Alejandra? You look exactly like our niece Carolina. Juan, doesn't Alejandra look like Carolina?"

Rosie sat down on the sofa, and hesitantly Alejandra sat down beside her, perched on the edge. Juan sat quietly at the other end. Jesús remained standing. He reminded Rosie of a master of ceremonies, organizing the conversation into a seamless performance. He *was* a performer, it occurred to her. He'd make a good salesman, and she wondered how many rugs he'd sold for Ahmad Shah. But now he was focused on Alejandra, on making her as comfortable as possible with an effortless, gilt-toothed charm tailored to suit a child. She couldn't tell yet what Alejandra thought of them and decided to stay put until Alejandra felt at ease.

"I need to make dinner," she said finally. "Would you like to stay and keep Jesús and Juan company?"

The little girl nodded and giggled, and Rosie excused herself. From the kitchen, she strained to hear as she chopped lettuce and onions into a bowl. She could make out Jesús's voice, lifting up from time to time in question. Occasionally, she heard her daughter's small answer. At one point her voice rose playfully and she laughed. Rosie relaxed. She oughtn't to have worried. Besides, the extra attention wouldn't do the child any harm. The Marrón brothers wouldn't be staying long.

After dinner, Rosie encouraged the brothers to return to the family room while Alejandra helped her clean up.

"Mama?" the girl whispered once they'd reached the kitchen. "Why does Juan wear that lady's earring?"

"I thought lots of boys wore earrings now," she said and put the last plate in the dishwasher.

"Some do, but little ones . . . Where are they from?"

"So many questions, Andrita. They're from Chihuahua."

"Like Grandma. That's a long way from home. I wouldn't like to live so far away from home."

"Neither would I."

The girl wandered out of the kitchen to the family room, where the brothers greeted her loudly and warmly. Soon after, Rosie joined them.

"Señora, do I have your permission to show Andrita the rug?"

Alejandra's eyes widened as Jesús unrolled the rug. Juan stood across from him, waiting. At a word from Jesús, each pulled his corner until the rug lay perfectly flat across the family room floor. Alejandra squealed when she saw the deer grazing along its borders and went down on her knees to touch it, tracing the outline of the animals. A moment later the little girl jumped to her feet and began dancing with delight across the Persian rug, crying, "Look at me!"

"Don't," said Rosie. "It's very expensive."

"Is all right," Jesús said quickly. "High quality rug. Alejandra can't hurt it. It was made for feet. Besides, it's a magic rug."

"Magic?" said the girl and stopped.

"Of course," he said with conviction. "Ahmad Shah told me about magic rugs. They fly through the air, take you wherever you want. If you know the right words and can command the rug."

The little girl turned her head to one side and gave him a long look. "Do you know the right words?"

Jesús shrugged, smiled, and closed his eyes. "No. It's difficult, you know?"

"Another time, Andrita," Rosie said quickly, stepping into the center of the carpet and taking the girl's hand. "It's time for your bath."

Every morning Rosie hurriedly cleared off the dishes and made beds, so she wouldn't find them made when she returned from work. At St. Francis she was aware of the brothers, somewhere in the building—upstairs, she hoped, attending the school. Usually they came down at 12:00 to say hello and then vanished for the rest of the afternoon. She hadn't told Al where they were staying, glad he never asked.

At noon on the ninth day, they came into the office. Al had just gone out with a client.

"Señora?"

She turned away from the letter she was typing. The word *señora* sounded so heavy. At the house they had started to call her *Rosalita*. Jesús stepped forward.

"We're leaving now," he said.

"You sold the rug?"

"We sold the little one."

She stared at him. "I didn't know there were two."

"Yes. The little prayer rug we kept in the trunk. Three hundred dollars. It was only four by two. We're going to California."

Rosie sat perfectly still, her hands folded in her lap. They were still in the house when she'd left this morning. She hadn't noticed anything unusual, no packing or bustle.

"Why not leave tomorrow?"

"The date, you know? If we wait too long, we'll be illegal again." He laughed. The gold teeth flashed for a second, then disappeared.

Rosie nodded. "Do you have your things?"

"Yes, in the car. We left your key on the kitchen table."

It was an effort not to drown them in the advice Al said she gave too freely. Each one came forward in turn to take her hand in both of his. Just as the brothers were leaving, Al stepped into the office.

"You are working, my friends?" His voice was jolly, and false. He stared at their hair.

"*Sí,* Beto," Jesús said. "But now we must leave Kansas City and go back to Los Angeles for the visas."

"I understand," Al said. "May I have a word with you before you go?"

Al took Rosie by the shoulders and steered her into the hall, speaking in hushed, rapid English.

"I haven't had a chance to talk with them. You know?" He raised his eyes upward and gestured, indicating the hair. "If you don't mind."

"Please. I'll stay out here."

"Good." He looked at her with appreciation and closed the office door. Rosie turned her back to the door and warmed herself on the memory of Al's smile.

She busied herself at the soft drink machine, bought a diet Pepsi, glancing once through the glass before walking a short distance away to sip her drink. She could hear Al through the door, his Spanish rummaging over the subject of their clothing and hair, each sentence carefully worded and utterly unequivocal. Rosie could feel her chest rise and fall.

Al opened the door and nodded at her to come back in.

"We're very happy for Señora Rodriguez's help," Jesús was saying as she entered the small room. "And for her gracious accommodations."

The smile of accomplishment that had lightened Al's face suddenly vanished. His mouth formed a straight line. She turned awkwardly back to the boys.

"I'll walk you to your car."

She brushed away their no's and led them down the steps and out the building to the parking lot.

"And after California?" she asked. "You have plans to come back? Finish the paper work and the one hundred hours of English? Become legal once and for all?"

"We'll be back, if we can find some work. We want to see little Alejandra again."

"We'll be waiting."

"*Un problema.* We must leave the big rug. I thought maybe we could leave it with you, Rosalita. Is okay?"

The front door made a hollow sound when she closed it. Her footsteps echoed when she crossed the living room floor. She dialed her mother's number and Alejandra answered.

"Don't leave yet," Rosie said. "I'll come and get you. I want to visit with Grandma."

"Can we stay for dinner?" the girl asked hopefully.

"Yes, if Grandma wants it."

"She'll want it."

Rosie hung up and leaned against the counter. When she finally went in to check the family room, the sofa bed had been made back up into the sofa. All traces of the brothers had vanished—the two vinyl suitcases, the hairbrushes they kept on the end table, the cheap shoes with the socks rolled neatly inside. All gone, except for the Persian rug, one rolled end visible behind the sofa.

It was dark when they left her mother's. Warm, humid air clung to her skin, without a hint of fall. She pulled the car into the drive and noticed a sedan parked across the street, the driver sitting perfectly still.

"Let me open the door," Alejandra said and took the key, running eagerly to the front while Rosie gathered their things and locked the car. She glanced at the other car and recognized Al. Her excitement turned to panic, and all she could think of was her hair and faded lipstick. He saw her looking, signaled with his hand and got out.

She waited as he approached. "Good evening, Ro-sa-li-ta." So, he'd heard the Marrón brothers calling her this. He must be teasing. "May I come in for a moment?"

"Of course," she said. "Would you like some coffee?"

He held the door for her. As she passed, she caught a faint whiff of alcohol. Alejandra had gone into the kitchen and turned on the TV. Rosie gestured Al to the sofa and sat opposite him in the rocker.

"What brings you over?" It took effort to remain calm, to behave with dignity and not drown him with smiles.

"How long did you have them here, Rosie?"

She felt confused. "Have who?"

"Come on! The Marrón brothers."

"Why are you asking me this question? For however long they were our clients. Less than two weeks."

"Why so defensive?" he said, breaking into a smile that flustered her. She threw her hands in the air, rose quickly, walked to the kitchen, and turned on the kettle.

"Would you go to the family room, Alejandra?"

"Why, Mama?"

"Alberto and I have work business to discuss."

The girl stared at her. Rosie seldom sent her daughter away, always included her, especially during the nine days the Marróns had stayed there. Rosie watched the pout form.

"Please, Andrita," she said and put her arms around the girl to soften the request. "Do it for Mama, okay? We won't be long. Business is very boring for young girls."

"You'll talk in Spanish, won't you," she said in a sulk and dragged herself up from the kitchen chair. "Can I watch on the big TV?

"Of course."

"Can I take some cookies and ice cream?"

"Yes," Rosie said, losing patience.

The girl moved through the kitchen with deliberate slowness. Exasperated, Rosie hissed. "Go now, like I say. Or I'll spank."

The girl whirled around, her mouth forming a large O.

"Go along. I'll bring the ice cream."

The child dragged herself out of the kitchen and said a mournful hello to Al as she passed. A moment later loud TV voices drifted out from the family room.

"Come in here," she said to him. "It's less formal." She put the two mugs on the kitchen table and sat in her favorite chair, the one with arms that used to be Miguel's. Al sat down across from her, his back to the wall.

"You came here to talk about the brothers?"

"*Más o menos*. Did you hear what Jesús called me? *Beto*. I thought nobody used that anymore."

Al shrugged and smiled down at the table. It bothered her that he looked so tired and defeated. She stared at him, waiting. Surely he hadn't come to tell her Jesús had insulted him with an unwanted nickname. Rosie felt her heart pounding. How often she'd daydreamed about Al being in her kitchen, drinking coffee, comfortable enough to share more of their lives than the office allowed. But something was wrong here, like a missed cue, a badly tuned note hanging in the air.

"You know, when I talked to them this afternoon, I felt I was speaking with two children," he said. "They're so eager to please." He laughed quietly. "Maybe they picked up their clothing style in Los Angeles.

Anyway, I told them it didn't work in Kansas City. And it probably does-n't work in Los Angeles either, but who are we to say? The trouble is, they're like everyone else who comes into that office, and even the ones who work there. No money." Al glanced up at her, leaned back in the chair, thrust one hand into his trouser pocket and pulled it inside out.

"Alcohol has loosened your tongue, Alberto."

He nodded. "Two beers. I never drink more than two."

"So?"

"We see all kinds, don't we, Rosie? We don't ever need to go to the cir-cus for entertainment, even if we had the time, which we don't. We don't need to worry about boredom on the job, just exhaustion. You know, in the front office they don't have any idea what we're up against. I told June if we didn't get some help, we'd both end up in the hospital. Then where would they be?"

He was rattling on, as lost as the Marrón brothers. She could not place herself in any of this.

"Why didn't you ask me to take them in?" Al said unexpectedly, his eyes focused on his cup.

"Because they were my clients," she said. "I have the room, and I know this: you would have said no."

Al lifted his arms in a gesture of resignation, shook his head. "You underestimate me."

"No, I don't think so."

"It's not professional, Rosie," he said, ignoring her answer.

The anger came out of nowhere—from the very tips of her toes and fingers. How hard she tried to do things right, to follow the rules, to cope. But here he was, telling her that nothing she did was right. *Nada.* She lifted her plump arm and brought the whole length of it down against the table, her hand in a fist.

"So what is professional?" she asked. "Do you think every problem we have comes with a ready-made professional answer?"

"You think too much from your heart."

"You've come all this way to tell me that? And in my own kitchen, too? You have a better way to think?"

"Don't get upset."

"Why not? You're upsetting me. I didn't ask you to come and give advice."

"Rosie, Rosie." He reached out, smiling, and clasped her hand, still lying on the table, clenched in a fist. It hit her then, what it was that seemed so off. What it was he wanted—the very thing she wanted and had thought about with longing in those loose, safe moments before sleep. But it was wrong. All wrong.

Did he really think just because he considered her a soft touch with clients that she needed to take any casual offer that came her way? She wanted to cry, to reach across the table with her trim, varnished nails and scratch out his faulty eyes.

You know, Al, she wanted to say but couldn't, *girls like us . . . we're not desperate.*

She pulled her hand away angrily. The mug shook when she lifted it. A small wave of liquid rolled over the side. She sipped carefully and stared, for strength, at the African violet on the table. No, she would not help him out.

"You're too sensitive, Rosie," he said, leaning toward her with his arms resting on the table.

"Really? How nice of you to drive over and say so."

She got up and walked away from him, to the sink. "Do me a favor, Al. Go home. I have a daughter to consider."

She kept her back to him, unable to see the startled look on his face. When she finally turned back, Al had gotten to his feet. She caught him straightening his tie, and when he saw her looking, he bowed slightly and spoke. "I'm sorry. Good night."

She pretended not to hear and turned back to the sink. When the front door closed, she shut off the water, sat down, and lay her head against her folded arms.

The next morning she arrived for work early. She needed time to collect her thoughts before he came in. She was Xeroxing documents in the front office when June, the bookkeeper, came over.

"Al called me last night about dinnertime," June said. "His wife kicked him out of the house again, threatened to call the police and tell them he was beating her, which is a complete lie. He won't be in today. Did he ever reach you? He said he was worried there'd be too much work for you, alone."

June turned away to speak with someone else. Hurriedly, Rosie took her copies, walked back to the staff lavatory, and locked the door. Breathing heavily, she braced herself against the sink with both hands and wept.

Had it been five months already? She hadn't been home but a few minutes when the doorbell rang. She opened the door and found Juan Marrón. The boy must have remembered her schedule, or perhaps he'd been waiting. Rosie stared at Juan's sandy hair, cut and combed straight up. He was wearing the earring again—the long, ludicrous silver teardrop with the turquoise cross at the bottom. *You want a job or don't you, Juanito?* she'd once asked him. *Then take the earring out,* por favor.

"Come in." She brought him into the hall, and a gust of crisp winter air followed him inside. "Where's Jesús?"

"I don't know."

"What do you mean, you don't know?"

He wouldn't look at her and stared at his shoes. Rosie followed his gaze. Juan's feet were covered with a new pair of high top sneakers in an ecstatic lime green. Her heart sank. The young man's gaze wandered up to her face, and when their eyes met, he looked away quickly.

"Start from the beginning," she said, bringing Juan from the doorway into the house, pointing him to the sofa. When had she first met the Marrón brothers? August? September? She remembered the days were still warm.

She went to the kitchen, took a can of cola from the refrigerator and brought it to him before sitting down in the rocker. He looked lost against the upholstery of the deep couch, his face pointed down to the sneakers that seemed to grow longer, brighter inside the house.

"Jesús and I took the car and drove from Los Angeles to Denver and then here. I had money. I've been working, you know. Here and there. He said he would drive to Chicago and then come back quickly." Juan looked up at her, his face puzzled. "Somebody in Chicago owed him money. Rough people, he said. So he wouldn't let me come. He said he wouldn't be gone long."

"And your things?"

"One suitcase." He pointed toward the porch. "And my money belt."

Why hadn't he called immediately after Jesús dropped him off? Why had he waited so long? Had he walked here? *¡Pobrecito!* What would he do without his brother?

"Do you have a place to stay?" she asked.

Juan shook his head and let it hang. "I call my mother every Sunday, and she says Jesús has stopped calling. She says she has a bad feeling."

"Bring it in," Rosie said and pointed in the direction of the suitcase left discreetly outside. "Stay here for the time being," she said.

He said nothing, shaking his head, his blue eyes pulling at her and suddenly bright with tears. He seemed undecided until Alejandra came home. Delighted to see him, she leaned against his chair, chattering on. "There is room, Juanito," the girl told him. "Better here than anywhere else!"

Juan sagged visibly into the sofa. She knew he couldn't bring himself to say no. There would always be room in her house for a good Mexican son.

That night she couldn't seem to fall asleep. Just as she was about to drift off, her muscles jerked. She dreamed she was falling out a window. Jesús appeared briefly, alone. He was animated, his arms moving in concert with his optimistic head, just like the afternoon he had charmed Alejandra.

She got up finally, peering at the harsh green glow of the radio clock. She tied her robe loosely around her waist and walked across the hall to check on Alejandra, staring for a long time at the sleeping form of her daughter. When she returned to her bed, she soon fell asleep.

Juan was still sleeping in the family room when she sent Alejandra off to school in the morning. She left him a note on the kitchen table before leaving for work herself. Lack of sleep made her jumpy. Drivers traveled perilously close or stopped too soon. Once a horn sounded so loudly she felt as if she were standing, unprotected, in the middle of the street. Rosie was trembling by the time she sat down at her desk, her hands moist, her body cold, even though she'd had the car heater on full blast. She kept her coat on until the heat of the office warmed her up.

Al arrived late, scarcely acknowledging her. Wife troubles, Rosie thought. She was learning to read the signs. He opened and closed file drawers with a snap and a shove that left a metallic hum in the air. He didn't appear to notice anyone or anything, as through he was too busy sorting through whatever thoughts had hounded him to the steps of St. Francis.

Any other day Rosie would have left him alone, but not today. She had to tell him. No one else would understand.

"Jesús has disappeared. Vanished."

Al looked up. "Who?"

"Jesús Marrón. Remember? Four or five months ago? The brothers with the hair? His little brother is back in town. Says Jesús has disappeared."

"Sold his rug and skedaddled, did he?"

"No. I have the rug. And he wouldn't do that. He wouldn't leave his brother. He wouldn't stop phoning his mother." Tears burned her eyes. She reached for a Kleenex.

As she explained, Al became more agitated and searched impatiently for something in his desk. The moment Rosie began to cry, he slammed the drawer shut.

"He was probably picked up for speeding in some godforsaken Missouri town," Al said. "'No moolah? No speaka de English? Into the slammer with you.'" Al leaned against the tall file drawers, his back to her, talking to the wall.

Rosie lifted her head, looking at him through her tears. He turned back to his desk, picked up a legalization form, and stared at it. Neither of them spoke. The room filled with cold, black silence.

"Better yet, Rosie. Just picture it." He waved the blank form, gesturing with it. "Jesús stopped on the shoulder to fix a tire. Jesús trying to cross the road. Along come some good ole boys in a pickup and its, Pow! Bull's eye! One less wetback. Jesús the roadkill." Furiously, Al wadded up the paper and threw it into the air. It arced and dropped and bounced against the floor, and rolled until it hit Rosie's feet.

She felt as though a rough sea had tossed her over the beach of her desk. A siren from the Avenue suddenly rose higher and higher, dropped into a loud tremulous wobble before rising again. Rosie covered her ears with her hands. She heard it coming toward her and closed her eyes. When she opened them again, she was aware of Al turning toward her. His face blurred, as if she were seeing him through simmering trellises of heat. His eyes widened. His lips formed words she couldn't hear, and he was moving toward her, around the desk, his arms outstretched. All she was aware of then was the color white, one small pearl button, the smell of an ironed shirt, a hand cupping the back of her head, and the hideous screaming siren that dropped lower and lower, into a sob.

Rosie faintly remembered someone helping her on with her coat, but she couldn't remember leaving the office or climbing into Al's car. She felt as if everything inside her had been scooped out and all that remained was husk. Then the car was moving. From time to time Al reached out and gently squeezed her hand, his own hand so warm it almost burned. She grew aware that he was talking, but she couldn't grasp the words. They arrived on the West Side before she could focus on anything he was saying.

"I told June you needed a vacation. A break. I'm taking you to La Posada's. Ever go there? Great mole. You need some mole. Chocolate's good for the soul."

The words kept coming, but she didn't feel the need to listen. The fact he was talking at all gave her comfort, and she closed her eyes. They felt so tired and raw.

"I phoned your mother," he said. "She'll take Alejandra."

And what about the boys? She couldn't allow herself to think of them, forcing her wild thoughts back inside the car. Then Al was leading her into the restaurant, speaking with a waiter, guiding her over to a booth. He helped her out of her coat and summoned the waiter again, ordering for them both. All the while he was watching her with an expression she had never seen before. He filled the booth with small talk, offering up an unfamiliar litany of comfort. How long had it been since anyone other than her mother had taken so much care? Maybe this was why she'd liked the Marrón brothers so much. For a moment she was afraid she might start crying and held her breath until the feeling passed.

She lost all sense of time, had no idea how long they stayed in the restaurant. Warmed by the meal, she began to speak of everything Juan had told her, and more, until she thought she'd finally recovered. Scarcely anyone was left when they put on their coats and left La Posada's. She mustn't worry about her car, he said. He'd fetch it for her tomorrow. When they reached her house, he parked in the drive and came around quickly to help her out.

"I'd like you to come in," she said. "Just for a moment."

"Of course."

She needed to know Juan was still here, and if he wasn't, she didn't think she could bear it. Once inside she noticed someone had left the kitchen light on and felt immediately relieved. The light seeped in and lay in a long yellow panel across the living room floor. Al remained in the entry hall.

"Don't go yet. I just want to check on him."

She walked down the short hall to the family room. Juan had left the door ajar, and she gently pushed it open. He was asleep on the sofa bed. She closed the door quietly and returned to the living room. She would have liked Al to stay but knew he wouldn't. Before leaving, he took her hands in both of his, reminding her it was all arranged: she was to stay home tomorrow and rest. He would phone in the morning. He paused, then, and said, "We'll find out, Rosie. I promise."

She watched as he climbed into his car and pulled out of the drive, disappearing down the dark street. She remained at the window for some time, gazing in the direction he had gone. Still she couldn't bring herself to turn the porch light off. Who knows who might need it?

She felt herself drawn back to the room where Juan slept. Noiselessly, she opened the door again and gazed down at the boy. Only then did she notice the Persian rug stretched out across the floor, and the sight of it made her catch her breath. All this time she'd kept it rolled up behind the sofa, and now it lay open. Had he pulled it out for Alejandra's sake, remembering how much she'd enjoyed it? She took off her shoes and tiptoed into the room. Streetlights glowed through the curtains and faintly illuminated the floral details of the carpet, the fragile deer grazing and drinking along its borders. *A magic rug,* Jesús had said, *if you know the words.* The room was too dark to make out its colors. She knelt down, running her fingers over the thick pile, and struggled to remember the startling hues: peacock, robin's egg, cobalt, and perhaps the improbable blue of the Marrón brothers' eyes.

Photo: David Remley

A fiction writer and playwright, Catherine Browder grew up in Ohio, Georgia, Oklahoma, and Michigan. She studied in England and later worked in Taiwan and Japan. She received a B.A. from the University of Michigan, studied at the Iowa Writers' Workshop, and completed an M.A. from the Professional Writing Program at the University of Missouri-Kansas City. Her plays have been presented regionally and in New York City. She's received fiction fellowships from the Missouri Arts Council and the National Endowment for the Arts, and her award-winning stories have been published in a variety of journals including *Prairie Schooner, American Fiction, Shenandoah,* and *Kansas Quarterly.* Her first story collection, *The Clay That Breathes,* was published by Milkweed Editions in 1991; and a *feuillet,* "The Heart," was published by Helicon Nine Editions. For many years she has taught English as a second language in both academic and refugee programs. She lives with her husband in Kansas City, Missouri, and is currently at work on a novel and a new play.